I0615245

LOVE'S LOST KNIGHT

ROBERT FEARNLEY

SilverWood

Published in 2026 by SilverWood Books

SilverWood Books Ltd
14 Small Street, Bristol, BS1 1DE, United Kingdom
www.silverwoodbooks.co.uk

Copyright © Robert Fearnley 2026

The right of Robert Fearnley to be identified as the author of this
work has been asserted in accordance with the Copyright,
Designs and Patents Act 1988 Sections 77 and 78.

All rights reserved. No part of this publication may be reproduced,
stored in a retrieval system, or transmitted in any form or by any means,
electronic, mechanical, photocopying, recording or otherwise,
without prior permission of the copyright holder.

This is a work of fiction. Names, characters, places and incidents either are
products of the author's imagination or are used fictitiously. Any resemblance
to actual events or locales or persons, living or dead, is entirely coincidental.

ISBN 978-1-80042-318-3 (paperback)
Also available as an ebook

British Library Cataloguing in Publication Data
A CIP catalogue record for this book is
available from the British Library

Page design and typesetting by SilverWood Books

NO AI TRAINING

Without in any way limiting the author's exclusive rights under copyright,
any use of this publication to train generative artificial intelligence (AI)
technologies to generate text is expressly prohibited. The author reserves
all rights to license uses of this work for generative AI training and
development of machine learning language models.

FOR MANY YEARS ROBERT FEARNLEY was the secretary of the UK branch of Pen in Exile, a part of International PEN, which was a centre for exiled writers. He has translated several books of both prose and poetry into English, one of which is *Latvian Tales of Magic*, a collection of old folk stories, which was illustrated by Maija Tabaka, an award-winning Latvian artist.

Love's Lost Knight, together with the recently published *Swan Flowers*, are his first original works of fiction and combine his two interests of fantasy and medieval England.

LOVE'S LOST KNIGHT

1

It was late spring, when April was merging into May. The weather, which had been bright and open for some days, had now closed in, bringing a dirty fleece of cloud to hang over everything. A friar, wrapped up against the early evening gloom, was walking calmly along the road out of Maidenhead. With each step of his left foot, the tall staff in his right hand came firmly down on the roadway, as if pulling him forward. His eyes, although perhaps inwardly fixed on Heaven, were outwardly gazing curiously at a youth who was sitting on a fallen tree trunk some yards ahead.

As he drew closer, he was able to see the youth more clearly. The hair, untidily straggling out from under his hood, was a very light brown, almost wheat-coloured. The face was round and full-cheeked with a tippy nose. The eyes were blue, like borrowed summer sky. As if for warmth, the whole body was enveloped in a coarse grey cloak that looked to have been made for a taller man, because the bottom lay in folds around the wearer's feet. The tip of the youth's right thumb was between his teeth, as if he were deep in thought, and he seemed unaware of the friar's approach.

The friar, who had slowed his gait slightly on his approach, stopped in the roadway. He was no more than a few paces from the youth, who now looked up at him, as if only just aware. The look he gave the friar was cautious, but there was an open friendliness in the beardless face that encouraged the older man.

"Good day, my son," the friar said benignly. "God keep you in his care."

"Thank you, Father. I pray he will."

The youth's voice was pleasantly melodic, but of a higher pitch than the friar had expected, almost as if it had not broken. The friar looked closely at the youth, who shifted nervously under the scrutiny, but the friar smiled.

"What do you out on the road here by yourself?"

The youth paused, then said, "I'm seeking my master. We became separated and I need to join him again."

"Indeed. And you seek him here, near Maidenhead?"

"He was last seen not far away, by the river, but two days ago. I fear he may be in difficulty."

"Is that so? And who is your master, my son?"

"My master is a knight – Sir Carlyon de Bernedeslaw. He's tall, of a goodly build, and has a fair mien with eyes as green as oak leaves. He's been on a quest set by his ladylove to find flowers of the swan, but I fear me it's not gone well. Have you seen or heard of such a man, good Father?"

The youth looked hopefully at the friar, who was struck by the bright beauty in the upturned face. He put his head on one side while he considered. The youth's speech had a strange accent to it. The vowels had an intonation that made the words seem to belong to a foreign cousin of the friar's own English, but he was able to understand it.

"I think me you're a long way from home," he said thoughtfully. "Your master too?"

"No, sir. My master took me into his service when travelling in the north-west. He's seeking his lady in these parts."

"Hm, is that so? I've seen no such person. Yet there is a castle not far away. If your master is a knight, then it may be that you'll find word of him in that place. I'm on my way there now. Come with me."

The friar had been leaning with both hands on his staff while he spoke. He now released the left hand and straightened up. However, he kept his gaze on the youth's smooth face, even though his body turned slightly, ready to set off. There was something about the young stranger that attracted the friar, and he was unaccountably pleased when the lad got to his feet to join him.

"I'm Friar Paul," the friar said, as they began to walk side by side.

"Ah, yes. I'm... I'm Stanford."

The friar's mouth pursed thoughtfully at the youth's hesitation, but he dismissed it as shyness. Somehow that pleased him.

At the castle, which was little more than a keep and a yard surrounded by a wall, Friar Paul rapped at a postern with his staff. Let in, they were taken across the yard and into a kitchen, where they were offered a simple meal of mutton stew and bread. Friar Paul muttered a brief grace and then set to with a will. Very soon, however, he turned to Stanford and, between mouthfuls, asked him about his master's quest.

"Pray, what are these flowers of the swan that he was sent to find?"

"A silly thing, I hold. Where a swan dies, flowers grow – special flowers, they say. My master's ladylove set her heart on some and sent him off to find them. He travelled into the north-west country, which is where I entered his service."

"I thought me so. Your voice told me you were from those parts. I once travelled there. A strange and wild land. It surprises me not that you came back to these parts with him. And did he find the flowers?"

"He did. He brought them back for his lady."

"I see. She is from these parts." The friar nodded, as if satisfied, and used his knife to cut off a piece of his gravy-soaked trencher.

Stanford had been eating more slowly, and he now paused to correct his companion's statement. "Not so, Friar Paul. She lives farther down the river. I fear me his love has not been rewarded. He travelled here two days ago – I know not why. So, I've come to seek him, in the case that he may need help."

"An interesting story. There's a tale to be told there. Ho, my good woman! A word, if you will."

Friar Paul had turned to call across the kitchen to the cook, who was busy with a large cauldron on the fire. She straightened up and padded over to stand complaisantly by the friar.

"My young friend is seeking his master, a knight," he told her. "What was his name?" he asked Stanford.

"Sir Carlyon de Bernedeslaw. He's come from Chertsey. Have you had a visitor these past few days?"

"Not at all. Not at all. My master, Sir John le Cerre-nore, is away in France with the King. He has forbidden his lady, Patrina, to receive any visitors."

"No one has called and been turned away?"

"No one of rank. No one to see my lord or his lady."

Stanford nodded and returned to his meal. Friar Paul, with a piece of his trencher impaled on the point of his knife, held it, while he looked at his companion. He thought he saw disappointment in the slump of the shoulders and in the desultory way that the food was being eaten. His interest in the youth increased, and he had a sudden suspicion that there was more to the story than there appeared to be. He looked back at his knife and almost unconsciously put the morsel into his mouth. While he masticated and swallowed, he wondered what he could do to help.

"What will you do on the morrow?" he asked at last.

"I must keep seeking. I sense that my master has some connection with this place, but I know not what."

"Think you he's in the castle after all?"

"No, he's not here. But I may find some direction on the morrow. I'll sleep and I'll pray."

"Yes. We can do that."

True to his word, the friar bade Stanford to join him in his devotions after the meal, and he said a special prayer that Stanford would find what he sought. Afterwards they went to sleep in a small room, which was made available for them above the stable. Friar Paul slept well, despite the bugs in the mattress, and the sun had been some half-hour risen when he awoke. He lay on his back and scratched himself for a few seconds. Then he turned his head to look over to where his young companion had gone to sleep. There was not a lot of light coming in through the small window, but Friar Paul was able to see that the mattress had already been placed upright against the wall, and a tremor of disappointment made his arms tremble. Then he heard Stanford's voice.

"Good morning, Father. I've brought in a pail of water, so we can wash."

Friar Paul looked at the door, which was just being closed, and called out a greeting, pleasure at Stanford's presence forcing out the gruffness that he usually displayed first thing in the morning. He stretched out his legs and clenched his arm muscles, relieving some of the stiffness in the joints. Then he pulled himself up into a sitting position. Calmly he observed Stanford, who had his back to him, while he washed. It had been a surprise to him the previous night that the young man had gone to sleep in his clothes, removing only his shoes. Even now, he had not disrobed to wash. Perhaps he was shy and did not want Friar Paul to watch him.

As he idly scratched at his chest, where he had been bitten in the night, it came into Friar Paul's mind that Stanford might perhaps be younger than he had first thought, to be so modest. It was almost as if he were a young maid. Thoughtfully, Friar Paul stared at Stanford, who still had his back to him, but who was now drying his face and hands. The upper part of his bark-brown tunic was very loose-fitting. Friar Paul had noticed the previous night how it fell in folds across the lad's chest and had thought then that it seemed as if it had been made for a larger man. He grunted and began to clamber to his feet, thinking again, as he did so, that the youth would have an interesting tale to tell.

While the friar, clad unselfconsciously only in his shift, stepped over to the pail of water, Stanford seemed to slip round him, hardly turning his face to him. By the time he had finished washing, Stanford had picked the friar's mattress off the floor for him, to place it neatly against his own, and had left the room to go across the yard to the kitchen.

In the kitchen, when he got there, Friar Paul found Stanford at the table with two of the manor servants, eating porridge from a wooden bowl.

"Ho, there, young Stanford!" Friar Paul heartily greeted him. "You were quick to leave me. Why did you not wait until I dressed?"

"I'm sorry, Father. I meant nothing, but I must be on my way."

"So soon?" Surprise and disappointment jostled both in Friar Paul's voice and in his posture, as he sat on the form next to Stanford. "Where are you going? I thought me we would travel together."

"If it's to be, so be it. I must find first where my master lies."

Stanford continued his meal, and Friar Paul left him to it, as he concentrated on his own, keen to get his fill. Meanwhile, Stanford quickly finished. Almost immediately he got to his feet, but it was not to leave. He went to the cook and asked for a shallow dish and some water. Carrying it carefully, he returned to the table. Friar Paul watched with one eye as Stanford sat down and pulled a linen kerchief from a purse on his belt. This he spread out on the table next to the dish of water. The kerchief had been bleached almost white and embroidered with dyed threads. Friar Paul paused in his eating and craned his neck to look at the design. It was intricately abstract, made up of lines, circles and whorls. At first, he could make nothing of it. Then, as he looked, it seemed to quiver and form shapes. Before he could recognise the shapes, he involuntarily blinked, and the design settled back. Again, Friar Paul concentrated, and again the design seemed to quiver and form itself into shapes.

This time Stanford interrupted. He had taken out a swan's feather, about a span in length. He placed this on the kerchief, and as Friar Paul watched, his curiosity still holding his hunger at bay, Stanford reached into his purse again. This time he took out a small flask. Removing the stopper, he sprinkled a few drops of colourless liquid over the feather. Quickly he put the flask back in his purse. Reaching out now, he lifted the kerchief with the feather and laid it carefully in the dish of water. For a few seconds he stared at it through narrowed eyes. Then he put the tip of his right thumb between his teeth and sighed thoughtfully.

"What is it, my son?" asked Friar Paul hoarsely. "Do you see something?"

"I see a town. Spires. A river. Many men in gowns. Do you know such a place? It can hardly be far from here."

"Hm. Many men wearing gowns? A monastery? But that would not be a town. Ah! Of course. I think me the place will be Oxford."

"Is it far?"

"No. Not more than two days, I'll warrant. It lies north of west from here."

"Then I must leave forthwith. My thanks for all your help, Friar Paul, but I must travel alone now. I wish for no company."

"Truly so? I thought me that we would travel together. But as the Lord wills. I am on my way to London. I want to be at St Paul's for Ascension Day. So be it."

Friar Paul watched as Stanford began to wring out his kerchief. For a moment he seemed about to resume what was left of his breakfast, but he lifted his head to speak again. Before he could do so, they were interrupted by the entry into the kitchen of a young woman in her late teens. She came in quickly, and her head moved anxiously as she searched the room.

"They tell me someone is seeking a lost knight," she cried out immediately. "I wish to speak with him."

"Here we are, my daughter," Friar Paul said, raising his hand to indicate Stanford. "Are you a member of this household?"

"Yes, Father. My name is Matty, maidservant to my lady. If you please, are you seeking news of a knight? I also."

The friar nodded. "Here is one who seeks his master, Sir Carlyon de Bernedeslaw."

"Sir Carlyon! What news of him? Is he in these parts? He was sent on a quest by my lady last December and we've heard nought of him since. Can you tell me about him, and about his squire, James?"

Stanford laid his kerchief down on the table and spoke calmly, as if reciting a litany. "I entered his service not long before Christmas last. He was searching for the flowers of the swan for a lady. By misfortune we were pursued for many days through the northern hills by a witch. She almost prevailed, but James bravely sacrificed his life to save his master and defeat the witch."

"James is dead?" Matty sat down on a bench on her side of the table, as if the shock had pushed her. "It grieves me sorely to hear that."

"I also was sorely grieved. And yet, I feel as though his spirit lives on somewhere."

"But Sir Carlyon? You say he's lost. Surely, he be not dead?"

"No, he lives yet, and I will find him. He returned to these parts with the flowers of the swan, to give them to his lady."

"So he succeeded in his quest. I'm right pleased at that. It was my mistress, Lady Patrina, who set him the quest. She's often had him in her thoughts and wished him a safe return. But he's not been here. Mayhap he's gone to her father's castle near Chertsey."

"No, he stayed not there. He came to these parts. I've felt his presence near the river. Something terrible happed there, but I think me I'll find him ere long."

Matty jerked abruptly to her feet. Her body was twitching slightly, and agitation was gripping her face. Friar Paul had been watching her with interest, intrigued by this lost knight who could provoke such reactions. He glanced at Stanford, who seemed to be looking coolly, almost aloofly, at Matty. Momentarily Friar Paul thought that it would be good to go with Stanford to seek out this knight and satisfy his curiosity, but immediately he decided to continue with his expressed intention and go to London. It was as though he knew that he could not go with Stanford. He looked back at Matty as she spoke, her excited words tumbling out.

"I must tell my lady this news. She's been waiting, hoping for Sir Carlyon's return. Would that he had come back sooner. We'll talk again."

She turned and bustled out of the room. Stanford barely watched her go. He tucked his damp kerchief into his belt and let it hang there to dry. Quickly he shook water off the swan's feather and placed it in his pouch. Friar Paul was surprised to see the cook hand him a small package of bread and cold meat, but he realised that if Stanford had spoken earlier to the cook, then he was serious about leaving. Friar Paul looked at what was left of his breakfast and decided that it could wait. As Stanford began putting on his cloak, Friar Paul stood up.

"Stay you not awhile yet? Her Ladyship may have something to tell you."

"No, I can't wait. There's nothing more for me here. This place is full of unhappiness. I want none of it."

"So be it, my son. God's blessing be upon you and may he guide you safely in your travels. I'll pray for you."

Friar Paul made the sign of the cross for Stanford, but the boy hardly acknowledged it.

"Thank you, Father. And thank you also for your help. But I think me you could pray for the people in this place. I sense a great need here." He bent and adjusted his hose in his boots, then, with only a smile of thanks to the cook, he lifted his pack and left.

*

As the dying rays of a setting sun picked out the tops of the buildings in Oxford, a cloaked figure picked its way wearily along the High Street, avoiding the piles of refuse which had collected there during the day. Although the stranger's clothes were dusty, as if after a long journey, the people who were still going about their business before nightfall offered barely a glance. The stranger walked along, looking round occasionally as if searching, and was soon walking along other streets. By the time that day had set its foot on night's neck, the stranger, seemingly still searching, was in Broad Street, where the looming buildings were daubed in shadow deeper than pitch.

Suddenly a flicker of light leaped out, as the door to a tavern opened and a large man roughly threw a younger man out into the roadway. "Get you gone!" he shouted. "And don't come back! You'll not fight in here!"

The young man lay where he had fallen for a few seconds, then quickly hauled himself to his feet. Even in the gloom, it could be seen that he was heavily built, and as he turned to stagger away, he bumped into the stranger, who had been trying to avoid him, while walking past.

"Forgive me, my good sir," the young man slurred, pulling himself up short. "I didn't see you there."

"It matters not, sir," said the stranger, softly but firmly. "No harm done."

The young man straightened himself up and tipsily tried to look in control of himself. "They don't want my business there. Ha! I had no mind to stay. They get such a low crowd in there." He tried to look closely at the muffled stranger in the moonlight. "Shall we go for a drink somewhere? I know a better place."

"Thank you, good sir, but I'm looking for lodgings. I'm a stranger in town."

"I can tell from your voice you're a stranger. And you seek lodgings? I've lodgings with some other students not far away. There'll be room for you, I trow. And they'll have some good ale. My name is Jan. Come you now?"

He launched himself off and the stranger fell into step beside him, seemingly content with the offer of lodgings. They walked in an eastward direction, Jan swaying slightly and occasionally catching the stranger's shoulder with his arm. The stranger, who was almost a head shorter than Jan, looked to be in danger of being knocked over once or twice, but they continued without mishap for some minutes. Then, as they turned into a dark alley, Jan's foot caught in a small pothole. Unable to prevent himself, he fell heavily onto his companion. Reaching out to hold the stranger and regain his tipsy balance, his weight dragged the two of them down onto the ground. This seemed to amuse Jan, and he began to giggle. The stranger, pinned down by his bulk, was not so amused, and tried to wriggle out. As if realising this, Jan drew up his legs to get to his knees. In doing so, one of his hands unthinkingly went under his companion's cloak, which had come loose during the tumble, and pushed on the chest. The material of the tunic was thick and coarse, but Jan clearly felt through it a soft, rounded female breast. He stopped trying to get to his knees and felt more carefully. It seemed that the stranger, whom he had assumed to be a young man, was in fact a full-grown woman.

"Ho! What have we here?" he said hoarsely.

The stranger, who had stiffened at his touch, now began struggling to escape once more. This seemed to excite Jan. He pulled at the tunic on the stranger's thighs and probed with his hand beneath. This confirmed for him that he was indeed dealing with a woman.

"Damn! A strumpet! Well met, I vow. I'll give you some trade." Roughly he tugged at the tunic to pull it over the hips.

His victim now began to kick out wildly with her legs, and to jerk her body. "Let me go! Let me go!" she cried, fear pushing her voice into a higher register than normal. "Leave me alone! I don't want this."

Jan seemed not to hear. His victim's tunic was now clear of her hips, but in the darkness there was nothing to see. Her legs were still flailing. Viciously he hit at them, and after several blows they lay still.

"Don't deny me," he grunted. "I'll take it now."

He roughly pulled her legs apart. Then he knelt in between them, pushing them farther apart with his knees. His victim had been crying out in pain during his onslaught. Now she reached up in the darkness and scratched at his face. At the same time, she began to shout.

"Help! Help me! Help me!"

In response, Jan poured blows onto her jerking head and body with both fists. One blow, sharper than the others, hit her chin and she slumped, unconscious.

2

She was unsure what it was that woke her. There was pain. The whole of her body was aching, and as she tried to move, to stretch, her legs seemed clogged with chains. She tried to hold herself still and collect her thoughts. She was in a bed in a room. Light was coming in through gaps in the window shutter, enabling her to see that she was in a somewhat sparsely furnished little room. She could hear sounds from elsewhere in the house. There were voices, rattles. Then her door opened, and a plump, middle-aged woman came in.

"Ah, my dear," she said with a calm smile, "you be awake now."

"I've been sleeping?"

"Yes. I gave you something to help you sleep, when you were brought in. You were moaning so much with the pain. You've been badly beaten."

"A sleeping draught?" she said, almost to herself. "The pain is hard. I was attacked. By a student, I trow. He wanted… I know not an' he did."

"Fear not, my dear. You were rescued in time, by God's grace. But you must still rest."

"I thank you for your kindness, mistress. May I know where I am?"

"This be my house, dear. I let out rooms to travellers. My name is Ursula, the widow Headington. You've travelled far, I'll warrant."

"I have. I'm Mary, the thatcher's daughter, from Lancashire. I seek a lost knight, Sir Carlyon de Bernedeslaw. He's in Oxford, I trow."

"There be knights here. They come and go. Mayhap you'll find him."

"I know I will." Then, bethinking herself, "What of the one who rescued me? Do you know his name?"

"Yea, and right well. It was none other than Robin, one of my tablers. You were lucky, I trow. Yester e'en he decided to go down to the river, and he was on his way back, otherwise he would have been in my parlour with his companion."

"I would fain thank this Robin. Can I see him?"

"Not until this even. He and Henry are goliards and they be out seeking money. You must rest. You'll see him then. I'll bring you some broth and we'll see to easing your pains."

Mary smiled, and a soft beauty limned her face in the dim light. She wanted to rest.

By evening she was feeling much better, although there was still a lot of pain in her legs, where the thigh muscles had been badly bruised by her attacker's blows. Her face and body were also signed with bruises, but their pain was a dull ache that only poked at her if she moved. When Ursula brought in a bowl of stew, Mary pulled herself up into a sitting position. Her facial grimaces and gasps of discomfort seemed to alarm Ursula.

"Don't you be doing anything silly, my dear. You still need rest."

"I want to sit up. I've been lying on my back all day. To move is good. I must get better soon and carry on my search."

"The morrow will be soon enough. Eat up now. Robin and Henry have returned. They're having supper, and I'll bring them in when they've finished."

Mary ate slowly, enjoying the food, and she had not finished when Ursula came back into the room. A man stood in the doorway behind her. Mary looked at him curiously. She guessed him to be in his early thirties, although his long hair and short beard may have made him look older than he was. His build was medium, and he had a friendly face which was lit up by a broad grin.

"This be Henry, my dear," Ursula told her.

Henry's eyes twinkled when he greeted Mary, and she smiled in response. Then, as he moved into the room, she was able to see the second man, who had appeared somewhat hesitantly in the doorway. He was more sturdily built than Henry, and taller, so that he had to stoop slightly to pass under the lintel. In the light from the unshuttered window his quietly smiling face could be clearly seen. Mary's body stiffened, her aches forgotten. Her heart jumped into her throat and seemed to push words out of her mouth.

"Carlyon! It's you."

The words seemed to have no effect on either of the two men. They continued to smile, almost tolerantly.

Ursula glanced at them and then bent over Mary, as if to reassure her. "That be Robin, my dear. He's the man who rescued you and brought you here."

"That's right," confirmed Henry, nodding his head in emphasis. "He was coming back here when he found you being attacked by that knave. He pulled him off and gave him a beating."

Mary's brow furrowed. Confusion was making her falter. Then she found words. "You are Robin? Do you not know me?"

"You're the poor woman I came upon last even," Robin said at last.

His voice was calm and well-modulated. Mary recognised it as clearly as she had the face. She refused to believe that she was mistaken, but caution urged her to tread carefully. She slowly shifted her legs under the blanket to make them more comfortable. The ache had returned.

"I've seen you ere this," she said. "I met you in Lancashire. Do you not remember?"

"Alas, no. I've no memories beyond a week or so gone."

"I've tried to get him to remember," broke in Henry. "It's as if he suddenly appeared in the river. Perchance he had been held by evil spirits in an underground cavern and had forced an escape. No matter. He was unconscious and like to drown when I came upon him. I pulled him out and cared for him. He had a wound on his temple, as if he had been struck, but no other harm, it seemed. Even so, when he spoke, he could remember neither his name, nor where he was from. So I gave him the name Robin, and we are waiting to see if his memory returns."

"Pray God, it will," said Robin, and Mary was struck by the note of anxiety in his voice. "I've no memory even of being in the river. Yet I oft-times feel strangely drawn to rivers. That was why I was out yester even. I had been taken by a sudden desire to go to the riverside and watch the swans. It was so calming."

"I call him Robin of the River," Henry said, smiling fondly at his charge. "Mayhap at some time he had been bewitched and had been changed into a swan."

Robin's eyes had had a faraway look while he had been speaking. Now he focused directly on Mary, who, despite herself, blushed slightly and momentarily lowered her eyes.

"I want to remember, whether it be good or bad. Do you know who I am? You say you saw me in Lancashire? What part of the country is that? Am I from there?"

"You are the one I saw. I know it to be so. You spent some months this past winter and spring in my mother's house. You are a knight, and you were on a quest to find the flowers of the swan. Remember you nought of that?"

Robin furrowed his brow and then shook his head. "Nought. Nought. There's nothing. Say you, I'm a knight?"

He sounded disbelieving, but Henry nodded thoughtfully.

"A knight? Mayhap that be so. The armour and the shield in the pouch will belong to you. And you had a fine sword belted round your waist. Do you know his family, my dear? Are they nearby?"

Mary moved her head slowly from side to side in negation. She was wondering what to do. This was not how she had envisaged her reunion with Carlyon. She decided to take things slowly, hoping that that would make the situation easier to control. "His father's house is near to London, I ween, but I know nought of his family."

"This be a strange tale," said Ursula, almost beaming in her interest. "Witchcraft lies behind it, I trow."

Robin looked nervous, but Henry laughed.

"I met a man one time on my travels. He had been struck on the head in battle and left lying with the dead. When he came to his senses, he could remember nought of the battle, nor how he came to be there. He wandered around for many months, begging for his food. Then one day, he was found by his wife, who had gone seeking him. She took him home, and, surrounded by familiar things, slowly his memory came back."

"Do I have a wife?" asked Robin, sounding almost hopeful.

"No," Mary assured him, "you are a bachelor." She decided not to tell him that he had been in love with the daughter of an earl. She had a fear of the consequences of his remembering that.

"There is your father's house," suggested Henry. "If that could be found, then mayhap you would remember who you are."

"Who knows if his father's house can be found?" said Ursula, folding her arms across her ample bosom, as if dismissing that idea. "Say you, Mary, that he spent some months at your mother's house?"

"Indeed so, Mistress Ursula. He spent a happy time there."

"That be it. We have it in our hand. There be no need to seek for it. Perchance if he returns there, he will remember it?"

"I think so also," agreed Mary. "My mother is a wise woman. She has many herbs and nostrums. I'm sure she'll be able to help."

Robin had unconsciously moved closer to the bed. He now looked into Mary's beautiful blue eyes and seemed to be drawing hope from her. "Can we travel there?" he asked.

"Assuredly. As soon as I'm recovered."

"Then I want to go. What think you, Henry?"

"I'd be sorry to part. You're a good goliard. You have an uncommon talent for rhyming. Even so, we must do what we can to restore you."

"So be it, then." Robin spoke decisively. "I'll be forever grateful that you pulled me from the river, but I would fain find out what kind of man I truly am. God speed your recovery, Mary, and we shall leave together."

He smiled at her, and despite the pain which still gripped her body, she smiled calmly back. Ursula also smiled, as if satisfied, and although Robin wanted to question Mary more, Ursula gently drove the two men out of the room, so that Mary could rest.

The rest seemed to help. By the next day Mary's condition had improved and she even took a few steps out of bed. Much of her body was patterned with a quilt of purpling bruises, but the aching was less, and she was confident of her recovery. In the evening, she joined the others for supper, and afterwards Robin sat with her to talk. He was curious to find out what she knew about him.

"I had nary a thought ever to meet someone who knew who I was. I thought I'd been plucked from the river after being bewitched and I had had no other life."

"Mayhap you *had* been bewitched. You were being driven by a force greater than you could resist."

"I think me you've broken that spell. I had accepted my life with Henry, but now I want to return to the life I had before Henry found me in the river. Who am I?"

"As I told you last even, you're a knight, the son of an earl, and your name is Carlyon."

He shook his head and said, "Carlyon? I've been thinking on it this past night and day, but it calls nought to my mind. But so be it. If Carlyon is my name, then I'll take it and bid farewell to Robin. That served me sufficiently, but now I'm Carlyon again."

He pulled himself up confidently, and Mary smiled, her happiness suffusing her face with a gentle beauty. His assumption of authority pleased her.

"Were you in service with my family?" Carlyon asked her.

"No. I'd been imprisoned by a wizard called Thomas, and you rescued me but last year, shortly before Christmas. Then we travelled through the northern hills, pursued by a witch, until you and your squire James killed her."

"An amazing tale. I wish me that I could remember it. But what was I doing in those parts?"

Mary did not answer straight away. For a second she paused, held by a hurdle of unsureness, but then she decided to tell him part of the reason. "You'd been sent on a quest by a lady who desired amusement. She had heard that special flowers grow where a swan has died. Nothing would please her, but that some of those flowers were brought for her. Ah me, there was a curse on anyone who picks such flowers. That, I ween, is why you have lost all memory of your previous life."

"Of course. I've been cursed. I understand. We must find a way to lift the curse."

"My mother will help. Mayhap in another day I'll be able to travel and we can leave."

Mary smiled encouragingly, and in response Carlyon smiled back, his wide green eyes bright with optimism.

Although it would take them many days to reach Mary's home, Carlyon and she were walking slowly. Carlyon had been impatient to leave, but now that they were on their way, he was caring towards Mary. At Ursula's suggestion, they were travelling as brother and sister, having agreed that that might be simpler. Carlyon had no way of proving his supposed lineage, so it would be unwise for him to claim to be a knight. Fortunately, the weather was in their favour. The winds were light, and the May sunshine warmed their backs as they walked. Carlyon let Mary lean on him, and he occasionally gave her a rhyme to help to keep their spirits up. Mary spoke to him about the time that he had spent at her mother's house, but he still remembered nothing.

"It matters not as yet," he said at one point. "I love to hear your stories. You have a beautiful voice. It plays so sweetly on my ear."

"My accent is so different from yours. There are folk in the south who find it barbaric."

He laughed. "They are the barbarians."

It was true that he found her accent attractive. He had no difficulty in understanding what she said, as if he were accustomed to such sounds. From time to time when speaking, he deliberately pronounced a word in the way that Mary would, and that amused her. He was pleased that he was able to make her happy, but he did not know why.

By the afternoon of the third day, however, Carlyon could clearly see that Mary was beginning to flag. He thought it best that they rest for a day or two, even though Mary resisted.

"I'm sure, if I keep walking, it'll help my legs. If we walk slowly, we can manage."

"If we walk more slowly, we'll be going backwards, I trow. No, there'll be no harm in taking a day to rest."

He spoke to a peasant working in a field and obtained directions to a monastery, which was less than a league distant. So, they left the highway and struck off through a bluebell-strewn wood. At the other side they followed a track which took them up a slight slope. The wood was on their left and grazing land for sheep on their right. As they approached the brow of the slope, they saw that a beech tree had fallen. It was partially intruding into the path, and Carlyon guided Mary onto the pasture, so that they would be able to walk by it. The branches ahead of them were thick with fresh green leaves, which surprised Carlyon, until he realised that the tree must have fallen only that day.

"Thank Our Lord, we were not walking past earlier, when it happened," he told Mary cheerily.

"I wonder why it fell?"

"Who knows? Mayhap a strong wind? But look there," he said, indicating the lower part of the fallen trunk. "We could sit on the trunk and rest for a few moments."

The severed roots, thick with pale brown soil, formed a solid halo round the now-horizontal base of the tree. Carlyon and Mary stepped round this and approached the smoky grey trunk, which was near enough as thick across as the length of a man's arm. They moved along until the trunk was low enough to sit on. Carlyon was about to lift Mary up, when a voice called out to them.

"Ho! You, there! A hand here, quickly."

They looked round, and as the voice peremptorily barked out the order again, Carlyon saw that it was coming from under the leaves farther along. He hurried over and, peering through, saw a young man lying there, trapped by the fallen trunk. He seemed of slight build, but he was well dressed in close-fitting silken hose, a deep blue tunic, and a long surcoat with tight, bejewelled sleeves. His face would have been handsome, had there not been a prominent wart above his left eyebrow.

"Stand not staring like idle kine," the man snapped. "Get me out of here."

"At once, Your Lordship," said Carlyon, and he grasped at a protruding branch.

His intention was to pull it up and roll it over, but he realised immediately that that was an impossible task. Nevertheless, with Mary's help he did pull at the branch. He noticed no difference, but it must have made the trunk move fractionally, because the young man squealed in pain.

"Hold clear, you oaf! Do you want to crush me even more?"

Carlyon and Mary stood back, and Carlyon looked up and down the tree. They would need to cut the man free, which would need an axe, and probably other men to prop up the trunk. He was about to tell the man this, when Mary tapped his arm.

"Use your sword," she said quietly. "I think me it will cut away this wood."

Carlyon glanced over at his pack, which was lying where he had left it, his scabbard tied firmly to it. Hurrying over, he grasped the hilt and pulled out the sword. Not since shortly after his rescue from the river, when he had curiously examined it, had he pulled out the sword. Now he hefted it, pleased at how comfortable it felt in his hand, and noting how light flashed up and down the blade in rippling streams. Lost in his pleasure, he would have continued practising feints, but the man called harshly to ask what he was about.

Carlyon moved back to where the man was lying. For a second or two he looked at the branches, then chose one. He swung the sword round, and the blade sliced through the wood as if it were soft clay. His eyes widened in surprise at how easily it had cut, and he paused momentarily. Mary was standing slightly away, with her arms akimbo. She smiled and nodded when Carlyon caught her eye. Raising the sword, he hacked at a few more of the branches. There was resistance to the blade, he could feel it. But the sword cut through them, whatever the thickness, as easily as it had the first branch. With five strokes he had cleared his way, so that he could get up to the trunk where the man was trapped. The man had made no sound of pain while the cutting was in progress, so Carlyon was encouraged to hack at the trunk. This time the man spoke, as Carlyon grasped the hilt with both hands and lifted it above his head.

"Have a care, you rogue! Don't shake the tree."

Carlyon paused, but then the sword seemed to tingle in his hands. Confidence seemed to flow down his arms and into his shoulder muscles like liquid iron. He knew that there was no other way forward. Almost letting the sword fall of its own accord, he brought it down on the fallen tree. The trunk was little more than twelve inches thick at this part, and the sword went in a good half-way. When Carlyon pulled, it came out with no resistance at all. Down again, this time at a slight angle, and he took out a V-shaped wedge. One more blow and the trunk was severed.

This time the man said nothing. He had tensed his body when the blows were struck, but the tree had not moved. Now he watched slyly as Carlyon walked round him and took two steps along the trunk to cut again. Three more strokes and the man was able to push the severed piece off his body. Carlyon helped him to move it away and then, with Mary's help, he got the man to his feet.

Having been rescued, the man's attitude became more gracious. "Blessings be upon you. A watchful angel sent you along this way."

He flexed his legs slightly, as he leaned on Carlyon, gasping a little from time to time. Yet despite the obvious discomfort he was in, he kept glancing – anxiously, so Carlyon thought – along the fallen trunk towards where the roots were poking upwards.

"How came you to be under this tree, Your Lordship?" Carlyon asked.

"I was doing some work there. This land is my father's – Lord Colhurst. I'm Martin, my father's eldest son. He'll reward you for this day's work."

"You're very gracious, my lord. My name is Carlyon, and this is my sister Mary."

Martin made no acknowledgement, as if the names of peasants were unimportant, so Carlyon went on.

"We'll help you back home now, if you're ready."

Without speaking, Martin removed himself from Carlyon's support and tried a couple of steps. He seemed able to walk, and he nodded, though seemingly more to his own satisfaction than to Carlyon's. With his face set, Carlyon picked up his sword and went to put it back in its scabbard. When he turned and picked up his pack, he noticed that Martin was looking nervously in his direction, but not quite at him. Glancing backwards, he saw for the first time that there were a pick and a spade amongst the roots. Thinking that Martin was worried about them, he put his pack down and went to get them out. As he pulled at them, he saw something else in the disturbed earth. Clearing away some of the soil, he pulled out a small wooden casket, bound with rusty iron bands. Before he could say anything, Martin had struggled quickly over, and it was taken from Carlyon's hands.

"That's mine! It belongs to my family. That was what I was seeking, when I dug at the roots and disturbed the tree."

Momentarily, Carlyon stood with his hands in the same position where they had been when holding the casket. Then his surprise at Martin's sudden action subsided and he let his arms drop. He had no grounds for complaint and no reason to doubt Martin's claim that a casket found on his family's land belonged to his family.

Martin spoke again, somewhat peremptorily. "I'll go home now. Give me your arm, my man."

Carlyon hung his pack on his shoulders and offered an arm. When they set off, he walked slowly, but more for Mary's sake than the young lord's. They had not far to go, however. In little more than fifteen minutes they arrived at a fortified manor house. It was a large place, almost a small castle, and when they walked through the gate into the yard, Carlyon looked around curiously as they walked across to the main house. To his far left he saw a cleared area of beaten earth. It was empty except for a pole firmly fixed into the ground. On top of the pole was a crosstree, with some sort of target board hanging from one end and a thick, dumpy bag from the other. Carlyon's brow furrowed over the purpose of this equipment. He had never seen such a thing before. Away to his right, there were empty animal pens, for use during the night, but Martin, leaning on his arm, obscured much of what else there might have been to see in that direction.

Martin had called out as they crossed the yard, and people came running. To one he gave the casket to carry. Another was sent to prepare refreshment for him. A third was sent for the pick and the spade, which had been left by the tree. When they were all in the main building, Martin brusquely told his personal servant to help him to his chamber. Then he seemed to remember his rescuers, who were now standing to one side.

"Take these two and give them food in the kitchen," he told a man. "I would speak with them later."

With no further acknowledgement, he leaned on his servant and moved away. Carlyon had observed Martin's behaviour with an impassive face since they had reached Martin's home. Nevertheless, he was oddly interested in how lords behaved, although he had no wish to behave like that himself. As a servant clicked his fingers to draw his attention, Carlyon smiled at Mary and offered her his arm for support. Together they followed the man and were soon seated at a rough wooden table in the kitchen, waiting for food to be served up to them.

"We can stay here and rest for a few days," Carlyon told Mary, looking round the kitchen. "It'll be good for us."

"Mayhap so."

Carlyon glanced at Mary, struck by the note of unsureness in her voice, and she went on.

"I don't feel easy in my mind about this lord Martin. I would not we waited here too long."

"We'll surely have nought but goodwill from him. But we won't stay here too long. We must continue to your mother's house. Rest you for a while now, and we'll make good time when we set off again."

He smiled and put a brotherly hand of reassurance over her smaller hand, which was resting on the table. She smiled back and did not move her hand until he took his away.

When they had finished their meal, they were sent for and taken to Martin's chamber. He was reclining on his bed, leaning back against silk-covered pillows. He languidly waved them over as they entered, dismissed his attendants, and then rested his gaze on the two of them, as they stood before him. Carlyon was slightly in front of Mary, and he looked curiously at Martin, interested again in how the nobility lived. Then he watched as Martin fingered a small leather purse on the bed beside him.

"It was well for me that you came along," Martin said graciously. "And well, i' faith, that you had such a sword to cut the tree. I doubt me I've seen the like. Where did you get such a sword?"

"I remember not for certain, Your Lordship. I've always had it." Carlyon was speaking truthfully, but a cautious feeling made him not want to go into details. "Mayhap it was my father's." It had crossed his mind to say that his father was reputedly an earl, but as he had no proof, he decided to stay silent on that. Martin would likely take him as an impostor, who was wishing to claim some inheritance to which he was not entitled.

"Hm, it is strange that a peasant should have such a sword, but perchance your father did some great service to a lord. No matter. I would that I had such a fine sword. I'll buy it from you. Here's a bag of nigh five hundred pence."

Martin picked up the bag and shook it. Carlyon heard the silver clink. It was a lot of money, over a year's wage for a labourer, and his lips tightened in thoughtfulness. Martin did not leave him much time for reflection.

"See now, my man, you can take this bag away with you. What need have you of a sword? Bring it up to me and the deal is done."

Carlyon acknowledged the sense of the words, despite the rather arrogant tone in which they were delivered. He was not fully convinced, but before he could say anything, he felt Mary lightly grasp his upper arm.

"I think it meet that the sword should not be sold," she said, looking at Martin, but speaking softly into Carlyon's ear.

"I think it also meet," said Carlyon. The firmness of his decision surprised him, it had come so suddenly, but he went on confidently. "I must keep the sword – until I find something I seek."

"Come now, my man."

A persuasive smile creased Martin's face, and it seemed to Carlyon as though there was a hand on his back, pushing him towards the young lord. The atmosphere in the room had become thicker, almost stifling. He wanted to leave, to get out into the freer air, but something seemed to be holding him. His gaze was fixed on Martin's face, listening to his baited words.

"The sword is nought to you. It's a knight's weapon. You'll have no use for it, I trow. Look now, with this money you'll be able to go home and live for a year or more. Mayhap you'll buy a small piece of land? You'll have a fine dowry for your sister. What say you? Bring the sword to me and all this money is yours."

The voice fell silent, but the words still seemed to hover around them like watchful flies. Before Carlyon could say or do anything, he felt Mary's hand squeeze his arm. His body gave an almost imperceptible jerk. It was as if a molten grain of gold had passed through his brain. He set his mouth and shook his head from side to side.

"No, Your Lordship. The sword is not for barter. We thank you for your hospitality and we're grateful for the chance to rest."

Carlyon prepared himself to resist further persuasions, but Martin's face changed its expression. The smiling friendliness became disdainful boredom. Martin turned his face away slightly, as if it had become tiresome for him to look at them. He let go of the bag of money, and it fell with a soft chinking onto the bed beside him. Then he limply moved his hand in a gesture of dismissal.

"So be it," he said, still not deigning to look at them. "I'll send you a small reward on the morrow. Stay as long as you wish."

Carlyon and Mary backed out of the room. In the passageway outside Carlyon looked questioningly at Mary, but she just shook her head, as if warning him not to speak. She touched his arm as a signal, and he followed as she began to move away. He realised that they did not need to speak about what had just taken place.

When he awoke the next morning, dawn had broken. He had been sleeping in a room with some of the manor's serving men, and they had already gone about their business. He got out of his bed and saw that a small wooden bowl of water had been left for him. Gratefully he wet his face and his hands. It was while drying himself that he noticed something amiss with his sword. It was with his pack at the foot of his bed, in its scabbard tied to the pack. It seemed to him that there was something different about the hilt of the sword. He stepped over and curiously examined it. He pulled the sword out of the scabbard and knew as soon as he touched it that it was not his sword. At first, he hoped that one of his fellow sleepers had taken the sword and mistakenly replaced it with another, but he knew that none of them had a sword. He anxiously examined the room, but there was no sign of his sword.

3

Carlyon was sitting on the end of his bed. There had been no thought in his mind that his scanty belongings would be in danger of theft. How could something so large as his sword have been stolen? His brow furrowed in thought, as he sat and considered what might have happened. It seemed clear to him that one of his night-time companions had stolen the sword. But he had no idea which one, nor how to prove such an accusation. Ill fortune had brought him and Mary to this place. He checked his pack, but nothing else had been taken. Not that there was anything else of value. Except for his shield. That was still there, and he picked it up.

He had a feeling that this sword and this shield went together, but he could not think how or why. Holding the shield in both hands, he rocked it to and fro slightly, while he sought for inspiration on what to do. The room was gloomy, and shadows were everywhere, even though the window shutter had been tied back. Suddenly, it seemed to him that there was a face on the shield, where the boss had been. He tried to look more closely, but there was not enough light. Then, before he could do anything, he seemed to hear a voice in his ear. It was low and sonorous, but the words were clear.

"The lord Martin has taken the sword. He is keeping it in his bedchamber."

As if spellbound, Carlyon asked softly, "Who are you?"

He again heard a voice as if in his ear.

"I am as familiar as your heartbeat. There is a task to be done."

"Do you know who I am? Can you tell me that?"

Carlyon had spoken clearly, but there was no voice in response. Straining in the gloom, he looked at the shield, but even the features of the face were gone now. If he had heard a voice, if he had seen a face, they were gone. He jerked to his feet and went over to the window. In the light there he examined the shield. It was no different from before. Its metal was smooth and shiny. Carlyon rubbed the palm of his hand gently over the boss. It was slightly cool to the touch, and unyielding. He looked thoughtfully across the room, as he leaned his back against the window ledge.

It was only a few seconds. He knew, almost without thought, that he must speak to Mary. Putting his left arm through the shield's straps and pulling it over his shoulder so that it rested on his back, he went off in search of her. He found her in the kitchen, where she was already eating some breakfast porridge with some other servants who had come in from their work. She smiled to see him. Then her face contracted slightly in puzzlement, as if surprised to see him carrying his shield. He shook his head as a warning, and she merely wished him a good day. As he sat down beside her with his bowl, he bent his head towards her.

"I would talk with you privily later," he whispered.

She nodded but did not have too long to wait. Most of the servants were soon about their business and they were able to speak in private.

Carlyon quickly told her that his sword had been taken. "Another sword has been put in its place, as if in hopes I would not notice it until we were far away," he said. "Lord Martin has taken it. It's in his bedchamber."

"How do you know?"

He hesitated. "My shield told me. I saw a face on it and heard a voice."

"Ah, yes. You've said your shield has spoken before."

"You know that?" He had been doubting the evidence of his eyes and ears. "What magic is this?" And he reached behind his back to touch the shield. "What is this shield?"

"I know not. But it is your familiar, your protector. It's good that it also wasn't taken."

"Hm. But I must get back the sword. It's part of my life before I forgot it. I can't let it go. It may help me to remember."

"That's so. You must reclaim it."

"How? I can't accuse Lord Martin of stealing it. He's too powerful."

Mary thoughtfully put her thumb between her teeth for a few seconds. Then she spoke. "We must steal it back. That's the only way."

"I think me you're right. I must get into his chamber and search for it. It surely can't be hard to find."

A servant girl passed behind them, about her business, and Carlyon stopped speaking. When the girl was out of earshot, he looked at Mary.

"It must be done soon," he muttered. "I'll watch for a chance."

"I also can watch, while you're in the chamber. It would not be good for you to be caught there."

Carlyon nodded thoughtfully. He drew in a breath, as if it were determination. Firmly he placed one hand on the table, about to push himself to his feet, but before he could do so, the steward came into the room. He caught Carlyon's eye and came over to him.

"My lord Martin has sent this for you, as a reward for your help yesterday. He wishes you well for your journey."

Leaning across the table, he laid a small linen purse in front of Carlyon. It clinked slightly, and Carlyon put out his hand to pick it up. Then, seeing the steward turn away to leave, he spoke quickly.

"We would rest today and leave on the morrow. Shall we see His Lordship this forenoon?"

The steward looked disdainfully at the two peasants sitting at the table. "My lord is unwell and will be keeping close within his chamber this day. His business with you has been concluded, I trow."

Carlyon inclined his head slightly in assent, but neither he nor Mary spoke until the steward had left the room. Then Carlyon glanced towards the end of the table, where a woman was preparing a chicken for broiling. She had stopped her work while the steward had been there, idly curious at what he had been saying to the two strangers. Carlyon bent his head close to Mary's and spoke softly.

"Let's into the yard. We must talk more on this."

Getting to his feet, he picked up the small purse left by the steward and pushed it into the larger purse hanging from his belt. Then he led the way out. The yard at the back was almost empty. The animals penned in overnight had been taken out to the meadows. A farrier was working near the stables, and a man was chopping wood over at the other side. Carlyon and Mary began to walk slowly round the yard in a large circle.

"This will be difficult," said Carlyon. "I'll have to wait until the midnight and hope His Lordship doesn't waken."

"He may be a light sleeper. I doubt me a search can be done so quietly. We need a sleeping draught."

"That may be so, but how to find?"

"My mother has taught me such things. I'll go out now to seek what I need."

Carlyon watched her go out of the gate and out of sight, before walking round to the front of the house. His way took him past the tilting yard, where two young men were practising. He stopped to watch as they took turns to canter down and strike the target with their lances. It was not long before he was rewarded, when one of the men missed his hit and the sack swung round on the pivot to give him a solid blow. Carlyon joined in the laughter of the other onlookers and then watched with renewed interest. There were more such misses, and as he closely observed the practice sallies, it seemed to him that the way to avoid being hit by the weighted sack was to hit the target directly in the centre. He found himself judging the expertise of the two men. The principle seemed simple enough, and he wondered how he would fare. Almost ruefully he shook his head and moved away, to continue his investigation of the layout of the house and grounds, ready for his and Mary's hoped-for departure that night.

It was almost dinner time before Mary returned. Carlyon was helping to spread straw at the stable when he noticed her come in through the gate. Leaning his fork against the wall, he hurried over to meet her. A smile lit up her face like warm sunlight as soon as she saw him.

"Did you find what you need?" he asked.

She nodded happily. "The woods nearby gave me enough. I must dry some leaves and grind some root, but I will be able to make a potion. We can then slip it into his food, or mayhap his drink."

"We must do that." He nervously pinched his nostrils between his thumb and forefinger as he thought about it. "Pray God, we'll have our chance."

"We must make it so. Then we can leave this place and go home."

"We shall do it. I've been to see Lord Martin's chamber. I'll be able to find it in the dark – I've made careful note of his door. Also, I've examined the postern. I've not been idle this morn."

"By my troth, that's so." And she gave him another smile of encouragement, which made his breath feel hot in his throat. "Let's in to dinner now. I'll prepare my draught this afternoon and then I'll help in the kitchen. My chance to slip it into Lord Martin's supper will surely come."

By evening Carlyon had perfected his plan of action. He would wait until the others in his sleeping chamber were asleep and then creep out. It crossed his mind that it would be easier if he took his pack out of the room beforehand and hid it somewhere else. That way there would be no unnecessary noise, should the pack or the shield knock on something. When he saw Mary at supper, she told him that Lord Martin's meal had been taken to his room.

"When will he be asleep?" Carlyon asked.

"Within the hour, I trow. Then he'll sleep till sunrise. If he awakens late, 'twill be blamed yet on yesterday's accident."

"I would it were sunset now. I'm burning for us to be on our way."

"I also." She laid a hand lightly on his arm. "But we must be patient and act carefully."

Carlyon nodded. He knew that she was right, but it made it no easier. Even when darkness fell and people began preparations for bed, time seemed to move as if moisture had got into the hourglass and clogged the sand. In the sleeping chamber, there was no eagerness to sleep at first. The men spoke across to each other, as they lay in their beds, retelling events of the day. Gradually, however, the comments became more desultory, as one by one the men settled down. In the end there was only one speaking, almost to himself, as he finished his story. The soft voice seemed to lull, and Carlyon's mind began to wander.

All of a sudden, he came to with a start. He had almost fallen asleep. The lone voice had stopped and there were now just the sounds of breathing and rustles, as people turned and moved, to stretch their tired limbs and drift away into sleep. Fearful that he also would fall asleep, Carlyon carefully sat up on his mattress, and in the deep darkness he pulled up his knees and waited.

When the regularity of the breathing made him think that it was safe to move, he reached for his overtunic, which was by his pillow, and got carefully to his feet. The shuttered window had a faint glimmer of light round it but gave no help to Carlyon. Fortunately, his bed was nearest to the door. A few steps and he was there. Except that, in the darkness, he had misjudged slightly. It was the wall. Gingerly he felt along it, and to his relief his fingers felt wood. Now he sought the door handle. There was a loud groan from the hinges as he opened the door, and anxiety stilled his movements. There was restlessness in the room, but he had to continue. Hopefully any disturbed sleepers would assume that someone was going to the privy. He moved the door again, and there was a gap through which he could squeeze. After closing the door behind him, he stood in the passageway and drew in a deep breath that was as much for relief as for respiration. Quickly he slipped his tunic over his head and fastened his belt round his waist. For a moment he stood and listened. There was no worrying sound. Keeping a hand on the wall for guidance, he set off down the dark passage.

He came upon Mary near the kitchen area. She had already lit the stub of a candle and was coming to seek him. After greeting each other in low whispers, Carlyon took the candle and led the way to Martin's bedchamber. At the door, he paused before opening.

"The hinges may squeak," he whispered.

"It matters not. The young lord will hear nothing."

Carlyon opened the door, so that he would be able to slip in. There was no noise. The young lord's hinges, it seemed, were kept greased. Inside the room, he held up the candle. Before he could do anything, he heard a low, ominous growling. Looking in the direction of the noise, he saw that there was a dog at the foot of the bed. It was on its haunches, as if ready to leap. Its lips were curled back, and Carlyon could see candlelight glinting off its teeth. He stepped quickly back out through the door and closed it.

"He has a hound in there with him," he told a surprised Mary. "If it doesn't attack me, it'll bark to bring the house running."

"Move away from the door." Mary took his arm to move him down the passage. When they stopped, she went on, "We must give the hound some of the sleeping draught. We'll find meat in the kitchen."

Carlyon let out his breath in irritation, but there was nothing else that they could do, so he led the way back to the kitchen. There, Mary knew where to look. Cutting open a small piece of meat, she inserted some of her potion.

"Put this inside the door and you should be safe."

"How long will it take to work?"

She shrugged. "Not long, I ween. We shall see."

"Time is passing. The longer we take, the more chance that we shall be discovered."

"Then let's about it."

Back at Martin's chamber, Carlyon opened the door enough to throw the meat towards the dog. He left a gap at the open door, so as to be able to hear the meat being eaten. The dog then came snuffling at the door, as if seeking more, but soon there was silence. Carlyon looked at Mary, but she shook her head warningly and he waited a few more minutes. At last, he pushed the door a little wider. Holding the candle, he looked in. The dog was lying on the floor. With a glance at Mary, Carlyon went into the room. The dog stayed as it was.

Carlyon looked around. There was no sign of the sword, but he had not expected there to be. He saw a wardrobe first, and he stepped over to it. It held only clothes. Apart from the bed, there was nothing else in the room except for a washstand and a large wooden chest. This stood on the floor under the window. It was knee-high and near as long as a small man's body. Disappointment beat painfully at Carlyon's brain when he tried the lid and found that it was locked. He looked around. The key must be in the room. There was only one place – the bed.

He moved across to the bed so quickly that the candle flame flickered wildly in the draught and almost went out. Cupping it with his hand, he went down on one knee to look under the bed. Then he got up and opened the curtain, so that he could feel under the pillow. Careful as he was, Martin nevertheless shifted restlessly. Carlyon stopped abruptly, but Martin did not awaken. Carlyon continued to probe but found nothing. As he withdrew his arm, the candle in his other hand tipped slightly and a blob of hot wax fell onto the shoulder of Martin's nightgown. Carlyon moved the candle away, angry at his carelessness. If the wax had fallen onto bare skin, the pain might have been sufficient to awaken. He sighed and began to pull back the bedclothes, hoping that the key was on Martin's person. It was. It was fastened to his left forearm with a leather lace. Relieved, Carlyon cautiously moved the arm to look at the knot securing the key. He picked at it with his free hand for a few seconds but could make no impression. It was too tight.

Suddenly his body gave a startled jerk, spilling another blob of wax onto Martin's nightgown. A noise from the doorway had intruded into his concentration and disturbed him, but when he nervously looked, he saw that it was Mary. He smiled his relief, and her presence seemed to calm his agitated heart.

"I was worried," she said, as she came over to him. "You were taking so long. Is the sword here?"

"I think me it's in yon chest. Here's a key. I've just got to cut the fastening. If you would hold the candle?"

So saying, he held out the candle and reached for his knife. But Mary held up her palm in a gesture of refusal.

"No. It would be better not to cut the key off. If we can take the key and replace it, Lord Martin will not notice aught amiss. It may be days before he looks to the sword, and we will be well away by then. Hold you the candle for me and my nimble fingers will loosen this knot."

Carlyon did as she told him, and she worked at the fastening. For a while it was difficult, and impatience again poked at him. Then suddenly it was looser, and after that it was quickly undone. He took the key and went to the chest. This time Mary held the candle while he opened the chest, and to his relief his sword was there. He took it out and held it as if it were an old friend.

Mary lightly touched his arm. "We must leave now," she said softly. "Lock the chest and I'll replace the key."

He nodded and put the replacement sword in the chest, before quietly closing the lid. Once outside the room, he slipped his sword into its scabbard. As it went in, the jewelled hilt flickered in the candlelight, as if sighing. Carlyon's lips also moved in a slight smile of satisfaction, and he led Mary away to where he had stowed his pack, ready for his departure.

When they were in the yard, they waited a few seconds in the shadow of the house. Carlyon was nervous about walking across, even though he knew that everyone must be asleep. He led Mary down the house and across by the stables. The stench of horses was heavy in the still air, and he found it comforting. It crossed his mind that he and Mary would be better off if they had a horse, and he wondered how easy it would be to ride one.

Then they were at the rear wall of the yard. There was only a short piece of ground to cross to get to the gate. They hurried over, and while Mary looked out across the yard, Carlyon pulled back the bolts on the small wicket, so that they could pass through. On the other side they stopped and looked at each other. Relief and happiness brought smiles to their faces, and for the first time Carlyon instinctively took Mary into a thankful embrace.

"That's it," he said, as he released her. "We must to your mother's now with all haste. They may come after us, so we'll travel by night until we're far away. Take my arm, and with God's grace we'll be kept safe."

Five days later they had crossed the River Mersey and were walking over the brow of a hill, when Mary pointed to some buildings in the far distance.

"There's Highfield village. We'll be at my mother's ere nightfall."

Carlyon looked eagerly, wondering if he had really seen those buildings before. "Is your mother's house in the village?"

"No, a little beyond, amongst those trees. My father was a freeman, and he left my mother one and a half virgates of land. My brother Ned lives in the village with his wife and helps Mama to till it. He'll welcome your help, I trow."

When they reached Mary's home, her mother, May, was weeding in her vegetable plot. She looked up on hearing their voices as they approached, and her lined face broke into a beautiful smile. Despite her tiredness, Mary ran to her and threw her arms round her. They were still embracing when Carlyon reached them. He had had time to observe the woman who he was hoping would help him. As mother and daughter separated, he saw that, despite her grey hair and plumpness of figure, May was still an attractive woman, with Mary's blue eyes and firm cheekbones. He smiled shyly in response to her welcoming smile.

"So, you've returned to us, Sir Knight," she said. "I thought me that would happen."

"You were right, Mama. He was in distress. He almost drowned, and his mind has been so struck, he's forgotten his very name."

May looked quickly at Carlyon, concern narrowing her eyes, and she listened while her daughter told her what had happened. Carlyon said nothing, content to let Mary speak for him. He looked at the two women, struck by how similar they both were, despite the obvious difference in their age. Their voices seemed soothing, and he felt comfortable there with them, safe.

"I doubt me it'll be easy to cure this," May said at last, looking at Carlyon, but speaking to Mary. "We'll have to wait and hope that time will heal." She nodded, and then, as if satisfied, she clapped her hands and rubbed the fingers of her left hand on the palm of her right. "Come now, we'll go inside and eat. Then I'll tell Ned you've returned safely."

Carlyon followed them into the cottage. Disappointment had flickered through him at first on hearing May's doubts about his cure, but, bending his head to enter the cottage through the low doorway, he suddenly felt happy. It was as if he had come home.

4

As the summer began to drift hazily into autumn, harvesting got underway throughout the land and livestock were being fattened up for winter slaughter. On his manor near Maidenhead, Sir John le Cerre-nore was out every day. The Michaelmas rents had to be collected and some of the tenants were having trouble meeting that quarter's demands. John had lost an eye while serving in the King's French campaigns that summer, but it was as if he had lost an ear. He was deaf to any excuses from the tenants.

Then there was the hunting. His father-in-law, who had provided the manor as part of his daughter's dowry, possessed a grant of hunting rights on a neighbouring covert owned by the King, and he allowed John to use them. John took his loaned rights seriously. Any infringements of the forest laws were rigorously punished.

John also took seriously his duties in the manorial court every fortnight without fail. There were always personal disputes amongst the tenants to be settled, and his zealous officers always produced people who were accused of committing minor offences against the law. However, on the morning of the first court that October, John was inclined to give it a miss. He had spent an uncomfortable night with abdominal pain, and his mood had not been improved when his servant had accidentally splashed him while taking away the water used for washing. It was an affront to John's dignity, rather than physical harm, but he gave the lad a heavy cuff about the head, nonetheless.

"On your way," he roared, "and don't come back!"

As the servant left the bedchamber, John broke wind heartily and it seemed to bring some temporary relief. Then the door opened again, and a servant girl came in, carrying a small beaker.

"Sally has made this, my lord. She says 'twill relieve the pains in your belly."

"God willing. But I think me I've been cursed by a witch in the village. She'll rue the day, when I find her."

He took the beaker of warm liquid and tentatively sniffed at it. There was a strong aroma of mint, but he also caught other unknown scents. When he took a sip, he could taste the bitterness of willow bark, but otherwise it was palatable enough. He drank most of it, but did not finish it, as he was beginning to feel better and thought that he had taken sufficient. In fact, he felt in a good enough humour to begin dealing with the day's business.

He saw the bailiff first, and then the other manorial officers. John dealt with it all, and then his steward informed him that one of his tenants wished for an audience. Nodding his head in careless acceptance, John had the man admitted. The tenant, with his head obsequiously bowed, began to thank him profusely.

John irritatedly cut him short. "Say what you want, fellow."

"My neighbour Mathew has brought a suit against me in the court today," the man hastily said. "He says that I have taken a piece of land which is rightfully his. It's a mere strip, less than a yard wide, and he says I've moved wrongly beyond my boundary. I say not. He wishes you to make a decision, my lord."

"So I shall. What then?"

"I say the decision should be in my favour, my lord. Please be so gracious as to accept this small gift."

The tenant pulled a handful of coins from his purse and laid them on the table. John quickly spread them out with his forefinger, counting them as he did so. Then he gathered them up and put them into a small casket by his side.

"Your gift has pleased me," he said, without looking at the man. "Leave me now."

The man started to thank him, but John jerked his head to look at him, his one eye glaring. The man closed his mouth and scuttled out of the room.

At the court session, John began with the minor offences against the law that were not being taken to the assizes. The first case was of two men who had been brawling in the village street. John listened to the description with great interest, guffawing wildly when it was told how one of the men had been knocked down and his head had fallen onto a fresh cow turd. The incident amused John so much that, whereas he had intended to fine both men, he let off the man who had pleased him more. That this was the bigger man, who had started the quarrel, was of no concern to him. His decision was final.

That, apart from the money that could be made from fines and bribes, was a particular source of pleasure to him. Knowing that he had such arbitrary power over the lives of ordinary people fired his blood with a force that at times almost made him grit his teeth. It was a similar sensation to when he had an opponent at his mercy on the battlefield or at a tourney. Of course, he did not have the power of life or death in the manor court, but the petty crimes and disputes presented to him were sufficient.

The third case which he heard that morning concerned a widow who was accused by a neighbour of theft. John thought her passing elderly, perhaps forty years or so, and she was plain in appearance. As he listened to the evidence against her, he wondered idly what her husband had seen in her. She was accused of stealing a plough, and her young neighbour explained with great earnestness what had happened.

"It's been the custom since my father's time that we ploughed the widow Thomson's field. This year her son, being now of age, took our plough and ploughed the field himself. Afterwards, his mother refused to give back the plough, saying it was hers."

Witnesses were produced, who testified that they knew these facts and that the plough had been found at the widow's house. John nodded at the end of this parade and was already wondering what to do. The widow could be fined, but it might be more amusing to have her placed in the cucking stool. That would teach her a lesson in front of her neighbours. Then the widow stepped forward, wanting to speak. John nodded.

"My lord, the plough was my husband's. In the time of the King's late father, he went with my lord the earl to fight for the King in Scotland."

John sat up and now listened with interest.

"Before he left, my man gave our plough to William's late father, William the elder, on condition that he ploughed our land until he returned. Sadly, he was slain in battle. The earl has allowed me to live rent-free, and because my son was an infant, I allowed William the elder to keep the plough, and he ploughed my piece. Now my son is of an age to plough himself, I desired back the plough, but William the younger says that the plough is now his by ancient usage."

The woman stood before John, twisting her hands together imploringly, and he looked at her in approval. To his mind, her history threw a completely different light on the matter. Her accuser might very well have a case according to ancient usage, but he, John, would not let a soldier's widow suffer. He drummed briefly on his table with the fingers of his left hand and gave an almost immediate decision. She would be set free, and the plough returned to her.

The rest of the session went well. John collected many fines, and at the end he was glad that his early morning gripe had not kept him in his chamber. He was looking forward to a pleasant evening, but late in the afternoon his father-in-law arrived on a visit. As the earl's small retinue came into the yard, John came out to greet them and himself helped his guest to ease his rheumatic limbs out of his wagon and climb down.

"Welcome, my lord," he cried, pulling his mouth into a respectful smile. "My heart's light to see you."

The earl stamped his feet on the ground, trying to loosen up his muscles. Then he straightened up and looked directly at John. "'Sblood, John! And it's a mercy my bones are still in one piece. It's not so easy for me to travel as it whilom was."

"But by Our Lady's grace, long may you be able to do it, Papa!" cried Lady Patrina, who had come out into the yard and was hurrying over to her father.

With a whoop of delight, the earl threw his arms round his daughter and kissed her affectionately. "I'll come to see you, and they have to haul me on a litter," he said. Then, pulling his head back slightly to look at her slim figure, he said without thought, "No sign of a grandchild yet."

Patrina blushed, and John pulled himself up stiffly, as if his want of prowess was being implied.

"It won't be long. We'll soon have news for you," he told the earl, pulling a broad grin across his face, but his words were more to support his self-respect than to spare his wife's feelings.

The earl made no further comment on the matter. He smiled warmly at his daughter and briefly hugged her again.

"Come inside, my lord, and take refreshment."

John indicated at the doorway with his arm, holding it out as if ushering his father-in-law towards the house. Patrina, hanging on to her father's arm, began to pull him, and, laughing, the elderly man began to move. Inside the house, he unconsciously began behaving as if in his own home, to John's barely covert irritation. He led the way into the great hall and went straight to his favourite chair. Setting his bulk onto the cushion, he placed his arms along the chair's wooden arms and stretched out his feet with a sigh of relieved pleasure. Then he took off his hat and rubbed the bald strip that ran down the centre of his crown. As if now ready, he put his hat back on and took a glass of wine from the manservant, while another began to remove his boots for him.

Later, after supper, John and the earl stayed in the hall to drink wine. Tapers had been lit to provide some light, and the smoke drifting upwards was swaying in the draughts that passed through the room. There was a silence, as subtle as a mid-May frost, for a minute or so. John was deferring to his father-in-law but wanting to get a conversation going. He was wondering whether to ask the older man if he was warm enough, when the earl suddenly broke the silence.

"A petition has been brought to me, Sir John. A petition from the tenants on this manor." He paused and his rheumy blue eyes looked directly at his son-in-law. "They are complaining of being treated harshly, and that they are being called to pay more than in my day."

John's body had stiffened while he listened, and it was with an effort that he had held his arms still. Now he put one hand on the table and leaned forward, as if about to stand up. "A petition, my lord? Who has done this? Who?" His brain raced behind his flickering eye as he tried to think of any of his tenants who might have been absent.

The earl, however, ignored the question, as though he had not heard it. "Old custom is not to be lightly discarded," he said. "What was sufficient for our fathers should suffice for us."

"I am my tenants' lord. This manor and all movables and immovables on it were given to me as part of my lady's, your daughter's, dowry. It all belongs to me now, to do with it as I wish."

The earl took a drink of wine, taking a few seconds to appreciate it, and then spoke in a tone which showed that he was unused to argument. "If tenants are made to pay too much, then they may not have enough to pay their dues."

"I only take what I should, my lord. If tenants can't pay, there are always others who can be given their land."

"It would grieve me sorely to see any of these tenants turned out, Sir John. I have known them for a long time – yes, many from their birth. I yet have a responsibility for them. By God's grace, we've been born into a privileged position. We must take what is rightfully ours, but privilege brings a duty to look after the less fortunate."

John shifted grumpily in his seat and tightened his lips, irritated that some of his tenants should have gone behind his back. He was conscious of the difference in rank with his wife's father, for his own father was only a baron, and he could pick up the command in the earl's words. He thought it good to try to change the subject and leave his dealings with his tenants until after his father-in-law had left. "I think me we'll have some good hunting tomorrow," he said abruptly. "The coverts are full. There's game and enough."

The earl looked at John and smiled, although it was not clear whether the smile was in acknowledgement of John's stratagem, or from pleasure at the thought of the hunting. "'Sblood! I must to my bed. These old bones will need a good rest if I'm to spend the morrow in the saddle. But you think over what I've said."

He drained his glass and pushed himself to his feet. John quickly got to his and called for a man with a candle to light the earl's way. He watched as the old man hobbled away on his arthritic legs, and then jerkily picked up his own glass to finish it. His bad mood stayed with him when he went to his own bedchamber, and a little later he carried it like a monkey on his back into his wife's chamber. She was in bed, lying back on her soft pillows, her bed curtains still open. Her smile of greeting froze on her lips when she saw the aggressive cast of his shoulders, as if he were forcing his way into her room. He spoke before she could say anything.

"Your father has been interfering in my dealings with my tenants. It pleases me not. If a manor's given as a dowry, then that's that. I can do as I please. And so I shall."

"Don't be hard on Papa, my lord. He's always kind to his tenants. That's his nature."

"My lord the earl is too soft-hearted. You know full, I like him much and his company pleases me. Yet I like it not when he interferes with my private business because of his gentle whims."

"I pray you be gentle also. You're a brave knight. Fearless. Everyone knows. It will be an even greater grace, and you're thoughtful towards those less fortunate than you."

John was standing with his feet apart, his hands on his hips. In his irritation, he had not even unbelted his dressing gown. "In faith, a weak man will do that. I didn't show any mercy to the King's enemies in France – save they were high-born, of course." He touched the scar on his face, which ran from his forehead, across the left eye socket, and onto the cheek. "I know not when I'll be able to fight again. I must fain now stay on my manor like a worn-out charger."

"You're not worn out, my lord. And you can go hunting still."

"Hunting? But even that bores me now. In fact, this whole manor bores me. I'll be glad when I get into my own inheritance." He caught the disapproving look on his wife's face, and quickly added, "God grant my father lives many years yet. I must take what God wills. But I miss Sir Carlyon. Were he here, we'd have some japes together." He looked at his wife, who was looking at him strangely. He took a step up to the end of her bed and stood there, thoughtfully scratching at a flea bite on his chest. "You should not have sent him away on a foolish quest to look for flowers. You're a silly woman. I wish I knew what had happened to him. It's almost a year since now. Even his father has heard nought of him."

"Indeed, Sir Carlyon is a gentle knight. I wonder sometimes where he is, and I am sorry if I sent him into danger. But it was a noble quest for a lady, not a foolish one. I also miss him. Humfrey told me he returned to Chertsey this last spring. He had a small pouch, which he carried carefully. Mayhap he had found the flowers. I wish I could have seen them."

John looked at her suspiciously and then broke wind, as if to show what he thought of her wish. Grunting his relief, he went on. "I doubt me he'll have found any. I doubt me there were any to find."

"I'm sure there were. I'm sure of it." She pulled herself up to a sitting position. "If anyone could have found the flowers of the swan, then Sir Carlyon could have."

"I'd have done it, if I'd have so wanted. But I fear me the flowers were cursed." John looked at Patrina, and a hard smile moved his jaw, as jealous wickedness forced words out from between his lips. "Sir Carlyon is most likely wandering about forlorn and lovesick, because he's lost your hand to another. Mayhap it's made him become a hermit in some lonely cave."

A thoughtful light shone in Patrina's eyes, as if such an idea pleased her.

John's face stiffened, and he spoke to hurt her, even though the words were casually tossed out. "Mayhap he's dead. I've heard such a tale."

"Oh, no, my lord! I hope not. Surely he's safe – pray God, somewhere."

John grunted and scratched at his groin. He had had enough of the topic now. It seemed to have made his situation even more boring. He looked at the candle by his wife's bed, which was slowly burning down and adding an acrid scent to the room.

Patrina's voice intruded gently into his introspection. "Are you coming into the bed now?" she softly asked. "The hour is getting late."

He began to move round to the side of the bed, but that seemed to nudge his mood once more. He stopped and looked at his wife, who had slipped herself down beneath her coverings. A little snake was eating at his heart, and the poisonous foam from its flickering tongue was trickling into his blood. His irritation again boiled up into his throat, to push out angry words.

"Why should I come to your bed? What use is there in bedding a barren woman? Why are you not giving me a son?"

"Surely it's early yet, my lord. You were away in France for a long while. There's yet time, an' we but try."

"I've tried my part. The lack is on your side. I should not have taken up with your family. You are all too soft-hearted and weak. You're a silly, useless woman and your father pokes his fingers into pies that are no longer his."

His fists were clenched by his sides, but passion had aroused him. He looked at his wife lying there, the candlelight throwing her long slim neck and neatly rounded chin into profile, and he decided to take his conjugal right. Quickly he began to unfasten the cord on his night robe.

Life for Carlyon in the north-west of England had settled into a pattern as the summer days rolled by. He was living in the cottage of May the thatcher's widow and had become part of the family. During the day he worked on the small piece of land that May owned by her cottage, and on the family strips hard by the village. With no memory of anything else, he threw himself into his new life, and Mary's company was like a summer-scented breeze blowing through all his new memories.

One evening, shortly after midsummer, their talk had come round to how the crops were doing.

"I thought me the ears of corn were filling out well, when I walked past this forenoon," said May.

Carlyon, who was using a piece of bread to wipe round the inside of his soup bowl, looked up and said, "We need more sun. Then they'll grow fat." He spoke like an expert, but he was repeating what he had heard other villagers say. "We have a lot of gaps. Was the sowing not done with care?"

"That was the heavy rain, as came the day after sowing. It scattered the seed, alas."

"But what we have is growing well, I trow?" said Mary, smiling encouragingly at Carlyon.

"Well enough," he responded. "Yet Old John says the crops are not so heavy as in his father's day."

"That may be so," May said with a regretful nod. "The land is growing tired. It's been worked so hard, even the fallow year is not enough. I know not what can be done."

"We must find new land, fresh land. What say you about that piece behind the cottage? Nought grows there but grass and thistle."

"I doubt me that will do. There are too many rocks and stones."

"I've seen that. Lots of black stones. Surely they can be cleared."

"No, the ground is full of them. My husband tried. If you dig, there's only more."

"Then mayhap we can make use of what the Lord has scattered so liberally. I've seen how they split well. Mayhap they can be collected and used for building or roofs."

May laughed. "I think me not. The stone is useless. It's sea coal, and if a flame is put to it, then it will burn."

"Surely not. I've never heard of that."

"Indeed so, Carlyon. It's well known in these parts. It gives good heat. Nobody knows why it burns, but if set alight, it burns slowly, and for a long time."

"Hm." Carlyon looked over to the lazy embers of the fire which had been used to cook their supper. "Then it could be used for cooking, instead of wood."

"No, we can't do that," May told him, shaking her head and wrinkling her nose in distaste. "When it burns, it gives off horrible fumes. It would kill us all."

Carlyon prepared to argue. He was sure that the smoke could be no worse than if green wood were put on the fire. However, before he could push his point, the women got up from the table, so he let the matter lie. Even so, he pondered over the business and even took a chance the following day to examine some pieces of sea coal more closely. He decided to try to burn some, so that he might check out the fumes for himself, but a spell of wet weather set in for a few days, and he postponed the test.

Before the weather cleared up, he went to see David the limer. He had been told that if lime were spread on the land after harvest, it would help to give better crops, so he wanted to order some bushels in good time. David was in the process of burning some limestone, and Carlyon watched as he stoked up the fire in his kiln with wood. After Carlyon had concluded his business, curiosity kept him there, and he asked David how lime was made.

"I burn up the limestone in my kiln here, see you. I must get it very hot."

As he was speaking, he was moving wood from his pile, ready to be added to the fire. Carlyon noticed for the first time just how much wood there was stacked.

"You seem to need a lot of wood."

"The fire must burn strongly all the time. I need more wood than stone."

"You need a substance that burns slowly. Have you tried sea coal?"

David straightened up and looked at him, one hand on his hip, as if supporting his back. "My father used it one time. I remember it gave good heat, but wood is easier to buy. My father couldn't get enough sea coal."

"I might have a good supply. If I can get it to you, will you use it?"

Carlyon stood there, smiling gently, while David looked thoughtfully at the kiln and then at the pile of wood. After a few seconds, David turned his head to one side and spat out a yellowish globule of phlegm and saliva.

Turning back to Carlyon, he said, "Yes. I can take sea coal. We can see how it be."

Carlyon's smile broadened, and the two men discussed the further details. Satisfied, Carlyon hurried back home to examine May's land more thoroughly and set up his part of the operation.

It was a few days later that Mary gave him something else to think about. May had just left the cottage and gone into the village to see one of her gossips, and Carlyon was about to go out and begin his day's work. As he was collecting his tools, Mary laid her hand gently on his arm. He stopped what he was doing and looked at her with an enquiring smile. Her eyes were as bright as sunlight on a stream when she spoke.

"Carlyon, my dear, I have to tell you, I'm with child."

He continued to smile, for at first her words seemed to have nothing to do with him. Then he understood what her words meant and looked at her abdomen. She seemed no different from usual. "How do you know?" he asked.

"Women know. And Mama says it's so. She says the infant will be born next spring. You'll be a father."

She looked at him shyly from under her eyelashes, and he suddenly realised how he was involved and what it meant for him.

He seemed to feel a strange glow spread through his chest. It was a feeling such as he had never had before. And he liked it.

"Ah, my love, these are welcome words. My heart's fit to burst. An infant! Of mine! We must hasten to have our marriage announced."

"We will. But will you marry me, even though you're a knight of noble blood?" she teased him in her happiness.

He was holding her in his arms, and he looked down at her upturned face. Although he sensed that she was teasing, he spoke seriously. "Perchance I am a knight of a well-born family, as you say, but I know nought of that. Mayhap I never will. I only know I love you and I'll love our child. This's what I want."

To seal his troth, he bent his head and kissed her rich, moist lips. He felt her body tremble slightly, and he knew that he wanted nothing more.

After the wedding, Mary gave him a ring. It bore a small, smoothly rounded stone, which at first glance he thought was a pale grey colour. Then as he moved his hand, it became a warmer pink or buttercup. Mary told him that if his heart was ever distressed, he must only touch it, and he would be eased. She would always be with him, as long as he wore the ring.

When the baby was born, they chose the name Stanford, which had been Mary's father's. Carlyon felt that it was also binding him more closely to her family. He found the three of them a cottage not far from his brother-in-law Edward's at the edge of the village and let his new responsibilities enfold him. Very rarely now did he think of his lost life and wonder if threads of it would ever return to tie him to his past. He had another future to dream about.

5

ay was alone in her cottage. It was early June, and she was preparing some herbal potions. Singing softly to herself as she worked, she looked up when a shadow appeared in her doorway. The stranger was of thin build, wearing a fur-trimmed robe dyed red and a felt hat with a brown feather. His features were handsome, except that, as May could not fail to notice, he had a large wart above his left eyebrow. He greeted her haughtily.

"Ho, goodwife! I seek a young man they call Carlyon, who's come of late to these parts."

"Seek you him, my lord?" May's tone was humble and polite. She was ready to help, but something about the man made her cautious. There was an air of menace about the way he stood with his shoulders pulled back, the way that he did not deign to look at her, the way that his left hand brushed at his tunic, as if knocking away dirt. She sensed that he meant ill and she drew herself in, pressing her clasped hands against her body just below her breasts. Nevertheless, her voice was still humble when she continued. "What business do you have with him, pray?"

"Do you question me, woman?" The man's eyes snapped onto her as sharply as his voice, but then something seemed to make him pause. His body relaxed and he smiled graciously. "I saw him last year, hard by Warwick. He did me a great service while he was there. He and his sister both."

"Say you so, my lord. And you seek them now, this brother and sister?"

"I do. They left my house before I could reward them. They were of great help to me, and I would fain now show them my thanks."

"It's like to have been a great service, that you should come all this way."

"I do what I must," said the man, irritation again tightening his face. "I've sworn a vow, and I must keep it. Do you know of this man and his sister?"

"Alas, my lord, your journey's in vain. They were in these parts some months since, but they've left and travelled south again. They said they were going to a town called Oxford."

"Oxford, say you. I know it well."

Without thanking her, the stranger turned and walked away. May stepped out of the doorway and watched him, her hands still clasped across her body. An uneasy feeling was clamping her fingers together. The stranger had made her worried. She decided to speak with Mary and Carlyon that evening. Slowly she turned and went back to her herbs, but it took her some time to settle.

Early that evening, May had just finished milking her cow when Carlyon bustled into her cottage. His hair was dishevelled, and distress was pulling his eyes wide. The baby in his arms was crying, a sound that May recognised as hunger.

"Oh, Mama, I can't find Mary! I don't know where she is! I came home for supper and Stanford was crying in his crib. Mary's gone."

"Calm down, dear. You'll upset the baby more. Mary has but gone to see a neighbour." As she was speaking, May took the baby from Carlyon and rocked it in her arms. Despite her words, though, she was worried. She could sense that something bad had happened. Mary would not have left her baby that way.

Carlyon seemed to be reading her mind. "No, she wouldn't have left Stanford alone so long. I've looked for her. She's not with any neighbours. Mistress Joan says she saw a stranger go into the cottage this afternoon. I fear me something happened to her."

"A stranger? What mark of stranger?"

"A young man, she says. In a red tunic and a hat. She'd not seen him before, but he seemed like a gentleman. He was not in the cottage long. Then he left the village. Oh, Mama, I fear me he's done ill to Mary."

"I fear me also."

She told him about that morning's visit, and Carlyon's brow darkened when she described the man.

"This is not good," he said. "That man will be the lord Martin, the one we told you about. He'll not be wishing us well."

"Did Joan not see Mary?"

"No. She wanted to ask her about the stranger, but her goodman came home and she was busy."

"There's witchcraft here. I like it not." May put a finger in the milk, still warm from the cow, and gave it to Stanford to suck. Her brow furrowed as she considered what to do.

"I ought to go out to seek her," Carlyon said, sounding as if he wanted confirmation.

"Yes, mayhap you could do that. I'll look after Stanford."

She thought it would be better if he felt that he was doing something, and she suggested that he start on the common. When she was alone, she glanced thoughtfully at Stanford and then quickly poured a little water into a basin. A sense of urgency was pushing at her shoulders, as she took off the baby's linen shawl and wrapped him in a woollen cloth. Holding the baby in one arm, she used her other hand to lay the linen shawl in the bowl of water. May looked into the bowl, narrowing her eyes slightly as she concentrated. There was silence, except for the slight sound of Stanford sucking at his grandmother's finger. A few seconds passed. Then shapes began to form in the water. May saw that they were trees. Lines creased her forehead, but as the vision became clearer, she recognised a nearby part of the forest.

With Stanford held protectively in her arms, she left the cottage. Outside, evening gloom was starting to wrap a cloak round everything. The sun had not yet set, but heavy clouds had boiled up to fill the sky. Birds were still singing, but the night was close by.

May stopped at the edge of a small depression. It was heavily shadowed by the surrounding trees, but she knew it well. In the banking on the far side there was a badger sett. Nervously, May peered into the gloom. She saw a crouching shape, but it was not a badger. She knew immediately that it was her daughter. Holding Stanford tightly, May hurried over. Mary was on all fours, like a badger. There was dirt on her clothes, and her hair was hanging loose about her face. May bent over her.

"What are you doing here? What's happened?" she asked.

"Mama! I'm so glad you've come. I can't escape. Help me!"

May quickly looked around, sensing witchcraft, but there was nothing. Even the birds seemed to have fallen silent. In the still air there was the faint stench of badger, but the animals had not yet come out. May crouched down beside her daughter. "I'll help you. But tell me what's happened."

"It was the young lord Carlyon and I met on our way home last year. That was an evil day, and yet we thought to do good. This was that lord who tried to steal Carlyon's sword. He came to the cottage today and wanted to buy the sword."

She paused, as if to take breath. Stanford began to cry with short, regular sounds, and May saw Mary shudder.

"Here, daughter. You must feed the babe."

She offered Stanford. Mary lifted herself to her knees and took her child, but then she lay down on her side like a badger sow, to put Stanford to her breast. This seemed to calm her.

"I told the lord the sword was not for sale. He offered more money, but I told him Carlyon would never sell. He went away, but unbeknownst to me, he sprinkled a potion on my bread before he left. I knew what he'd done at my first bite, but it was too late. It made me come here to live amongst the badgers. I want to leave, but I can't. There's a power holding me here."

In the gloom, May saw Mary turn her face imploringly towards her. She gently laid her hand on her daughter's shoulder and stifled a sigh. "You've been bewitched. But I'll seek a way to break the spell. God will defeat this evil."

She sat down beside the mother and child and waited, motionless. Into the silence came a slight rustling. An old male badger poked its head cautiously out of a burrow in the banking. After a few seconds it came fully out and waddled over to snuffle in some undergrowth. Soon it was joined by other badgers, seemingly oblivious to the huddled group of three humans. May also ignored the badgers. She knew that the task ahead of her would not be an easy one, and an icy fear of failure was hovering at the back of her head.

When Stanford had been fed, Mary handed him back to her

mother. "You must leave now, Mama. I'll be safe with these animals tonight. If you come to me tomorrow, I pray you'll have the power to free me."

A sigh trembled through May as she took her grandson. She did not want to leave, but she knew that she would not be able to help if she stayed. She leaned over and kissed Mary's brow. "God keep you, daughter. I'll return on the morrow."

With Stanford in her arms, she slipped out of the dell, unsurprised that the badgers seemed not to see her. It was as if she were not there. Anxiously she hurried home, where she cleaned Stanford and settled him down in a cradle to sleep. She had just finished when Carlyon came in. His face was haggard, and a great weight of sorrow seemed to be pressing his shoulders down, making him stoop slightly. He looked at May and told her that there had been no sight of Mary. She stepped over to him and held his hands in hers. As she told him where she had been, his shoulders straightened, and a bright glint came into his eyes. When she had stopped, he squeezed her fingers, as if in thanks.

"I'll go to Ned," he said. "We'll get some men from the village, and we'll bring her back by force."

"No! No!" In her agitation, May clung impulsively to his hands. "You mustn't do that. It'll only send her mad. I have to find a way to break the spell. Only that will save her."

"Say you so? There is one other thing. I'll find Lord Martin and offer him the sword, if he'll but restore Mary to us."

"I'm sure you mustn't give up the sword. Mary's been bewitched because she refused to do that. You must not betray her. Look you, stay here with me and Stanford. Fear not, I'll find a way to set her free."

Carlyon released himself from May's hold and went to slump

on the bench by the table, as if he could think of nothing else to do. May looked at him and wondered at the strange power that was working amongst them. She cut him some bread and cheese, but he left it untouched, and during the night she heard him moving restlessly in his bed, as she lay in hers, wrestling with the problem.

The following morning dawned with sunshine, but the mood in the cottage was no brighter than the night before. While May was preparing some milk for Stanford, Carlyon suddenly spoke.

"I want you to take me to Mary. I want to see her."

"We can't do that. She won't be out during the day. We must be patient, and mayhap by this eventide I'll know what to do."

"I pray you will." He restlessly moved about the small room, and then, as May began to feed Stanford, he said, almost as if to himself, "I must work for Lord Dalton this day. I'll say my wife is grievous sick and tell the bailiff I'll come on the morrow."

"No, son. I think me it'll be best if you work today. Perchance also it would be best if we say nought about what has happened to Mary. Should someone ask, say she's with me. Go now, I pray you. I'll look after Stanford and find a way to get Mary back."

Carlyon still seemed reluctant, but under May's gentle urging he at last left the cottage. May finished feeding her grandson and, after laying him in his cradle, she stood in thought for a little while. Then she clapped her hands together and drew the fingers of her left hand over her right palm. Picking up a shawl, she fashioned a sling round her neck and, placing Stanford carefully inside this, she set off for Mary and Carlyon's cottage.

Their livestock had not been attended to, so May checked on the pig and milked the cow. Then she turned her attention to the cottage. It seemed to have been undisturbed since the previous night. Everything was in its place. May recognised her daughter's tidiness.

There was just one thing: on the table was a pot of honey and a piece of bread. May remembered how Mary had said that she was about to eat when the stranger came. Carefully she placed the bread into her basket and, after a final look round, she left the cottage.

Back home, she settled the still-sleeping Stanford into his cradle and then sat at her table to examine the piece of bread. She brought it up close to her face and drew in a long sniff through her nose. There was the smell of the bread, and of the honey. But there was something else. It was familiar, flitting at the back of her memory, but she could not quite pin it down. She held the bread slightly away and peered at it intently, moving it about in a shaft of sunlight which was coming in through the door. Again at the table, she spread out a small bleached-white cloth. Then with a knife she gently tapped at a part of the bread where the honey had not been smeared. A brief grunt of satisfaction left her lips as she saw some grains of powder fall onto her cloth.

For the rest of the day she let most of her normal work go by, as, except for caring for Stanford, she tried to find an answer to her problem. Towards evening she was still seemingly no nearer and was wondering what else she could try. A restless call from Stanford interrupted her and she decided to take him to see his mother.

The badger sett was as secluded as the previous evening. Mary was crouching there alone. There was more light on this occasion, and May could see that her daughter was looking much worse. Her face was smeared with dirt, and her tunic was heavily soiled. She looked haggardly at May, but seemed too weary even to show her relief that her mother had brought her baby. May passed him over to her, placing him in Mary's arms as she lay on her side. Then she knelt and watched. At first, she had been too overcome by her daughter's appearance to be able to say anything, but at last she could speak.

"This's not looking good, daughter. It's powerful witchcraft that's holding you."

"I know, Mama. I can feel my strength leaving me. I seem not to be here in this body. I know not where I am."

"Alas, my darling child, it grieves me sore to see you like this. But have faith. I will find a way to free you."

When Mary had finished feeding her son, she lay back, exhausted. May folded Stanford in her arms, and as she looked down at Mary, alarm held her face in a tight grip. Mary's eyes were closed, but her breathing was regular. Then her eyes opened and she looked up at her mother. May saw her lips move, and she bent a little lower to catch the quiet words that came out.

"There's not long to go now before it's all over. Death will free me. Look after Carlyon and little Stanford."

Mary closed her eyes again, while her mother murmured a few words of comfort. May knew that she could do nothing if she stayed. It was as if the creature lying before her was no longer her daughter. Holding Stanford close in her arms, she got awkwardly to her feet and hurried home. She was trembling with the fear that she might not be able to save Mary.

She said nothing of that when Carlyon came home. He immediately asked for news, while still standing in the doorway. May told him that she had been to see Mary, but she did not say how bad things were looking. Carlyon seemed not to notice the lack of convincing detail in May's words. He looked outside, where there was still plenty of light left by the setting sun, and said that he wanted to go and see Mary.

"No, son, that would not be good. It'll sore distress her, and she sees you. Hold fast yet another day. We'll have it all resolved ere the morrow's nightfall."

May laid a hand on his arm, hoping to comfort and trying to hide her worry that the next day's resolution might not be a happy one. She sensed Carlyon's restlessness travel into her own arm, and let him move away. With her face tight, she watched as he walked about the room. He pinched a thumb and forefinger over his nose and then turned and looked at her.

"This lord Martin is the answer here," he said. "I'll seek him out and make him release Mary from this spell. If not, I'll kill him."

"Softly, son. You know not where this lord lies. How to find? And you do, how know you he'll do as you ask? It may not be good to kill him before we know what has bewitched Mary. Trust me." May sighed. "Look now, go you home and see to your cow. When you come back, bring me Mary's holy day shift. I'll have need of it."

Carlyon seemed reluctant to leave, but he went without further argument. May stood for a moment after he had left. She had no need of Mary's shift, but she had thought that it would give Carlyon something purposeful to do. On his return, they sat and talked for a while but covered no new ground. When the last embers of daylight had died, May was relieved to receive Carlyon's agreement with her desire to go to bed. That night she whispered a prayer of thanks when, after some restlessness, she heard his regular breathing and knew that he had fallen asleep. For her, sleep was longer in coming, as her fevered mind shook with its search for an answer to their trouble.

In the morning, after May had awoken, she lay in her bed and continued to think things over for some minutes. She called back the ideas that she had had before falling asleep, and examined them. She sensed that she was on the threshold of a solution. One push and the door would open. However, before she could step into the light, Stanford woke up. His questioning cries for attention brought her to her feet, but as she busied herself with him, her mind still worked in the background.

By the time that she had prepared some milk for Stanford and was about to feed him, Carlyon had washed himself and dressed. He too seemed to have been thinking in the night.

"I shan't go for today's boon service," he announced, making May look up at him. "I'll seek out this lord who's brought such harm to my wife. If you fail and all goes not well, then I shall make him rue it."

"I doubt you should seek him, Carlyon. If he sees you, he may do something untoward. You must do your work for Lord Dalton. It will keep your hands and your mind busy."

"No, Mama. I must do something for Mary. I'll send Paul to do the work. He'll do it for a penny. Worry not. I'll be careful. I'll be sure not to be seen."

May sighed. She was thinking now that perhaps it would do no harm. "So be it. I'll be busy this day. There is an answer here, and pray God, I'll find it."

Carlyon went out of the cottage before May had finished feeding Stanford. Left with her grandson, she looked down at him. He was calmly looking up at her while he sucked at the improvised teat, and the fingertips of one little hand were moving against the leather, as if comparing it with what he could usually feel. A flush of love suffused May's body, and she remembered how she had held Mary at that age.

"Don't worry, my darling," she told Stanford softly. "We'll have your mama back with you today."

She spoke with conviction, as if the baby would understand her words, but she knew that there was still far to travel. During the day she continued to grapple with the business. She had a good idea of the narcotic powders which had been included in Lord Martin's potion, but she was fearful that there was yet another substance undetected. It was difficult to concentrate, because that day Stanford was unusually fractious, as though he knew how urgent the situation was becoming. Then, early in the afternoon, while he had fallen asleep in her arms, she let her mind drift. She floated through her unconsciousness like smoke through a room, and she seemed to hear Mary's voice.

"Death will free me."

She had said that to her mother the previous evening. May had accepted it as true, but now she remembered how Mary had seemed already absent from her while saying that. Mary also had told her that she seemed not to be in her body, but in an unknown place. Drifting with these thoughts, it came to May that death would indeed free her daughter: the death of the power that was holding her.

There were a good three hours left before sunset when Carlyon returned. He brought some milk from his cow, but May could see from the slump in his shoulders that his spirits were not high. His face lightened slightly when he saw how his son, sitting in May's lap, smiled to recognise him.

"How has he been this day?" he asked.

"Restless, I fear. He needs his mama, but I'm hopeful we'll have her back this even."

"I also hope so. Fortune hasn't been with me. Lord Martin isn't staying with my lord Dalton. They've heard nought of him at the manor house. No one else has seen him. It's as if he's an invisible sprite."

"Evil is often not so easy to spot. It works secretly. But come, we must move swiftly now. Time is short, but the time has come, I trow. You must do exactly what I say and, God willing, we'll prevail."

"Of course, Mama. What must I do?"

"First, go back home and bring your sword. We shall have need of its strength. Meet me anon at the crossroad and we'll go to free Mary."

Carlyon glanced at May, but asked no other question. She watched him leave, then she wrapped Stanford in his mother's holy day shift and, with him in her arms, she picked up a small pouch. For a moment she stood, said a few brief words of prayer, and left the cottage. Outside it was overcast, thick clouds having gathered in from the west, and May shivered slightly. Bowing her head, as if to protect her grandson, she set off for the crossroad.

When she was joined by Carlyon, she took him to the badger sett. They spoke little, for there was little to say. The gloom under the trees as they walked through the forest seemed to be settling on them, almost as if it were a physical presence holding them back. At the edge of the clearing they stopped.

"Wait here by this tree," May told Carlyon. "Make no noise. Come when I call you, and do exactly what I say."

He nodded, and she stepped out into the small clearing, which was darkly shadowed by the closely surrounding thick canopy of leaves. At first glance it had seemed deserted. Although deep in shade, it was still too early for the badgers to come out. However, May had seen a crumpled shape lying by the far side. Up close, she knew that it was Mary. And yet it was hardly Mary. She was almost unrecognisable, smeared in mud and dirt, so that, in amongst the gloom, she almost blended into the banking. Her clothes were also missing, and she was covered with a badger's skin. May lowered herself carefully onto her knees. She knew that there was very little time left.

"Hist, Mary," she whispered urgently. "I've brought Stanford for you to suckle."

She held Stanford out to her, but weakness seemed to be holding Mary immobile, and she gave no sign of accepting her son. Stanford also seemed to take fright. He uttered a piercing wail, and May felt his legs kick, as if he were trying to escape. She pulled him back in close to her.

"Yes, my darling," she muttered. "You know she's not your mama now."

Stanford's reaction had confirmed what she had been thinking. With her free hand she felt in her pouch and pulled out a small flask. She sprinkled liquid from it onto the neck of the silent form lying before her. Quickly, she soundlessly asked for God's help. Then she struggled to her feet. Stepping away two paces, she turned and indicated to Carlyon that he should come over to her. He came, and she saw that his eyes were wide in helplessness.

"Hold fast, Carlyon," she told him. "That's no longer Mary. Fear not."

It was true that in the deceiving darkness the shape on the ground at their feet looked just like a badger. Carlyon was looking at it as if held in fascination. He gave a start, when May touched his arm.

"Quickly, now. Time is passing. Take out your sword. You must kill this creature, cut off its head."

"I can't do that. It's Mary."

"Not any longer." May looked down. Sometimes the beast looked to have a human shape, sometimes an animal shape. The more she tried to concentrate, the more it moved from one shape to the other. "Mary will only be freed if this turnskin is killed. Do it now, I pray you."

Carlyon took the sword out of its scabbard and stiffly raised it above his head. There he held it, as if reluctant to move.

"Be brave, son," May hoarsely told him.

Suddenly the sword moved downwards. With a clean slice it took off the head of the dark figure lying motionless on the ground before them. A groan forced itself out of Carlyon's mouth. He straightened up, holding his sword in front of him.

6

Carlyon had not wanted to kill his wife, to cut off her head. Even if it was to free her from an evil bewitchment. He had known May long enough to know that he could trust her. And yet it hardly seemed possible that she would tell him to kill Mary. He wanted to refuse. He thought that he would just nick the back of her neck. Perhaps that would suffice. Let out the bad blood. He was judging how to do that safely when matters were taken out of his hands. Before he knew it, the sword had begun to swoop down, dragging his arms.

Now he stood there, unable to move. Anguish was holding him motionless, his sword pointing out in front of him like an accusing arm. He looked down at what he had done, but uncontrolled tears made it difficult to focus. Then he sensed May move beside him. As he watched, he saw her bend over to examine Mary's crumpled body. She was holding Stanford with his face close to her breast, but Carlyon could hear him crying. May abruptly straightened up.

"See, Carlyon," she said. "It's nought but a badger."

He did not quite understand, unsure why a badger was there. May tapped his arm and he lowered his sword.

"Look! See for yourself," she told him.

He bent down and peered into the confusing shadows.

Tentatively he reached out to touch the severed head. He grasped it and lifted it clear of the ground. His brow furrowed. It was indeed a badger's head. "I don't understand," he said.

"It matters not." May tugged at the shoulder of his tunic. "Come! We must leave this place. Mary's not here. We must away home quickly. She be not safe yet."

She turned and set off hurriedly through the darkening forest. He looked at her, and then at the dead shape on the ground by his feet. Suddenly, as if pulled, he began to move and he hastened after May and his son. When they reached the highway, May headed for the village. She was not slackening her pace, even though Carlyon could hear her breath coming in quick gasps. Stanford was quiet, as if the motion had sent him to sleep. Carlyon asked what had happened, but May breathlessly told him to ask no questions.

May's worried sense of urgency passed itself to Carlyon. Her anxiety was almost like a yoke holding him in tandem with her as they hurried along the road. All of a sudden there was a break in the cloud cover, very low on the western horizon, and a beam of sunshine shot out through it. It illuminated clearly their village nestling on the hillside, still some four or five furlongs distant. Not quite for a minute, and then the light faded, as capriciously as it had come. Even so, Carlyon's heart had been enlightened by it.

At their cottage Carlyon released the fastening on the door, but was unaccountably nervous about opening it. At May's urging, he pushed it wide and stepped inside. It was too dark to see anything, but as May came in behind him, he reached on the shelf by the doorway and took up a flint. Striking it, he lit a candle. With it held out before him, he turned to look round the room. There seemed to be no difference since that morning…then May drew his attention to the far side of the room. Holding the candle to show better, he saw that there was someone lying on the bed. He strode over so quickly that the flickering candle almost blew out. Leaning over the bed, he looked down at his wife. She was lying flat on her back, one arm across her midriff and the other bent close to her head. At first Carlyon feared that she was lifeless, but then he saw the regular rise and fall of her breast.

May confirmed. "She sleeps. We're in time. We must wake her gently."

She laid Stanford carefully in his cradle, where he stirred slightly, but did not awaken. Carlyon was at the bedside, and he tentatively reached out his hand to touch Mary's shoulder. She gave no sign of movement, so he shook her slowly and softly called her name. This time she moved on her own and a low sound came out through her lips. He shook and called again, and her eyes opened. His own eyes closed momentarily in relief. When he opened them again, he saw that Mary was looking at him as if somewhat mazed, as if unsure where she was and why. She closed her eyes, and he thought that she had gone back to sleep, but they opened again after a few seconds. Now she smiled, and in the flickering candlelight, beauty like a humming bowstring enlivened her face.

"Mary," he said, "you're back again."

"Back?" Her voice was very low, and he had to strain to hear it. "I've dreamed a strange dream."

"You've been bewitched. It was no dream. You've been running with wild animals."

"Say you so? My limbs ache and I can scarce move." Then a look of fear crossed her face, and she cried, "Stanford! Where's my baby?"

"Fear not, my darling. He's safe and well," her mother soothed, coming over to the bed. She had a beaker in her hand. "Drink this and you'll recover your strength."

She had taken some of the morning's milk from the pail and stirred in a powder which she had brought with her. Now she told Carlyon to hold Mary in a sitting position, while May held the beaker to her lips. Mary dutifully drank and then lay back, seemingly more comfortable, as the effects of the narcotic delusions drained out of her system.

"I know not where I've been," she said, her voice already firmer. "At times I seemed in my body, at other times I was elsewhere. Even now it's fading."

"So it will. You were possessed and have been wandering while a turnskin took your form. It's over now."

"Is it so?" asked Carlyon. "Why should this happen to us?"

"Evil came for you. I know not why, but I fear me, you must still beware."

Carlyon looked over at the sword, lying on the table where he had placed it. "What is this sword?" he muttered, almost to himself. "I wish I knew why it seems so special to me."

"It'll come, son. We'll be thankful we've got through this. We must talk more on the morrow."

May clapped her hands together, as if satisfied, and rubbed her palm with the fingers of the other hand. Silently she picked up the beaker and took it over to the table. Carlyon smiled down at Mary and then carried the candle to put it in a holder. As he straightened up, he saw movement out of the corner of his eye. A man loomed in the open doorway of the cottage. The man stepped inside, and the candlelight picked out his face.

Carlyon stiffened when he saw who it was. "Lord Martin!" Despite the deferential title, Carlyon held his head straight and looked directly into the intruder's face. The strength of his anger was almost tangible, and the candle flame seemed to flicker in the emotion. "So, there you are at last!" he continued. "You dare to come here?"

"Did you think I'd be thwarted by a peasant? I offered you a fair price for that sword of yours. Other lords would have taken it as their right, for surely such a weapon belongs of right to a lord and not a common churl."

"Common I may be, but you'll regret what you've done."

"How so? Your sister has gone off mazed and killed herself. What's that to me? You should have sold me the sword. It's taken me trouble enough to find you, and it'll be worse for you, and you don't give it to me now."

Martin stepped farther into the cottage. Haughtiness was pulling him up, making him seem taller than he was. He opened his mouth to speak again, but no words came. A look of disconcerted fear spread over his face, as he seemed to be looking at something beyond Carlyon's shoulder. Carlyon turned his head to look. Mary had got out of bed and was standing with a blanket draped round her. Martin closed his mouth and gulped. Then he was able to speak.

"You! I hadn't expected to see you alive. Hah! You think you can escape. I'll not be denied." He raised his arm and pointed a finger at Mary. Then his narrow eyes moved to look at Carlyon. "I have the power. You will give me the sword. There's silver in my purse. I'm not a thief. If you give me not the sword, it'll be the worse for your sister and her infant – and also for you!"

While Martin had been speaking, a volcanic rage had been bubbling inside Carlyon. For a year he had always been humble in the presence of nobility, knowing that that was expected. It had not come naturally to him, but it had not been difficult. Yet from the moment that Carlyon had seen Martin in the doorway of his own house, he had felt an urge to stand up to him. He had already told Martin that he would regret what he had done to Mary. As a river, after being blocked, breaks out even stronger, now Martin's final words seemed to open a trap in Carlyon's chest. He pulled himself up to his full height of a good four cubits, and moved over to the table.

"You threaten me and my family," he snapped. "In my own home! I'm a free man, and what's mine is mine. If you want the sword, you can have it!"

He reached out and picked it up off the table. The hilt seemed to leap up into his hand. Turning, he brandished the sword at Lord Martin, who was standing his ground, as if disbelieving what was happening. Carlyon's intention was to beat Martin with the flat of the blade, but that did not happen. As Carlyon brought it down, it twisted and lunged. Before anyone in the cottage knew what was happening, the sword was deep in Martin's chest. The young lord's face froze in horrified surprise, but death was almost instantaneous.

Carlyon was also held by surprise for a second or two, until Martin's weight pressing down on his sword began to push his arm downwards. He stepped back. The sword slid out, and the body dropped to the floor. The event seemed to have surprised the women too. May had let out a scream and was now exclaiming her consternation as she fluttered her hands. Mary too had let out an involuntary gasp. Then she moved over to stand near Carlyon.

"Is he dead?" she asked.

"I fear me so. I didn't expect that."

"What're we going to do?"

They were interrupted by a cry from Stanford. The alarmed voices of the three adults had woken him up. Mary went over to rock his cradle and say soothing words. The other two adults lowered their voices and spoke more calmly.

"He's the stranger who came to my door," May said.

"Yea, a dark day. He's the lord we told you of last year. He tried to buy the sword, and then he tried to steal it."

"A sword so powerful can't be stolen. It must be given or bought, else it will lose its power."

"I didn't mean to kill him. The sword seemed to move of its own."

May glanced at Carlyon. He looked down at the sword still in his hand.

"The sword was not to be taken by him," she told him. "It sensed some evil, I trow."

"Evil, well enough. Now we may find it falling on us. A lord's death is not a simple thing."

Mary left her son, who had settled back to sleep, and came to join them. She looked down at the dead body. Nervously she crossed herself. "We must act quickly," she said. "I don't want an evil spirit in this house."

"Fear not, daughter. I can ward that off."

"I must take the body away." Carlyon spoke firmly, having come to a decision. "I'll wait until later in the night. Then I'll take it into the forest and leave it in a secluded spot. If it's discovered, then men will think he was slain by robbers."

"I fear me you may be seen taking the body. Mayhap we can go to the sergeant and tell him that I was being attacked by a stranger. You came in and killed him to defend me."

"Yes, we could say that. No jury of good men would say aught against that."

"Hold. We must think more on this," May warned. "If we go to the sergeant, there'll be an enquiry. The coroner will want to know who he was and why he was here. Especially if it's suspected he was no wandering vagabond."

"We could remove his clothing and dress him in simpler clothes," Mary suggested.

There was silence for a few seconds. May seemed to be saying a prayer. Carlyon looked down at the body, wondering if they would have anything to fit. Mary stood with her thumb-tip between her teeth, as if it would help her to think. Then she spoke.

"I wonder where he was lodging, and where his horse may be."

Carlyon glanced anxiously at her, but her mother seemed not to have heard her at first.

"I think me the assize won't go well for Carlyon if this man is found to be a lord," she told them. "Carlyon is but a commoner in the world's ken. An' he claim to be a lord, they'll think him crazed and not listen to his evidence. No. It would be better if the body is hid in the forest. Should any soul come to ask questions another day, then we must deny all knowledge of him. Why should we know this lord?"

"I agree," said Carlyon, glad that May was supporting his first suggestion. "It'll be good to get him away from this house. Why should it be thought he had business in our village? I doubt me he was lodging hereabouts. I would have found him this day. He'll have been staying by Warrington or Salford, I trow."

He took up a cloak and covered the body, then stepped round it and closed the cottage door. Standing with his back to the door, he looked at the two women. May smiled reassuringly at him and he went to pick up his sword again. He sighed regretfully and got a cloth from the cupboard to clean off the blood and polish up the blade. While he sat there doing that, Mary got herself ready to feed Stanford and May got out some bread and cheese. Were it not for the blanket on the floor, the cottage had assumed its usual domestic calm.

When the time came to remove the body, Carlyon got up almost reluctantly and went outside to check the area round the cottage. On his return, May said that she had been considering where best to hide the body.

"I know just the place," she said. "It may be that no one will find him."

Carlyon nodded in acknowledgement, but did not want to speak. He knelt by the body and then paused, as he was about to reach out. Giving his head a shake, as if to dispel hovering fears, he pulled at the cloak to wrap it more fully round the body. Mary came to help. Together they rolled Martin into the cloak, until it was tightly round him.

"How will you carry it?" Mary asked.

"On my back. There's no other way. Come now, help me. Can you lift?"

He crouched down on his haunches, resting the fingertips of one hand on the floor for support. Mary and her mother pulled up the body. Both grunted as the exertion forced breath out of their lungs, but they were able to lay the burden on Carlyon's slightly bent back.

"A mite more over my shoulder," he told them, and with his free hand, he helped them distribute the weight better. "Good. Now, a hand, I beg you."

They helped him upright, albeit leaning forward a little, and he stood for a moment or two, accustoming himself to the burden. He let out his breath in a sigh.

"So be it. Pray God, this'll be the end of it." He turned his head to look at Mary. "Bar the door when we've gone, and open to nought till I return."

"I will. Go safely. And you, Mama."

Carlyon went out through the open door, followed by May. Mary watched them set off, then quickly pushed the door to. Outside, it was quiet. Much of the earlier cloud had been blown away, and the starlit June sky had enough light for them to see their way. As they went onto the road a dog barked somewhere nearby. Carlyon tensed, but there was no response, and it seemed to settle back down again.

May walked in front, leading him in the direction of her cottage. It was difficult to talk, as they were walking one behind the other, but Carlyon had no wish to say anything. Eventually they turned off the road into the forest. Here it was difficult to see much, but May seemed to know her way. Carlyon began to struggle with the weight on his back. As he forced his way through undergrowth and amongst the trees, branches and twigs held at his face like ghostly fingers. He began to have the feeling that Martin was moving and clinging on to him. It was as if the corpse did not want to be abandoned in an unmarked grave. Carlyon pushed on, but at last he had to stop. Struggling with the awkward bundle on his back, he called softly to May.

"Mama! Can you help here? It's slipping off my back."

She came round behind him, and with her help, he pulled Martin higher up. The clinging sensation disappeared, as if May had taken it away, and the body became simply the dead weight that it was. Even so, Carlyon felt uncomfortable. He tried to look at May, but in the darkness he could see nothing of her face. There was only a vague shape.

"Is it much farther?" he asked.

"Not too far now. We'll soon be there."

"I like not this place. Are you sure there're no evil spirits abroad?"

"Spirits there may be, but they won't harm us. Were you to see this place at midday, it would seem the most peaceful place you could imagine."

"Mayhap. But at midnight I only see what there is. And sense. I wish I'd brought my sword. What and this lord Martin's spirit follows us?"

"Fret you not, son. I'll protect you and Mary from that. But come now, let's press on. It'll soon be over. And see, a moon is rising now to give us a little guidance."

She moved back in front of him, and they set off again. This time it was not long before May stopped again. Carlyon saw a small hollow, clear of trees, so that there was some glimmering of light from the open sky. The hollow had a pool of water on one side. In the deceptive darkness Carlyon was unable to judge its size, but it barely seemed large enough to take a man's body. Involuntarily he shivered at the thought that Martin might pull him down into a bottomless pit of water. He let the body slip off his back to lie on the ground.

"How deep is this?" he asked.

"No more than a man's arm, I ween. But 'twill do. Look you, just by here."

Carlyon looked to where briars were growing over in an ever-falling fountain of leaves.

"We can put the body under them. No one comes to this spot. A young maid was killed here in my father's time. Her spirit is said to haunt the place, enticing men."

Hearing that, the hairs at the back of Carlyon's neck began to prickle, and he wondered that May had brought him there. Looking across the pool, his tired eyes saw shadows twisting and twining as if alive. In the short time that they had been standing there, he had heard snortings and rustlings around them. He knew that such noises would be coming from small forest creatures that came out at night. Even so, it was unnerving to hear and not be able to see.

May seemed to sense his unease. "Quickly, now. Let's get this done." She pushed her way through some undergrowth and used her staff to hook under the briars and lift them a little. "Can you push it under there?"

Carlyon picked up the body, still wrapped in the cloak, and moved up to May. It was very difficult to see what he was doing. As he got to the edge of the pool, one of his feet slipped over and went into the water. He could not prevent a shout of fear, but the water came little more than halfway up his calf, and May's hand on his arm steadied him.

"Have haste, now. Push it in."

Using both hands on her staff, she again lifted the briars a little. He pushed the body under them. When the briars fell back, they pressed the body into the water. Thankfully Carlyon climbed out, heedless to the scratches. He began to shake his foot, to get rid of the water, but May immediately pulled his arm.

"Come. We'll leave this place. I'll come back after sunrise and see that all's hidden."

"I'll come with you also," Carlyon said as they moved off. He would bring his sword with him. "We may need to move the body."

"No. I'll come on my own. I know this place well. I think it best you stay away and never come here again. You go home now and comfort Mary. She'll be fretting at your lateness."

Carlyon agreed. As far as any future visit was concerned, he doubted that he would be able to find the place on his own. Now he kept close with May, almost touching her as they walked. Soon the forest thinned out, and through the trees a broad moon chequered the ground to mark their way. Unlike their arrival, he was walking more easily as they left. The removal of the physical weight from his back seemed to have moved a weight also from his spirit.

He accompanied May back to her cottage. After embracing at the door, he set off for home, eager relief driving his legs to run at times. Mary was waiting up for him when he arrived. It had been an anxious wait, and his return showered her in warm joy. She impetuously threw her arms round him and kissed him before he could even close the door.

"Went all well?" she asked breathlessly. "Is Mama safe?"

"All's well. I took Mama back home." He shivered. "God grant I have no such night again."

"Amen. We've overcome something fearsome this night."

She let go of Carlyon but stayed by him as he closed and barred the door. When he turned back, relief was warming his smile for her. At last he felt secure. Silently he stepped over to look at his son, sleeping peacefully in his cradle. Mary came to stand beside him. For some seconds they stood looking down, then Mary put her hand on Carlyon's arm. Her touch was as gentle as dawn slipping out of night, but he felt it. He turned his head to look at her.

"Come now, Carlyon. Let's to bed."

"Yes. All's safe now."

As the following days passed into weeks, the body was not discovered. Apart from the first few days, they did not talk about it. May had told them that the body was well hidden and that they should rest easy. Carlyon's mind took some time to become eased, for he could not prevent himself from often thinking over what had taken place. He had been greatly disturbed by what had happened to Mary. His memories only went back for little over a year, to the time when he was rescued from the Thames by Henry the goliard, and so he had few experiences for comparison. The turmoil of his thoughts churned away for several days, bringing to the surface emotions which he had not experienced before, like carp pulled, thrashing, from a millpond. These emotions were firmly concerned with Mary and Stanford. Knowing that he had almost lost Mary, he realised how lost he himself would be without her. His love for her and his son became a strong bond that he vowed would never be broken.

Through the summer months he worked hard, tying himself into the life of his local community, for that was his life now. During the previous spring, before sowing got underway, he had thought up a short drama, which he and three of the other village men performed to great entertainment during the May Day festivities. A few days before midsummer, the village priest came to talk to him.

"Your play caused some amusement last May Day, I trow," the priest said. "And yet such lewdness is surely not proper. The Church does not approve of such things."

Carlyon pulled in the corners of his mouth, as if contrite. He said nothing about having seen the priest laughing with everyone else at the ribald sallies in the drama.

"And yet I think me you have a talent the Church can use," the priest went on. "Where did you learn your letters?"

"I was taught when I was a boy. Before I came to these parts," said Carlyon. As far as he knew, he was telling the truth.

"Mayhap you had been placed in a monastery as a foundling and were destined for the Church?"

"That may be so, Father," said Carlyon, although he knew it not to be so, "but fate has brought me here and I must accept God's will."

"Amen, amen. And that's what I wish to talk to you about. Your talent can be used for the Church to enlighten other men. I wish you to write another play, but this time to be performed in honour of our church's patron, St Oswald, whose day falls in August. Know you the blessed St Oswald's history? No? We shall speak this Sunday after matins, and I'll tell you of his life. There will be lessons for men to learn."

Carlyon nodded, intrigued, and in due time he produced a moral, uplifting drama which was performed in the churchyard that St Oswald's Day.

So the summer passed. Materially Carlyon's family was well provided for. Since making his deal to supply sea coal to David the limer, he had also made deals to supply two forges. As required, he hired a labourer to dig out the black mineral, and with the profit he was able to rent extra pieces of land for growing crops. He was even able to lend out money on occasions.

Then one evening, some two weeks or so before Michaelmas, when he was talking to Mary over supper, he broached something that had been in his mind for a few days. "The harvest has not been so good this year. Everybody's talking about it. It seems to me also that last year's was better."

"At times harvests are bad. But we always have to eke out the flour, ere spring's over. At least the pigs are getting fat."

"We've been giving them extra food. They'll see us through the year. I think me not, my love, that we ourselves have need to worry. But there are others who'll be in debt. This may serve us, because some will be willing to sell land. It'd be useful to get another piece that has sea coal. And I would like to have a larger house built – with two, even three rooms."

"That would be lovely." Mary's eyes sparkled in her pleasure, and Carlyon trembled to see how he could make her so happy. "I'd like a room of our own, free of animal stink at night."

"I also." He paused and smiled, then went on. "I have me an idea." He indicated the oak chest against the wall, where they kept their money and their few more valuable possessions. "There's armour in that chest – good-quality mail and plate. A smith would pay fair money for it."

"You think to sell it?"

"That's so. I know not where it came from, and I can think to have no use for it. It'd be good to sell it."

"You may be right. I can't say. Mayhap there'll be no need of it. It was another life. You have this one now."

"This is my life – you and little Stanford. I want no other and nothing will call me away. We'll sell the armour. It's nought but a sign of a life I've left behind." The firmness in his voice was emphasised by a light tap on the table with his extended forefinger.

Mary met his smile with her own. "And yet you will not also sell the sword?" she asked slowly.

"No." Carlyon had already considered that. He looked over at the chest and spoke as if to himself. "I feel I must keep it. When I touch it, I can sense a strange power in my arm. There's magic there, I trow, but it's good magic."

"Magic indeed. The sword has brought us some trouble, but it has also been of great help. I've often wondered whose it was, before you found it."

"A valiant knight's, no doubt. It's not a thing to be able to sell to an ordinary man. I'll keep it. Mayhap Stanford will have use for it one day. I'll speak to the smith about the armour when I take him his sea coal."

"I think me you would get a better price an' you went to Warrington. There are more smiths there."

Carlyon nodded thoughtfully and took a drink of his beer.

It would mean a full day, but he could see the benefits in Mary's suggestion.

One day the following week, Carlyon left the house while it was still an hour to dawn. The armour had been packed away into a stout leather pouch, and Mary had prepared some food for him. Almost as he was about to leave, he decided to take his sword.

"It'll serve me well, and I meet any robbers on my way," he told Mary, who smiled.

"I pity the robber who meets you," she said fondly.

Tenderly he kissed his sleeping son and then Mary. She wished him well and he slipped quietly out of the house, knowing it would be the following day when he returned.

There was a slight September chill in the air, but he thought that the day would promise fair. The darkness was silvering away in the dappled east, but he knew the road out of the village well and he strode along confidently. Not long after daybreak, however, he saw a sheet of rain come flapping towards him through the trees like a dirty grey flag. The storm was heavy enough to make him take shelter, but the worst of it lasted little more than thirty minutes. When the rain lessened, he set off again but found that the road had been turned into a quagmire. He struggled on for a while, but then thought that it might be better were he to strike off for some higher ground that he could see to his right. He went through a wood and found the going easier, though still wet.

Fortunately, it was not too long before the rain died away completely. He strode on in high spirits, buoyed by the fresh scent in his nostrils that the rain had released from the surrounding vegetation. The sun was out, and he could feel it warm on his face. His thoughts began to wander, and as he walked, he slipped into a daydream about his future plans for him and Mary.

This was interrupted when his path took him by the lip of a quarry. His attention diverted, he stopped for a moment to look over. The quarry was not deep – little more than the height of three men, he judged – but it was broad, and he could see men working on the far side. He had heard the tapping of their tools before he came upon the quarry. For a few seconds he stood and watched, taking the opportunity to draw breath. Taking a final deep breath, as if drawing in calmness from the tranquil scene, he turned to continue his journey.

As he twisted his foot round, it slipped in the muddy soil. He struggled to recover, but the weight of the pack on his back made him overbalance. Before he knew it, he was tumbling into the quarry. It was all happening so quickly that he had no time to react. There was a weird sensation of floating. He knew nothing of how one of his hands ineffectually scrabbled for the side of the quarry as he turned upside down. Nor did he know anything of how his head struck against protruding rock on the quarry floor, and there was nothing more. No awareness of anything, no sensations, only blankness.

7

Out of an empty, blind darkness, Carlyon began to sense movement around him. This was overlaid by pain. There was aching in his body, but most of all, it seemed, in his head. He had no idea what was happening or where he was. Suddenly he was frightened. He thought that he was in water and like to drown. He must have cried out, because he heard a voice in his dream.

"Calm thissen, brother. There's no water here."

A realisation came to him that he was lying on the ground, and he tried to think how that had happened. He should have been in water. Perhaps he had been pulled out and was on the riverbank. His eyes, which had been open for some seconds, at last made connection with his brain. His brain also now began to make sense of the sounds coming into his ears. They were the voices of two men; voices filled with concern. He understood, despite their rough accents, that they were asking how he was feeling, and could he sit up? Slowly he moved his head and a spasm of pain struck at the back of his eyes. Then it was gone, and when he opened his eyes again after their involuntary closure, he saw two men, one on each side of him. They were dressed in rough grey peasant tunics, their hair was dirty and unkempt, and he could smell the sweat from their labour. One of the men pushed an arm beneath his shoulders and lifted him up slightly. The movement brought a grunt from his throat, but his head seemed clearer, and he was able to take in more of what was happening.

"We were working over there," one of the men said, "and we saw thee fall. That were a tumble."

"Yea," said his companion. "I thought tha werest a bird. How dost feel now, brother? Better?"

"I think me so, good men. I fell here, you say?"

"Right there." One of the men pointed up at the quarry lip behind them, but Carlyon could only turn partly to look.

"I can't remember falling here," he said. "Are we far from the river?"

"Not far. Half a league."

"Nay, less," added the man's companion. "Thou crossed it, I trow. We heard thee say as tha werest drowning. Hast travelled far? Thou beest not from round here. Where from, brother?"

"From? Oh... I've come from Chertsey."

"Churt's Eye? I know not that place. Dost mean Chester?"

Carlyon pulled himself up a little more, so that he could wriggle his arms out of his backpack. He was strong enough now to sit unaided, and when he spoke again, his voice was firmer. "Tell me, good fellows, how far are we from the town of Maidenhead?"

The men, kneeling on each side of him, looked across him at each other. One licked his lips nervously and edged slightly away. The other crossed himself but seemed determined not to flinch.

"There be no such place in Christendom, I trow. Who'd live in such a meanly named place? What do men call thee, stranger? Beest thou a Christian man?"

"Of course! I'm the knight Sir Carlyon de Bernedeslaw. My squire must be hereabouts."

The men seemed a little reassured. One spoke to the other, as if Carlyon were a child. "He's mazed from his fall, poor soul. He thinks he be a knight."

His companion laughed as his body relaxed. Carlyon looked suspiciously at him and then glanced down at himself. For the first time he noticed what he was wearing. His boots were well made, but of undecorated leather in a clumpy design. His tunic was of plain brown wool and his cloak also seemed homespun with no pattern. His rich clothing had disappeared. His immediate thought was that the two men had attacked him and stolen his clothes, but almost straight away he realised that they would not have dressed him again.

"I don't understand. My clothes have gone. How did I get here?"

"We know nought o' that. We saw thee fall from up there." The man pointed, and this time Carlyon turned and saw the top of the quarry wall. "How thou got there, only God or Satan knows."

"What place is this?" Carlyon asked. "Is there a town nearby?"

"Yea. We be no more than an hour from Warrington."

"Say you so? Warrington?" Carlyon knew the name. He also knew that it was in north-west England, not far from the Wirral Forest. His brow furrowed as he fought with his confusion. He'd thought that he had returned to Chertsey, and yet here he was still in Lancashire and dressed as a peasant. It made no sense. It was as if he had been dreaming. "Is this my pouch?" he asked. "I've dropped no other?"

The men moved their heads to look around, but there was nothing else to see. Carlyon opened the pouch, but there was only armour inside. His sword was fastened to the outside. It comforted him to touch it, but it was of no help in explaining his present situation. He looked inside his small pouch, but that contained only a little food. Nothing else. No flowers of the swan. Again his brow furrowed. He was at a loss. He remembered finding the flowers, picking them, and taking them back to Chertsey. He was sure of that, but he began to wonder if it was all in his imagination.

His two helpers had stood up. While seemingly happy at an interruption to their toil, they were now becoming restless.

"Wouldst like a drop o' ale?" asked one. "I'll fetch thee some."

While he went over to where he had been working, Carlyon's gaze was caught by a tree that he could see. It was a crab apple full of fruit.

"What time of year is this?" he asked tentatively, almost fearing the reply.

"Harvest time, brother. It's nigh to Michaelmas."

Carlyon drew in his breath. Michaelmas – but struggle as he might, he could remember nothing since spring. Yet he must have been wandering around all summer. Perhaps he had been bewitched?

The man returned with an earthenware flagon and offered it. Carlyon took out the wooden stopper and raised the flagon to his mouth. As the cool, sweet liquid slipped down his throat, he still tried to remember how he had returned to Lancashire. Thoughtfully he lowered the flagon to his lap. However, the beer had at least refreshed him physically, and he handed it back with gracious thanks.

"We must back to work now," the man said. "Rest thee here awhile."

Carlyon nodded and again thanked the men. He watched them trudge away across the quarry floor, then looked at his pouch. There was still a slight ache in his head, but he pushed himself to try to remember where he had been since spring. He could clearly remember taking the flowers of the swan back to Chertsey. At least that had happened. He remembered well being told that Lady

Patrina was married and living near Maidenhead. So, he had gone there and walked by the river to scatter the flowers. He remembered them floating away, and then he'd stumbled and fallen into the swiftly flowing water. After that, it was a blank. Try as he might, there was nothing more. Angrily he banged his fist down on his pouch in his frustration. He forcefully blew out a breath. There was no help for it. He looked down at his clothes. Perhaps he had been robbed during his wanderings, and he had only been able to get a peasant's clothing. At least he still had his sword. He touched it reassuringly and then spread out his palms to look at them. They were sunburnt and lightly calloused. His brow furrowed. Could it be that he had been engaged in manual labour? Surely not? He was a gentle-born knight.

On one of his fingers there was a ring. He looked at it closely, seeing how the colour of the single stone seemed to change when he moved his hand. He wondered how he had acquired it, where it had come from. He rubbed his fingers gently over the smooth stone. As he did so, he felt a strange sensation, which started in his stomach and moved into his chest. It was a pleasurable sensation, but there was something regretful about it, as if there was something missing. He pulled in his lips and let his hands move apart into his lap.

The tap of the quarrymen's tools broke into his introspection, and he looked over at them. It came to him that they would be unable to help him anymore. Judging by the fresh mire on his boots, he had walked far already that day. He had not been staying in the neighbourhood, so no one would know him or know why he was there. Tightening his lips in determination, he came to a decision. What had happened, had happened. There was nothing to keep him in Lancashire and he should return home to Hertford. His family was there.

Gingerly he felt his head, just to the side of the temple. It was painful, but it was not bleeding. Nor did there seem to be any other injuries elsewhere on his body. Grunting quietly, he pushed himself to his knees and then stood up. At first he swayed, as his head began to swim. He held out his arms, as if seeking support, and took in some deep breaths. His head cleared and he looked around carefully, but steadily. There was still a slight ache in his head, but he took a few steps to test and found that he could walk without any other discomfort. He picked up his pack and put it on his back. For a second he paused, and then he walked over to the quarrymen, who had stopped work to watch him.

"I bless you for your kindness, good fellows," he said. "I know not how I fell, but, thank the Lord, I seem no worse for it. I must be on my way now."

"Are't ready to leave, brother?" asked one of the men, concern showing in his face.

"Indeed. I've far to go. Where lies the road to Warrington?"

Convinced by the firmness in his voice, they gave him directions, and he set off.

When he came upon Warrington, its buildings crumpled together in a bend of the River Mersey, he sat under a tree to rest before entering the town. For some seconds he allowed himself to relax. Tenderly he felt at the side of his head. It was no longer aching, but there was still a little pain to the touch. He decided to have his dinner, and he pulled out the cloth-wrapped package. Having unwrapped it, he examined it curiously. Bread, cooked meat, some cake. He wondered where he had obtained it, who had prepared it with such care. Something was nagging at him like a cord flapping at his back. He knew that it was important, but try as he might, he was unable to reach behind him and grab the cord. He had to leave it.

When he had finished eating, he looked in his purse. There were a few pence, and he considered how long they would last. Then he shrugged. He was sure that he would manage. Slowly, but purposefully, he pulled himself to his feet, fixed his pack over his shoulders, and set off again. He knew that he had several days in front of him.

Four days later he had crossed much of Staffordshire. That evening he found lodging for the night in a monastery, grateful for their charity. A blister had come up on one of his feet and he was finding it painful to walk. On arriving at the monastery, he went to the infirmary and spoke to one of the brothers.

"How far have you walked, my son?" the monk asked.

Carlyon told him, and added that he was travelling to Hertfordshire, where his home was.

"That's a long way distant. How came you so far?"

"I know not, Father. There's a hole in my remembrance, as if five months of my life had been scooped out and discarded."

The monk looked at him dubiously, and Carlyon went on.

"I've tried to remember. I came through these parts last Advent season, and I can remember returning south afterwards come springtime. Unless perchance that was a dream and I've been wandering around until I came back to my senses but four days gone."

"A strange tale. I have heard of people being transported into an ecstasy and remembering nought when they awoke. But not for so long a span. Have you felt the Lord's presence?"

Carlyon shook his head, and the monk looked disappointed.

"I've seen strange things," Carlyon said, "but I know them to be real. I'm afire to get back to my father's house. Mayhap the answer lay there. It's a long walk yet. Do you have a salve for my feet?"

He pulled off his boots, and the monk washed his feet for him. The good brother seemed to have seen much worse, because he made no comment. He rubbed an ointment on them and bound them with clean linen cloths, finally blessing Carlyon and sending him back to the guest room. After evening prayers, Carlyon sat on his bed and reviewed his progress. He flexed his aching limbs and came to a decision. He would see if he could exchange his armour for a horse. Even an aged palfrey would make it easier for him.

However, when he awoke the next morning, his feet seemed much eased, and he thought that he would keep his armour yet. He had had another idea, just before he fell asleep. He could sell the strange ring. After dressing, he tried to slip the ring off his finger, to examine it more closely. To his surprise, it would not move. Nor could he even twist it round on his finger, even though it had always moved easily until then. He tugged for a while, but then gave it up, thinking to try later.

He continued southwards that day, and towards late afternoon he found shelter in a cottage. To repay the hospitality, he went out with the man to help him gather firewood. When they returned to the cottage, a horse was tethered outside.

"What's this?" said the man, as much to himself as to Carlyon. "So late a stranger."

He put down his end of the tree and, gripping his axe, went into the cottage. Left outside, Carlyon lifted one end of the trunk and pulled it round to get it out of the way, ready for cutting to size. Then he rinsed his hands in a pail by the doorway and splashed some of the water onto his face. The evening had turned cooler, and now that he was no longer working, he felt the chill through his clothes. He shivered slightly and thought warmly of the supper that his host's goodwife would have prepared. He bent his head under the lintel and entered the cottage.

It was gloomy inside, but he saw the visitor standing with his back to him. He was almost as tall as Carlyon, and even in the dimness Carlyon could see that he was well dressed. The clothes had been tailored to fit the body, his belt was decorated, and over his blond hair he was wearing a hat instead of a hood. Carlyon realised that the man was a person of rank. He stopped just inside the doorway, and his host, who was standing in front of the stranger and a little to one side, glanced at him and then spoke to his new visitor.

"Here's the fellow I just told you of, sir. He's travelled down from Lancashire."

The stranger turned his head towards Carlyon and, as if habitually speaking to a peasant, he began to ask Carlyon if he had seen a knight on his travels. Carlyon, standing with his back to the doorway, had a shadowed face, but light was falling on the stranger. He was a young man, and Carlyon recognised him immediately. He was his squire, James Morton. Surprise swept away his tiredness, as if a cloak had been snatched off him.

"James!" he cried. "How came you here?"

James drew his head back and he looked suspiciously at Carlyon. Then recognition flashed into his eyes. "Is that you, sire?" He stepped up closer and raised his arm slightly, as if about to touch Carlyon in order to confirm that he was real. "You seem changed."

"Mayhap so. I fear me I've had adventures since we parted, and here I am, dressed as a peasant. But say, how came you here?"

"Your father has sent me. No one knew where you were. It was as if you'd been spirited away. When I left you by the Thames, I went into Maidenhead and found lodgings for us, but you came not. I searched for you, but there was nothing and no one had seen you. I thought me you had gone back to your father's, but they knew nought when I got there. So I went back to my father's house and waited for you to come. Three weeks since, your father sent for me and asked me to search for you. I thought me you may have gone back to Lancashire. I'm on my way there. Is that where you've been? Why did you stay silent?"

"Ah, James, I know not what to tell you. But come, we're keeping these good folk from their supper. Let's sit and we'll talk."

The peasant and his wife had been listening to what was being said, clearly interested in it. The wife, who had been interrupted in her work by James's arrival, now picked up the pot of stew from the fire and carried it to the table. They all sat down, the woman took her toddler onto her lap, and they took it in turn to serve themselves. After a grace had been said, James added more.

"Thanks to the Lord for helping me to find my master, who was lost."

Carlyon also added his amen to that. Then, before beginning to eat, he had a question for James that he had been nervous to ask. "Is it true, James, that we went to Chertsey and discovered that Lady Patrina was married to Sir John?"

James paused in his eating and confirmed it.

Carlyon nodded in regretful acknowledgement. He had not wanted to believe it. "I thought me that might have been in my imagination. We went to Maidenhead, did we not? I went by the river and scattered the flowers. So much trouble in their getting and so little effort in their casting away. And then, alack, there's nothing. I must have been bewitched. Yet somehow the spell was broken a few days ago. I came to my senses dressed as a peasant in Lancashire, but not knowing how or why."

"So, you went to Lancashire? Mayhap you went to seek Mary? Did you find her?"

"Mary – the thatcher's daughter? She is a pearl, but I doubt me I would have gone seeking her." Carlyon shook his head. "I know not why I returned to the north-west. I've no memory at all of what I may have been doing these past five months."

"Five months?" James put the fist holding his knife onto the table and looked at Carlyon with puzzlement wrinkling his face. "What five months?"

"Since we parted at Maidenhead this last springtide. I say, I can't remember where I've been since then."

"It was not this last springtide. It's nigh two years since we set off on the quest for the flowers of the swan, and it was a year last springtide gone that we parted. Knew you not that?"

This time Carlyon laid down his knife. He sat with both hands on the table, pressing as if trying to prevent himself from falling forward. "Our quest was last year, you say?" He looked at his hands, but they seemed no older for their missing year. Except that they were unusually suntanned. "I can't think that. What can I have been doing? I must have been wandering as a beggar."

Disconcerted, he stopped speaking. Learning so suddenly that he had lost another year of his life made it seem worse. His brain was swirling like a boy's Shrovetide spinning top, and he had to blink several times to clear his vision. The two peasants were looking at him and James with great interest, clearly amazed at the story that was unfolding before them. Even their toddler child was silent.

James began to speak, as if noticing nothing odd. "Mayhap there've been adventures. Who'll be able to say what you've been doing? Yet I ween there'll be nought of import, else you'd be able to remember it."

"Hah!" said Carlyon. "Mayhap. And yet…" He shook his head, feeling a little more sure of himself. "Pray, James, tell me what you did when we parted."

"I found lodgings in the town and then waited there, as you told me. When you came not, I went back to the river to seek you. I searched all around. I also made enquiries of the lady Patrina's household, but no one had seen you. I thought me you had gone home, so I went to see your father."

"How is my father? And my dear mother?"

"Well. Both well, sire. They were most pleased with our adventures on the quest and eager for your return. I went back to my father's house and waited for you to send for me. Then nigh St Helena's Day last it was your father who sent for me. He entreated me to go out and seek you. I was to discover what had happened to you…" James paused and then went on. "If it had been God's will that you had died, then I was to bring your remains home."

Carlyon crossed himself at the thought and involuntarily glanced down at his body. "Thank the Lord, it came not to that," he said, smiling a little ruefully. "But what did you discover about what had happened to me?"

"Very little, I fear. I travelled first to Maidenhead and made enquiries. No corse of your description had been found, so I was hopeful that you were yet alive. I found me a herdsman, who remembered that a man had been rescued from the river. He was near drowned, and when he came to his senses, he knew nought of who he was, not even his name. No other man knew who he was. He was a stranger. I asked about for more news, but I learned only that the man had gone away with his rescuer."

"I must have been that man. I wish I could find my rescuer and thank him. But mayhap I've already done it a hundred times over.

I must have been wandering the land with him. If we found him, he would say where I've been this past eighteen months."

"I knew in my heart also that you were the stranger. But where to find? I thought to travel northwards, asking if aught had been seen. One woman told me of a man who seemed like you, but he was travelling with his sister, so it was not you. Then I found you here, like a miracle."

"Truly a miracle." Carlyon sat up straight, as confidence like strong arms raised him. He was feeling more himself now. "I can scarce believe it myself. We must give our thanks in the church tomorrow, before we leave. Then home. It matters not what I've been doing since we parted. It can't be important. I suppose I was living as a vagabond, a peasant. Yet it surely did me no harm. I doubt it could have been a bad life. Mayhap I even enjoyed it. But now it's past. I must think of the future. On the morrow we set off for my father's, and I can take up my life again."

Carlyon grinned his happiness at James and reached for his beaker of beer. As if accepting that the wondrous tale was over, the peasant's wife got up from the table and took her toddler to prepare it for bed. Shortly afterwards the man went out to bring in his chickens and the household prepared to settle down for the night.

The following morning Carlyon made as fond a farewell to the peasant and his family as if he had been living there for a month, rather than overnight. In some way he felt grateful to them, almost feeling that they had brought him and James together. Now the two of them set off southwards, Carlyon taking the horse.

"We'll go to Lichfield," suggested James. "It's not far distant. We'll be able to buy a horse there."

"And some proper clothing for me also," added Carlyon. He looked down at his drab clothing, eager to dress in the richer cloth to which he was entitled. Then, as they went along Watling Street, he remembered something. "A cousin of my uncle Richard's wife has an estate by Lichfield. We'll visit there and he'll provide us with all we need, I trow."

They sought directions, and when they reached the manor house, James said that he was the squire of Sir Carlyon de Bernedeslaw and that he wished to speak to the lord about his master. Taken to see Lord Walter, James showed him the letter, which he carried from Carlyon's father, requesting that he be given all assistance.

"I bid you welcome, my boy," said Lord Walter, after reading the letter. "I've heard somewhat of your master's disappearance. Think you he's in these parts?"

"Indeed so, my lord. In fact, here he is." James indicated Carlyon, who was standing by his side.

Walter looked at him suspiciously, as if surprised that a peasant should be so forward as to be by the squire's side.

"I came upon him but yester even. He's been wandering mazed this past year and more, but we return now to Hertford."

"This man is Cousin Carlyon?" asked Walter, speaking to James as if he were more sure of his identity at least. "Is he not an impostor?"

"Not I, my lord," said Carlyon, speaking boldly and clearly. "I am my aunt Elizabeth's nephew, and I pray your help to return to my father."

Lord Walter squinted closely at him and then examined the seal on the letter. Satisfied as to the genuineness of that, he asked some personal family questions. Carlyon put a halter on his impatience and answered the questions. He could not understand why Lord Walter was asking after the family instead of giving them refreshment. However, out of politeness he humoured the elderly man.

At last Lord Walter's eyes crinkled in a warm smile of welcome and he opened his arms to embrace Carlyon. "Welcome, cousin," he said. "This is a strange thing, but happy I am to see you. You must stay here with me and rest. I'll warrant you've many an adventure to tell for our amusement. I'll send a messenger off this day to your father to give him the good news. Now, we must see about some clothing for you."

The next day, in new breeches and chemise and with a warm overtunic of dyed wool, Carlyon felt totally at home. He was at ease in a society that was as familiar to him as the warm breath in his body. He and James stayed with his relations for over a week. By day they went hunting, and in the evenings they played chess or backgammon. Lord Walter's son, a few years older than Carlyon, was excellent company. His wife had recently had a baby son, and Carlyon, who had never before had any close association with babies, was strangely entranced by the little fellow. He tickled him with his forefinger to make him laugh, and the baby would look at him with wide, enquiring eyes. It gave Carlyon an odd feeling, that he could not understand. James came upon him one afternoon with the baby on his lap. He had been singing a little song that seemed to have come from nowhere.

"My lord Walter the younger is practising swordplay in the yard, sire. Do you desire to join us?"

"Of course. Straight away." Despite the eager tone of his words, it was almost reluctantly that Carlyon handed the baby back to the nurse and got to his feet. "Come, James, let's give our arms some work."

"He's a bright little fellow," said James as they left the room. "He's taken to you, I trow."

"I love him dearly, though I know not why."

Carlyon bit at his lower lip thoughtfully. He had been surprised that he was so attracted to the baby, and he thought that it might be because he felt that he should be married to Lady Patrina and be a father in his own right. A wave of sadness hit him, and ebbing away it left him with a sense of emptiness, as if he were missing something. While walking to his chamber to get his sword, he absently rubbed at the ring on his left hand with the fingers of his right. Unaccountably, the image of Mary the thatcher's daughter slipped into his mind. Her eyes were alight with warmth, and her welcoming smile brightened her face with gentle beauty. He almost faltered in his step, thinking that she was there in front of him. It seemed odd that he should be thinking of her after so long, but he wondered where she was and if she were contented. He smiled to himself and shook his head. She would no doubt be with her mother, or perhaps even married by now.

When the time came for Carlyon and James to resume their journey home, Carlyon was astride one of the best horses from Lord Walter's stable. It was warm Michaelmas weather, which suited the mood of the travellers as they went down Watling Street at a relaxed pace.

"I'll be glad to get back home," Carlyon remarked. He had pulled his hat low over his forehead to shield his eyes from the sun, which was almost in front of them. He bent his head sideways to look at James. "I've had a surfeit of adventures for the nonce."

"Truly so, sire. Pray God, nothing now hinders our journey."

"I doubt anything can. We're but a few days from home with stout steeds. I look forward to the feasting there'll be when we arrive." Carlyon grinned at James, then looked at the road ahead, seeing his home in his imagination.

James was silent for a while, and then spoke, hesitantly, as if unsure. "Will you now settle down at home? Content yourself with hunting and the like?"

"I think not. Once I had such intentions – had affairs turned out differently. But, my love has married and there's an end of that. For me, there's a restlessness in my body now. I feel strangely that I've left something undone. So, I'll bide at home this winter season, and then next spring, I'm sure the King will be campaigning. We'll join him and that should keep us busy. Mayhap I'll find a new lady to court."

"There'll be adventures enough, and we go abroad, sire. It may be campaigning will ease your mind."

"Hope you so? I doubt. Danger surely holds no refuge, nor war no peace. I only hope that keeping my arms occupied will keep my heart from dwelling on lost time."

"Amen to that. I'd fain go with you to serve the King."

Carlyon smiled to himself. He realised that James had been anxious about his own situation. He thought to reassure him. "To be with the King will be good, James. There'll be opportunities for advancement there, I trow. Then when we return at the end of the year, it'll be fair to speak about your investiture."

James muttered words of thanks, but Carlyon good-naturedly cut them short. He could sense his squire's embarrassment and understood it. He knew that James had always felt some awkwardness over the fact that his father was a merchant, albeit a rich one. To become a knight would be a fine advancement for his family, and Carlyon felt good about being able to help. As they rode along together now, he remembered the slightly awkward fourteen-year-old who had first entered his service. The James who was riding beside him was a different person. Carlyon had been surprised at the change in him since they had parted at Maidenhead. James, almost eighteen years of age, was now a man. His body had filled out, and he carried an air of confidence with him, as if it were a second skin. In faith, thought Carlyon, he'll make a good knight.

The following day they were travelling down the border between Warwickshire and Leicestershire, and as the sun began to wester, they left Watling Street and went a few miles northwards to find a monastery for the night. On leaving the next day, their way back to the highway took them past a cottage set amongst the trees. It was a tumbledown affair. Carlyon saw immediately that the roof had known better days, and he appraised it as if he knew about such things. Wattle was sticking out of the walls, and the open door was hanging on only one top hinge. A few hens were scratching on the threadbare mat of grass which covered the yard, but there was no sign of any other livestock. Raised voices could be heard from inside the hovel. Then as they drew nearer, a raggedly dressed man came out through the doorway as if thrown, and fell in a crumple on the ground. Two men dressed in scarlet livery came out and began to beat at the peasant with thick staves. Carlyon was going to ride by, but it seemed to him that the men were taking pleasure in the beating. He saw a weeping woman, equally raggedly dressed, appear in the doorway, and he impulsively reined in his horse.

"Ho! You fellows!" he called. "What goes on here? Stop that!"

The men did stop, and looked over at Carlyon and James, still several paces away. One man kept his staff raised, as if ready to resume the beating. The other straightened up and partially lowered his staff.

"Who interferes in my lord's business?" this man asked boldly.

"I do, Sir Carlyon de Bernedeslaw. I say again – what goes on here?"

"This knave owes dues to his lord. Nought else."

"That's no reason to give him such a beating. Lay off now."

"We've authority to beat an idle knave. We take our orders from our liege lord."

The man shifted his grip on his staff and turned his back on Carlyon. The peasant on the ground cowered and a whimpering sound came out of his mouth. The staves again came down on his body. The man who had spoken to Carlyon raised his arm for a second strike. It began to come down but was unexpectedly halted. Carlyon had moved his horse across, and he now held the man's arm in a tight grip.

"I won't have this! Enough!"

He twisted the man's arm and pulled the staff out of his grip. Raising it now, he brought it down on the man's shoulder. The man tried to move out of the way but tripped over the peasant and also fell onto the ground. His companion stepped back a pace and looked nervously undecided. Carlyon dismounted and lifted the staff to give its previous owner another knock but was interrupted by a loud voice.

"Who interferes with my men?"

8

It was an authoritative voice that held Carlyon's raised arm just as he was about to bring his staff down onto the fallen caitiff. The voice was also laced with anger, and yet it was somehow familiar to Carlyon. He let the arm holding the staff fall to his side, as he turned his head to look towards the direction of the voice. Its owner was astride a well-built horse of a good fifteen hands in height. The saddle and trappings were of fine quality, and the tossing of the horse's head seemed to indicate the animal's own pride in its appearance. Carlyon took all this in as his gaze flicked across, but it was the sight of the rider that made him loosen his grip on the staff, which fell unheeded to the ground. The new arrival was a large, somewhat beefy man, his and his horse's height making him tower over the small group as he came, almost aggressively, nearer. He was wearing a fine green overtunic, which was held in at the waist by a decorated leather belt. His hood was pulled closely over his head, allowing only a few wisps of dark brown hair to straggle out, but Carlyon could clearly see his face. The familiarity of the voice was confirmed. It was Carlyon's old friend, Sir John le Cerre-nore.

"John!" Carlyon cried out, delight arm in arm with surprise. "By Our Lady, you're here!"

There was no mistaking John. He looked just the same to Carlyon. His strapping body was topped by a round, cheery face that was seemingly ever ready to break out into hearty laughter. The only difference was a scar on his face. It ran from his brow over the crumpled left eyelid and down the cheek. Carlyon wondered at the swordsman who had dealt such a blow.

John had leaned forward slightly at the sound of Carlyon's voice. His good eye was now peering at Carlyon as if unsure. Only for a second or two, then suddenly his face broke into a broad grin, crinkling the lower edge of the scar. Quickly he scrambled off his horse, which shied at the unexpected movement. On the ground he ignored the horse, which stamped a few times before settling. John seemed to have forgotten his men. Roaring out his pleasure, he strode towards Carlyon. "By Christ's blood! Carlyon! Where've you been? There's been no word of you for so long, I was feared you'd be dead."

He threw his arms round Carlyon, almost squeezing out his breath. Carlyon, although slightly shorter, returned the embrace with the same strength and fervour. He was about to speak, but John's voice boomed out first.

"I feared me you were dead," he repeated, "you've been lost so long. I can't tell you how good it is to see you here. I couldn't have had a better gift, no, not if the King himself had come here with his treasury. Man, we'll have some good times together now, I swear it."

He paused, as if thinking of what they would do. His grip loosened somewhat, and Carlyon managed to speak.

"I also am joyed to see you. I scarcely expected it. How come you here?"

John seemed not to hear Carlyon's words. He rolled on regardless. First, he took his arms from Carlyon and released him.

Taking a pace back, he looked him down and up in one glance. "You're looking well, thank the Lord. You must have had a good time. Plenty of fighting, I trow. You'll come home with me now. I want to hear all about your adventures. Then we can get out. There's much good hunting here."

Carlyon gestured his thanks, and would have spoken, but John forcefully carried on, as if his words were a thrusting gale.

"You must say where you've been this past time, what you've been doing. But we must away to home. My lady will be so full of joy to see you. Even though you have no flowers for her." He gave out a good hearty laugh at that last sally, his body shaken by the amusement. Still chuckling, he turned as if to go to his horse but spoke to James. "How now, Master Morton! It's good to see you. You'll have tales to tell also, I trow. But to your horse, Carlyon, and let's get home. Mount up, mount up, so we can be off."

John was at his own horse in three strides and hauled himself into the saddle. There was not even a glance at Carlyon. It was as if he expected his words to be obeyed. Carlyon, who had smiled ruefully at the reference to flowers, but had not been amused, was pleased at the prospect of staying for a few days with John. However, before going over to where James was holding his horse for him, he looked across at the peasant. The man was still on the ground where he had first fallen. It seemed that he had not dared to move, although he was watching the behaviour of his betters with wide eyes.

"What of this poor fellow?" Carlyon asked, gesturing in his direction. "What's being done here?"

John looked contemptuously over at the man, as if the matter was an irritating interruption. "The knave owes rent. I've been lenient long enough. He claims he's no money, no goods. Ha! A good beating will be bound to beat something out of him, I'll warrant."

Carlyon looked back at the peasant. It seemed to him that the man was telling the truth, although he did not know why he had such a feeling. "I'll pay you what he owes, John. How much is it?"

"You've always been soft-hearted. It'll be your downfall one day," said John. His tone was almost scornful, but then he laughed. "So be it. I'm right pleased to see you again. By Christ's blood, I'm so pleased, I'll let this knave off." He looked over at the man, who looked bemused, as if he had been listening to exchanges spoken in a foreign language. "Get you to your prayers, fellow, and give thanks. You've been very lucky, but you won't be so lucky come next quarter day. Mark you that well."

As Carlyon began to move towards his horse, John shifted his neck to look at his men.

"Leave this," he snapped. "Haste you home and tell Master William to prepare for honoured guests. Away now!"

They began to run, and Carlyon mounted his horse. By the time he was comfortable in the saddle, John was already following his men. Carlyon glanced over at the cottage. The man had hobbled over to the doorway and was standing there with his wife, looking at his benefactor. Carlyon nodded to James, shook his reins, and prodded his horse into motion. Cantering slightly, he caught up with John and fell into a slow step beside him. The Michaelmas sunshine was warming his body, and his spirits were soaring. He was still amazed at how fortuitously he had met his old friend on the road.

"How come you to be in this part of the land?" he asked.

"My father has died. I'm now the baron."

"Say you so? It grieves me much to hear of your father's passing. He was a fine gentleman, and I always held him in great honour."

"He always spoke well of you. He was fond of you. But he's now dead and I have all the property."

Carlyon noted John's matter-of-fact tone but was not too surprised. He knew that John and his father had often quarrelled. He was pleased that John had come into his inheritance, but he was genuinely sad to hear of the old baron's death. He asked John when it had happened.

"But two days after this last Christmas. It wasn't expected, but I think me he ate too much. The priest shrove him before he died, and Masses are being said for his soul each month at St Mary's in Hornsey. So I moved to this manor shortly before this last Candlemas. You'll like it here. There's good hunting. I can't tell you how much I've missed you. Have you been missing me in your adventures?"

"In faith, John, there've been times when your strong right arm would have been truly useful. I've had adventures enough and I've tales to tell. Yet some adventures, if there were, I can't remember at all. Perchance the strangest tale lies there." Carlyon shrugged then, as if shaking it off his shoulder. He changed the subject. "I was told you were fighting with the King in France. You also will have tales to tell, I ween."

"Tales there be. The campaign went well. I saw much action. Then I was wounded." John put his gloved hand up to touch the scar. "It was only a slight skirmish, nothing of import. A knave caught me with a battleaxe. I was fortunate I moved my head in time, but I lost my eye. I came home to recover, and then I came into my inheritance. So since that time, I've been making do with what excitement I can find hereabouts. I hope I can still serve the King in his battles yet. Mayhap next year. This home life here is not for a man."

As they rode up to John's home, Carlyon looked at it with mingled feelings of curiosity and nervousness. Outwardly it was a large, fortified manor house surrounded by ramparts and a water-filled ditch. Carlyon's first impression was that it looked easy to defend. And he knew what was inside it that should be defended, for he had once had dreams of having that treasure. Now that he was about to meet Lady Patrina after almost two years, he was almost wishing that he could ride on by. They had parted with such high hopes and rosy dreams, but this time their situations were utterly changed. His hands tensed on his reins as he wondered how their meeting would be.

His horse carried him over a drawbridge side by side with John, and into a courtyard in front of the house. Men ran out to help them dismount, but after reining in, Carlyon stayed stiff in his saddle, as if ready to turn and ride away. John dismounted without a word or a sign of acknowledgement to his groom. He looked at Carlyon, who smiled and quickly jumped down. With a nod to the servant, he turned and walked with John towards the door. The steward moved aside to welcome them in, but the doorway was suddenly filled and the baroness hurriedly stepped over the threshold.

For a moment Carlyon's mind seemed grasped between iron plates, and his breath was snatched from his mouth. Unconsciously he had stopped, as if his legs had taken their own independent decision. Then, before he could do anything else, Lady Patrina was upon him. She seemed to have leaped the few steps from the door. Ignoring her husband, she threw her arms round Carlyon, crying out her delight. He bent his head slightly and she stretched up on her toes to give him a welcoming kiss. She released him, and her body seemed to move back a pace.

"I'm so pleased to know you're still alive, Sir Carlyon!" she said immediately, her words bubbling out like pebbles tumbling down a cliff. "I've prayed for your safety so oft. I could scarce believe my ears when they said you were coming here. It seemed my prayers had been answered." She turned her head to look at her husband, who was standing with his left arm akimbo and impatiently watching. "How did you find this lost knight, my lord? Oh, I'm so glad!"

She hunched up her shoulders and pulled in her mouth, which pushed up her cheekbones. Carlyon recalled that unforced gesture of pleasure which had always amused him to see. The effusiveness of her welcome surprised him, but her delight seemed sincere.

"I'm pleased to see you looking so well, my lady. I could scarce believe my eyes at first, when I saw your lord but a few minutes gone."

Carlyon continued to smile at her, yet he was being buffeted by surprise at how he was not feeling as he had expected. Two years had passed, but he could clearly remember the excitement that he had felt, simply by being in her presence. At such times he had wanted to embrace and kiss her. It was because of his feelings for her, and his dream that those feelings would be returned, that he had left on his quest. Now it was as if he had lived another lifetime. She did not seem to be the same person, even though she looked the same. She was still slim, with her pert mouth, her long neck, and her small, unblown breasts held up under a close-fitting bodice. Her long hair was the same shade of brown, except that when he had last seen her, it had been hanging loose upon her shoulders. This time, under a hastily knotted scarf, it was tied up on the top of her head, which brought home to him the fact that she was a married woman. Yes, she was physically the same, but she seemed elusively different, older.

"Did you find the flowers of the swan, my lord?" she asked, almost bouncing excitedly. "Did you bring any for me?"

Carlyon caught the glimpse of girlish excitement in her voice and movements. It was hard to believe that he had once found that alluring. Her face was full of interest in him, but he knew that her heart was quite empty. He disdainfully drew his head back, as if to show that he was beyond such feelings. However, before he could say anything, John straightened up and moved to put a hand on Carlyon's shoulder.

"Leave such fripperies, wife," he told Patrina authoritatively. "Carlyon will have much better tales to tell than that. Tales to be told over wine. Come, let's inside."

His hand was still on Carlyon's shoulder when they began to move, but it was more his force of personality that was pushing, rather than the hand. They entered the house and John called out for wine to be brought. Carlyon furrowed his brow at the loud harshness so close to his ear, but he knew that John always had that tone when giving orders. The retainers also seemed accustomed to their lord, for wine and refreshments were already being hurried into the hall. John led Carlyon to the table and the three of them sat down along one side, Carlyon between his host and hostess. Then, as wine was poured out, Carlyon became aware of another presence in the room.

While they had been out in the bustle of the courtyard, Carlyon had been half-conscious of a black figure hovering in an alcove just on the edge of his vision. However, he had been so distracted by Patrina and John that he had not focused on it. He had ignored it, swollen as his mind had been by John's exuberance and Patrina's pleasure. Now he saw that this same black figure had come in after them and was standing silently against the wall nearby. Looking properly, Carlyon saw that it was a man in a friar's habit. He was standing motionlessly with his hands in his sleeves across his abdomen. His head was bowed a little, almost as if humbly praying, and yet Carlyon saw that he was watching what was happening. He was like a brooding shadow, hanging there, looking slyly out of everywhere eyes, as if suspiciously.

Patrina saw that Carlyon had noticed the man. She called to him to join them at the table. "You must come and take a little wine with us, Friar Godfrey. It's not good for you to be standing apart there."

She got up from her seat and went over to him. Carlyon could not help but see how humble she was towards the friar, and he watched curiously as she leaned over and solicitously offered to show him to the table. The friar kept his head slightly bowed, but the still-watchful eyes gave him an air of almost disdainful superiority, as if he were receiving his due. Patrina guided him to a seat on the bench beside her, keeping a little behind and to his left as they walked, and with her hand at his back, but not quite touching it. Carlyon was not sure whether Patrina was being so careful because of the friar's age and infirmity, or because of reverence.

"This is Sir Carlyon de Bernedeslaw, an old friend of mine and my husband's," she said, then turned to Carlyon. "I want you to meet Friar Godfrey. He's a great help to me. We're lucky to have such a holy man in the house."

Godfrey acknowledged Carlyon with the barest inclination of the head that seemed part blessing and part condescension. Before resuming her seat Patrina served out some wine herself for the friar. Carlyon was surprised at her behaviour, and he took the opportunity to observe Godfrey. He was not a tall man, being little more than Patrina's height. His build, under the voluminous habit, seemed to be wiry, and Carlyon suspected that he had been wrong about Godfrey being infirm, or indeed quite so aged. Just before Patrina sat down and blocked his immediate view, he had time to note that amidst Godfrey's thin black hair there was a bald patch on the crown. It almost looked like a tonsure, but it was not so neat. All in all, there was something about him that seemed familiar to Carlyon, but his few seconds of observation did not allow him to dwell on it. John, who seemed to be ignoring his wife's behaviour, was speaking to him.

"Come now, Carlyon, I want to know what you've been doing these past two years."

"Oh, yes," said Patrina eagerly, then turned to Godfrey. "Sir Carlyon has had many bold adventures. We must hear them."

Carlyon took another sip of his wine and said, "Truly, I know not how to begin. So much time has gone by. So much has happened. Ah me, and yet I still recall the chill of that morn when James and I set off to seek the flowers. But we travelled on, at times going astray and wandering hither and thither. On our journey I bought a sword that a peasant had found in a field. After that, we were followed by the owner of the land, an old dame. She was laying claim to the sword, and I would fain have let her have it, but it seemed to me she was a witch with uncanny powers. She pursued us through the northern hills for some time, striving to do us ill. I have tales to tell there on an autumn eve by the fire. At times I feared we would scarce escape her evil desires. Then, by God's grace and James's bravery, we overpowered and killed her on some desolate moor. James almost lost his life in the doing of it, but thank the Lord, he was spared."

"Hah!" broke in John, turning to James, who had been seated beside him, and giving him a hearty clap on the shoulder. "I always thought me he was a man of the right kind. I'll be right glad to have you fighting beside me in battle."

"I also," agreed Carlyon. "There'll be no truer companion.

I know not what would have become of us, if not for James. He was prepared to give his life to save me from the witch, and I also thought he'd perished. He disappeared and I had to continue my quest alone."

Patrina twisted her body and bent forward to smile down the table at James. "James should tell his own tale. It seems to me there's much of interest there."

"Indeed so, my lady," James said modestly. "I have a tale to tell, although not so strange as my lord's."

Patrina smiled again, and Carlyon thought that she was looking at James as if she had realised that he was no longer the callow youth whom she had barely noticed before he set out on the quest.

Carlyon continued his own tale. "I travelled on through the north-west country, and I received much help from a maid and her mother, a thatcher's widow. They saved my life and nursed me when I took a sickness. It was they who told me where to go to find the flowers." Unaware, he paused, as his mind continued in the north-west, thinking about the flowers and about the few fleeting weeks that he had spent with Mary and her mother. He was reluctant to say much about them: it seemed personal and private, not to be shared. Unconsciously the fingers of his right hand moved over the ring on his left. A surge of warmth blew through his body like a loving breath.

"But you found the flowers, didn't you? Were they as lovely as they say?"

Carlyon jerked back into awareness, as if Patrina's impatient words were a handful of grit thrown into his face. He rubbed his thumb and forefinger over his nostrils and went on. "I travelled into a wild forest, where I saw a swan. I followed it, and so I found the flowers growing in a small clearing. It was a beautiful sight, and it should have been left unspoiled. Well, there, I wanted to take some back for you, Patrina, so I dug up some half-dozen or so. I carried them to Chertsey, to your father's house. There they told me that you and John were married. That was a great surprise to me, for I had scarce expected such a thing in so short a time."

John guffawed and banged a clenched fist on the table in his amusement. "I warned you I'd not be idle while you were away. I warned you, and there you are!"

Carlyon smiled somewhat ruefully and equably said, "A good man has won a perfect lady's heart. I give you my congratulations, John, and I wish the two of you a fruitful life together."

He nodded first to one and then the other. Patrina laid a hand lightly on his arm and thanked him for his good wishes. He looked into her soft-fringed hazel eyes and thought that he saw genuine compassion that he should be feeling disappointed. He was searching for words to ease her, when he suddenly saw her expression change, as the muscles around her eyes and mouth became enlivened. She wriggled on her seat and clasped her hands together under her milk-white throat.

"But what about the flowers?" she asked excitedly. "You picked them for me. I want to know what happened to them. Say what happened, I beg you."

"There's little to say. After I learned of your marriage, I thought to go to Maidenhead and give you the flowers. I know not why I didn't do that. Some other power seemed to be holding me. I scattered the flowers on the river and watched them float away."

"Ah me, that's so sad. You brought them so far and failed at the last. I do so wish you had come and given them to me. Or even left them with a servant. Could you not get some more, now you know where they're to be found? Oh, that would be so marvellous."

She had turned to look at Carlyon, her hands still clasped imploringly in front of her throat. Carlyon looked into her animated face and sadness shook him that she seemed more disappointed at not receiving the flowers than concerned about his feelings. He wondered that he had ever been attracted by such an apparently shallow person. Now she was asking again about bringing her some more flowers.

"No," he said firmly, making no attempt to soften his refusal. "I wish with all my heart I'd never heard of the flowers of the swan. There's a curse on them and I'll run no such risk again."

"A curse?" asked Patrina, and Carlyon felt John stir with interest. "What curse?"

Carlyon dropped his voice slightly and spoke with a grim seriousness. "Whoever picks the flowers is cursed with ill fortune. What happened to me was most strange. I had been forewarned of the curse, but at first I seemed to have escaped it. I got out of the forest safely. I found James, that I thought was dead. We made good speed back to your father's house and encountered nothing ill on the way. Alas, at your father's house I was told that you and John were married. There was an end to my dream, and I truly thought me cursed."

Patrina let out a sentimental sigh, and at the sound, Carlyon, who had been looking meditatively at the table, looked round at her. She met his glance with a sympathetic, almost apologetic expression. He felt her touch his hand, and then saw her glance move to look beyond him at John. As he straightened, John guffawed.

"Think you that to be a curse on you, Carlyon? Hah! Had I known what trouble marriage is, I would scarce have bothered myself with it. You're lucky still to be single, old friend. I wish me with all my heart I'd gone on that silly quest with you."

"Nay, John, I protest, but you've been far luckier than I. You've won a queen amongst women." Carlyon made an effort to be gallant, as was proper. Yet there was a wonder at the back of his mind, as to why he had had such dreams about Lady Patrina. Perhaps because it was expected that a knight must have a ladylove, and he had known Patrina since they were children.

John laughed derisively and said, "I can't see what can be so cursed about being unlucky in love."

"A man can indeed be unlucky in love without being cursed. Yet I believe in my heart that it happened to me because I picked those few flowers of the swan. I wish I'd let them be. No, wait!" Carlyon forestalled John's intervention. "There's more. Losing my ladylove wasn't the only misfortune. Straightway after I had scattered the flowers and seen them float away down the river, I was yet cursed by having my mind taken away. For a year and a half after that I've no memory of what happened to me in that time. I remember well being by Maidenhead a year last springtide past, and then I awoke but a few days ago near a town called Warrington, dressed as a peasant. All else is black as dreamless night."

"A strange thing indeed," said John, managing to break in. "I'd heard that you were lost, and nobody knew where you were. Say you that you know not where you were either? I can scarce believe that."

"Yes, I was truly cursed. Whether I'd been placed in a deep sleep or had been wandering the country with my wits mazed, I can't tell. I only know that when I recovered my wits, I was in good health, and I had no injuries to my person. And, although I was dressed as a peasant, I had my armour and armaments in a pouch by me."

"Who could believe such a thing?" said John, shaking his head. "I'd fain like to know what you had done."

"Mayhap the good brother can help here," Patrina said, indicating the friar, who had been covertly watching from the side of his eye without moving his head. "Friar Godfrey is one who can do wonders in healing the worries of flesh and spirit. He's a great help and a comfort to me. Truly, I know not what I'd do without him. He has many wonderful potions to cure ills. Even talking with him, when I make my confession, can make my heart and mind feel lighter. His voice is so soothing and calm." She now turned to the friar and asked, "Tell us, Father, will you be able to do something to help Sir Carlyon?"

Her hands were clasped beseechingly, as if in humble prayer. Carlyon rested one of his hands on the table in support, as he leaned forward to look round her. Patrina's air of subservience had a strange confidence to it, and it made him hopeful that he might receive some help. Friar Godfrey sat immobile with his hands together but hidden by his wide sleeves. He was looking down, as if praying. The four others waited, and at last he spoke.

"This is an interesting case. Yet, in despite of what men say, I'm not a miracle worker. I doubt me in my heart whether I should help here, even were it in my power to do so. It may be that there are memories that should not be recalled."

While speaking, he had continued to look downwards, as if refusing to look into Carlyon's face. His voice was calm, but to Carlyon the tone seemed to be almost contemptuous. Carlyon was keen to get back his memory, but there was something about Friar Godfrey that made him pause. His withdrawn manner and disinclination to look directly into anyone's face seemed more furtive than humble. Now, as Patrina respectfully pressed him to help, the friar sighed.

"Very well, my child. I'll commune on this matter. If I'm told what can be done, so be it. If not, then it must be left so."

He lifted his head at that, but looked away, disdaining to look at the others. Carlyon felt that the friar did not want to talk more about him. However, John broke the silence.

"I say the past is past. What's gone is gone, and we should leave it there. We've other things to do." He turned to Carlyon. "I want to show you my horses after dinner, and tomorrow we'll go hunting. For now, I've business to attend to."

Carlyon caught a note of irritation in his voice. He wondered if it was because John did not approve of his wife's interest in him, or whether it was because of the friar. He did not want to cause trouble, so when John began to get to his feet, Carlyon also stood up. John called to the steward to have the guests shown to their chambers, and then left without speaking to anyone else.

9

*I*n his room, Carlyon washed himself and changed his travelling clothes. His mind was working grudgingly at the elusive atmosphere in the household. He had known his two friends since they were all children, but something had changed during their parting. He had been away less than two years, and he knew that he himself was now a different man. Even so, he could not catch what was making his friends seem different. Yet he sensed that there was something amiss, and he resolved to discover it, for the sake of their friendship. Before he could pin anything down, he was joined by James.

"I was wondering about our stay here, sire," James began almost immediately. "Your father will be eager to see you. Your mother also, I ween."

"I know that, James. But I did not expect to meet with Lord John. I'll have a messenger sent to Hertford. I know not how long I'll stay here, although I doubt it'll be long. Yet I feel me in need of some pleasure. I'll enjoy being with Lord John. He's rough, I grant you, but he's excellent company, an amusing man."

"And the baroness, sire? You were much enamoured of her."

"You say true. It was because of love that I wasted my time on an unwise quest. But – hey-ho! – no man, at the same time, can both love and be wise."

"Will it not seem strange, to know her love is another man's?"

Carlyon smiled and shook his head. "I no longer have those feelings for Lady Patrina. In truth, I can't say from where they came. It's as if I never had them."

"The baroness is still beautiful. To me she is a wonderful lady. I would hope to win the heart of such a lovely lady one day."

Carlyon smiled again, this time indulgently, and said, "I'm sure you will, when the day is ready." Then, as if speaking to himself, he went on, "Lady Patrina is indeed a beauty. I doubt me there's many a fairer. I hope she'll be happy with Lord John. And yet, I find it strange that she will prefer him to me." He shook his head, as if his thoughts were drops of water on his hair and abruptly changed course. "The air in this house hangs thickly. I fear me we have unhappiness lurking. What think you of this friar?"

"I think me he be not so humble that he should be. There's something about his carriage I like not. He has a fearful mien, even though there's nothing to see. I feel uncomfortable in his presence, as if he can see into my heart and read things there that I know nought of."

"Hm, that's so. He moves about this house like a dark planet in the sky, gazed on and feared by mortals. I too felt uncomfortable when I felt his eye on me. There's something about him that I've seen before. Mayhap I have seen him ere this."

"Yes, sire, there is something familiar about him, but it may be all friars are like that. He didn't seem to know us."

"You may be right. We've met many people on our travels. Yet somehow Friar Godfrey is different from other friars I've seen."

"It may be he's very holy and not of this world."

"Holy is as holy does, I trow. Yet my lady is very solicitous towards him, so we must take him as she finds. But, James, let's away to dinner."

Carlyon noted that Friar Godfrey did not join them for dinner, and when he remarked on it, Patrina told him gaily that he was out of the house, "doubtless away on some holy matter, ministering to the sick or the like". He left it there, pleased at the friar's absence, yet sorry that he did not have the opportunity to observe him more. After the meal he went round to the stables with John, who pointed out to him a horse that would be better for hunting than the horse which Carlyon had received from his cousin.

"There's some rough country hereabouts. He'll take you through it. Have yourself a ride. Try him out."

Carlyon thanked his friend and said he would ride round the yard. While the horse was being saddled up, John took his leave. He said that there were manorial matters to deal with, and so Carlyon trotted round the yard on his own, getting used to the feel of the ride. He was pleased with the horse. It reminded him of Champion, his own horse waiting for him at his father's. The brief visit to the stables had given his spirits a cheerful lift, and after handing the horse back to the stableman, he decided to take a walk through the garden that lay off to the side.

He looked approvingly at the cabbages and root crops that were still growing well in the warm autumnal days. On the far side there was a wall, little more than a man's height. Seeing an opening, he went through and found himself in a secluded garden that was, from his first glance, for flowers only. There were some small pollarded trees and several bushes, none of which he was able to recognise without their blossom. He took a few steps into the garden and then stopped. He was not alone. Lady Patrina was there, in a pale green dress, with a shawl over her shoulders.

"Ah, pardon me, I beg of you," he said graciously. "Please forgive my intrusion, I didn't know this was your garden."

He turned to leave, but she told him to stay.

"No, wait. Please let me welcome you to my little island. I'd fain talk with you."

"But I interrupt," he said, and indicated the small shears which she had in her hand.

"Not at all. I've been cutting a few twigs to decorate my chamber. I have enough now." She handed the shears to her lady-in-waiting, who put them in the basket with the stems that she had cut. "Come over here and sit with me awhile."

She showed Carlyon a bench-shaped mound covered in turf, that was in a part of the garden that was still receiving the afternoon sunshine. They walked across to it, and after the servant had laid a cloak on it, they sat down. Patrina turned to Carlyon. Impulsively she hunched up her shoulders and pulled in her mouth, pushing up her cheekbones. He sensed her pleasure and smiled in response. Somehow, he felt that he was with the old Patrina.

"It was a surprise to me to find you here in Leicestershire," he began straight away. "It's so far from London and the court. Surely John has property in Middlesex?"

"Indeed so, but John preferred this manor, and so here we are." She smiled, a little helplessly, Carlyon thought, and added, "John desired to be not so near to my father. They've not been as friendly as before. His thought was, that my father would interfere too much with our household. So he moved us here and I don't see my father so often now."

Carlyon saw a brief shadow of sadness cross her face, and

he pressed her forearm in sympathy. He had not expected such a confidence, but he knew how fond the old earl was of his daughter and how he had always indulged her. It crossed Carlyon's mind that perhaps she was missing that. "It is a long way for your father to travel. And yet, there is your uncle and aunt not so far away towards Leicester town, I trow."

"Of course, less than half a day, but John is not so keen on visiting them."

"He seems to be very busy with his estate here. And you also, you must have much to occupy you, now you're a wife and mistress of a household."

"Truly, there's little enough to do. John and his staff do all that's necessary. He won't let me do too much." She laughed shortly. "He thinks I'm too precious. I must be kept safe and sound. I'll be pleased when I have an infant."

Surprise pushed Carlyon's back straight, and he asked, "When is that? Will it be soon?"

She blushed, as she moved her hands over her midriff in response to Carlyon's glance, and said, "Oh, there's none yet. But I'm hopeful before too long."

Carlyon looked at her milk-white fingers holding in her abdomen and could not help remembering how once they had seemed to hold his heart like mighty cords. Now those were snapped, and, to his surprise, it was as if he had never been caught. Patrina herself was caught, and seemingly hopeful of being with child. He nodded and cast around for something else to talk about. "How did you find your priest, Friar Godfrey? Is his house nearby?"

"He was priest to the household when we came. He had not been here long, I trow, but a twelvemonth or less. As to his own house, he said he came from a friary in the north-west."

"Ah," commented Carlyon thoughtfully, wondering if perhaps he had met Friar Godfrey during his travels in that region.

"We're most fortunate with him," went on Patrina enthusiastically. "He's a great comfort. I know not what we would do without him. He has cures for sicknesses, and I swear he can divine the future. He's said he can cure my childlessness. That's why I'm sure it won't be long."

Carlyon kept his face impassive. In truth, he found it hard to imagine Patrina as a mother. However, she seemed to want to leave the subject, for she turned towards him and smiled positively.

"I'm truly pleased to see you, Carlyon. It gives my heart such joy. I hope you'll stay a good while. We've few guests visiting yet."

"I'd fain stay here, but I need to see my father before too long."

"Of course. And yet it's love for you that makes people greedy for your company. I know John will be most unhappy when you leave. He'll tell you so himself, I'm sure."

Carlyon also was sure that John appreciated his company, as he himself did John's. The hunting that he did with him the following day seemed to put John into a genuinely good mood. His hounds brought down a magnificent stag, which he himself was able to finish off. Carlyon enjoyed the chase too. John had been right to claim that there was good country around his manor. Afterwards they laughed and joked together, as they rode back home. This jollity continued when they met in John's parlour to relax over wine before dinner. The talk came round to John's time in France, and he launched into a tale.

"We were quartered in a small town – I know not the name – and His Majesty was negotiating with the French King. The weather was foul, much rain, and it was difficult to make up a tourney for our amusement, or even to go hunting. So, one day Lord Stephen

Calow and I paid a couple of harlots to wrestle each other in a pit of mud. By Christ's blood, I can't tell you how funny it was. So, they fought together a good while, and were fair daubed all over with mire. You could scarce tell one from the other, so we knew not which our money was on. Then one of them ripped the other harlot's shift – so not to be outdone, that one did the same."

John laughed at the memory and paused to take a draught of wine. Carlyon smiled indulgently, imagining the scene. However, he was not destined to hear the end of the story, because before John could begin again, they were interrupted by the entry of a servant.

"What do you want?" snapped John, although seemingly only mildly irritated.

The man merely bowed and explained that John had told him to report immediately if there was any tenant that would not pay. Carlyon guessed that the man was used to being spoken to roughly by his master. He lightly fingered his glass and thoughtfully watched the man as he gave details.

John paused a few seconds before answering. "I'm occupied now. I'll go with you early on the morrow and we'll get the money, or we'll turn the man out. Away, there!"

Carlyon recalled what had happened the day before, and as John's servant left the room, he asked John why he was so hard in collecting his dues from his tenants. He knew that John should not be poor, because his father had been a wealthy man. The John that he had known, although often indifferently cruel, had a generous side and had not been overly concerned about money and material things.

John looked at him with what was almost a sneer, and said, "I must collect my dues. I need to collect as much silver – yea, and gold – as I can."

"Why? What's going to happen?"

"It's needed. I must do it. My stores must be built up."

"Be that so? Yes, money will be short this year, I trow. There'll be many a soul going hungry. The harvest is as bad as last year's."

"Say you that?" John's brow furrowed in surprise. "What are harvests to do with us? Peasants must pay what they owe. Friar Godfrey tells, it's their duty."

"To tell the truth, John, I know not what harvests are to do with us. Yet I feel somehow there may be importance there. As for Friar Godfrey, I think his advice is not so Christian as his friar's habit gives appearance of being. There'll be much sorrow amongst the poor this winter. It's harsh to press so hard upon the poorer folk, think you not?"

"I think me there're worse plagues in this world than tears. We must all accept the position into which God has been pleased to place us, and we should behave according to our rank."

"Verily so. Yet rank brings responsibility also. Our lieges pay us their duties in return for the protection we give them."

"And so, I protect my tenants – if they pay their dues. And pay they must. Friar Godfrey wishes it so."

"What do you do with all the money you collect? Do you have a counting house here?" Carlyon moved his head from side to side, sweeping the room with a scornful glance, as if seeking a door to the counting house.

"Yes, there is a treasury. In truth, though, I know not where. Friar Godfrey is keeping the money safe, all with my family's gold and jewels, until called for."

"When will that be?"

John shrugged, and Carlyon wondered if it was because he did not know the answer. He was about to press John but decided that it was none of his business. He moved to ask John about something else that had been at the back of his mind.

"The lady Patrina seems much beholden to this friar. He has great influence over her."

"Friar Godfrey is a wise man. He gives good advice. He tells her what her duties are to her husband. It's good that she follows him. He knows much – and can do much. I've seen him do wonderful things. He's said he might be able to cure this eye of mine and bring back its sight. It'll be marvellous and he do that. I'll be able to fight properly then. I find it hard to judge distance now. I can't explain. I'm fine in close-quarter work, but I can't use a lance or a bow. By Christ's blood, but that'll be a day! Look you here, Carlyon."

John turned his body towards Carlyon and began to pull up his sleeve on his left arm. On the upper part there was a small cloth poultice, held on with a leather patch. Carlyon leaned forward to examine it and then looked questioningly at John.

"That's a magic potion. Friar Godfrey puts it on for me. He says it'll help to restore my sight. He says I must only be patient."

Carlyon nodded his understanding. Even so, he did wonder why the poultice was on the arm, rather than over the eye. He supposed that Friar Godfrey knew what he was doing.

After they had all had dinner, Carlyon ordered horses to be prepared, and he and James went out for a leisurely ride around the manor. Although he had been out all morning, he felt a restless need to be away from the house. It had been fortified in order to provide a defence from attack during the civil disturbances of the previous century, but Carlyon had a feeling that the fortifications could keep people in as easily as keeping them out. The house had an unhappy air that seemed to fill his nostrils, making the air beyond the walls seem even fresher.

Even the horses seemed frisky at being outside, and they went at a canter for the first few minutes of the ride. When they were walking, Carlyon looked about him and found his earlier impressions confirmed. Although the fields were being well tended, there was evidence of lack of care elsewhere. Many of the cottages they passed were in a sorry state.

"There's need of a good thatcher here," he remarked to James. "There's many a roof here won't keep out the winter rains."

"Perchance the people are so poor, they can't pay for such work."

"Their lord should be looking after that," Carlyon muttered, as if to himself. Then, in a normal voice, "Surely they could do much for themselves. Look you at that cottage wall yonder. A few pails of daub and it'll hold against any wind or weather."

James looked at him but said nothing. Carlyon also fell silent, and as they rode on, he pondered over what he was seeing. Compared with the manors and hamlets through which they had passed on their way south, there seemed to be a lot of poverty. It did not seem to fit with what he had seen in the manor house.

He pulled his horse gently to a stop by an open field. The last late barley was being harvested, and he looked over at the scythed stalks, splattered with the bleeding heads of severed poppies. Some men were resting nearby with their sickles, while a few women and children were gathering the barley into stooks. Carlyon clicked his horse into movement and went over to the men. Then, leaning on his pommel, he spoke to them.

"Goes the work well, good fellows? How's the harvest? Better than last year, I hope."

He thought at first that no one was going to answer him. The men had watched him and James approach, but when he was near, they had lowered their heads, or looked away, as if no one wanted to draw attention to himself. Carlyon was used to deference, but this seemed different. It was almost as if they were afraid of him. He noticed that the women and the children, out in the field, had stopped work and were watching him. He smiled and spoke in what he thought was an encouraging voice.

"Come now, fellows. How's the harvest this year?"

At last, one replied, although he kept his eyes lowered. "Not so good, my lord. Last year was poor, but this one is worse."

"Yea, there'll be some folks hard put to get through this winter," said another man, emboldened to speak.

"It grieves me to hear that," said Carlyon. "But see you, the harvest will soon be home. There'll be a supper this coming week, I trow. You'll have some celebrations and then you'll be able to rest."

"No rest for us, my lord. We'll be hired out, to get the money to pay our debts and our dues. We mayn't fail there."

There was a general murmur of agreement, and Carlyon remembered the heavy treatment that he had seen John's men give out. He pursed his mouth and sighed.

"You have a hard lord, I ween."

"Pray God and we don't have a harder. Yet 'twas not the baron brought these hard times."

"No, by God," said another man, bitterness twisting his face. "It began under his father, God rest his soul. The steward became as hard as flint. We suffered then, we suffer now. He was the one who raised the rents and imposed the amercements."

"Did the old baron order him to do that?" asked Carlyon. "Was His Lordship oft here?"

"He was not here so oft of late. Not after the baroness died, bless her soul. But he was a good lord. I remember that."

"Yea, he was a good lord. And Steward William also was a good man. Until the friar came."

The men fell silent, and it was as if they were withdrawing inwardly. There was almost a physical shrinking.

Carlyon cocked his head in his surprise. "What has the friar to do with all this?" he asked, knowing immediately which friar was meant. "He's but a priest to the household."

"And it were good, were he only ministering to their souls," said one reluctantly. "But 'tis said he's the one making my lord greedy for wealth. Nobody can do anything. He has magical powers. Indeed, he cursed Joseph's son for an offence, and the lad took sick and died. Ah, 'tis well not to offend the friar."

Carlyon was about to question farther, but one of the men got to his feet, muttering that he had to get back to work. As if taking the hint, the three other men joined him and were quickly out in the field. Carlyon watched them go. It seemed to him that they did not want to talk about Friar Godfrey. He looked at James and then set his horse in motion.

"These folk seem afeared of Friar Godfrey," he said.

"There is something fearful about him. As if he can see sinful thoughts hidden deep inside a man's heart."

"He has a way of looking at a man that makes me uneasy also. It seems to me that people here are more afraid of Friar Godfrey than of Lord John."

"He has much authority hereabouts, I trow. Mayhap he does have magical powers. If that be so, then he may indeed be able to discover what happened to you while you were lost."

Carlyon shook his head doubtfully. "I think what happened to me is of little account now. If God grant my memory return, then so be it. But I would not desire to put myself in Friar Godfrey's power.

I have a strange feeling about him. For all his holy words and cast, I sense something evil hovering about him."

"I've been raking in my mind, to try to think if I've seen him before."

"I also. It crossed my mind that perchance I'd met him in my lost wanderings, but as you said, James, mayhap all friars look the same, dressed as they are." Carlyon blew out his breath in exasperation and pulled his horse to a stop. Looking round, he set off again, almost at right angles to their previous direction. "I think me this'll get us back to the house most quickly. I like not the influence this friar has on Lord John and Lady Patrina. I have a feeling he means no good to them. I'd fain take a look inside his chamber, if I can. Come, James, let's to it."

Back at the manor house, Carlyon sent a servant to enquire after Friar Godfrey. Told that the friar was not in the house, he nodded at James and the two of them set off for the friar's chamber. At the top of the staircase Carlyon told James to stay and keep watch. Then he went quickly along the passageway. Outside the door to the chamber, he paused. After an assuring glance back at James, he put his hand on the door ring and turned it. The latch lifted and he pushed the heavy door open. Ignoring the squeaks, he slipped through the opening. He could not prevent a little gasp of relief when he saw that there was no one in the room, but it was momentary. He closed the door and looked around by the light that came in from the window.

He saw the bed, and by it, a small table with a candlestick on it. On one wall there were shelves holding bottles and wooden boxes. He stepped over and peered at them. Some of them had writing on them, but when he tried to read the markings, he was unable to understand their meaning. The writing was a mixture of symbols and what seemed to be an unknown language. Carlyon had a knowledge of Latin and French, and it was clearly neither of those. He opened a few of the containers. Some held liquids, others powders. Tentatively he sniffed as he opened them but recognised nothing. The liquid in one bottle made his mind momentarily cloudy, and he swayed. Quickly he replaced the stopper and took in a few deep breaths.

He decided to leave those things for the moment and look around farther. The trunk of a tree, upright in the corner of the room, caught his eye. He went up to it and touched it. To his surprise, the bark seemed flexible, like a lightly starched fabric. He drew his finger away, and once more it looked exactly like solid wood. Examining it again, he saw that there was an opening. It could be pulled apart far enough for a man to get inside. It came to Carlyon that, if it was taken outside, amongst trees and bushes, it could be used to spy on someone's activities. He wondered why a friar would have need of that.

He continued his examination of the chamber. There was a chest under the window, but when he tried the lid, he found it locked. He turned his attention to a bench. It was marked and stained and cluttered with equally stained dishes, together with a pestle and mortar and a crucible. This was obviously where the friar mixed his potions. Carlyon pulled in his lips and his brow furrowed. He had found nothing that would help him to work out what Friar Godfrey's true nature was. Indeed, he was not even sure what he was looking for. And yet there was something about the chamber that was niggling at him. Something was not right. He turned and looked around the room at the stale rushes on the floor, the opulently curtained bed, the bare stone walls. Then he realised. There were no religious symbols in the chamber. It was more like an alchemist's room than a priest's.

While he was considering that, he heard the sound of footsteps on the stone flags in the corridor. The steps were slow, almost a shuffle, so he knew that it was not James. He needed somewhere to hide. Desperately, he looked round. There was only one place, and by the time that the door was scraping open, he was inside the tree trunk. He found a knothole which he could look through, if he bent his knees somewhat. With that, he was able to see that it was Friar Godfrey who came into the chamber.

The friar walked across the room and dropped what seemed to be an empty shoulder pouch onto the floor by the bench. Then he sat on a stool and for a few seconds he breathed heavily, as if collecting his breath. Seemingly recovered, he looked suspiciously about him by moving his eyes from side to side but barely changing the position of his head. With a grunt, he pushed himself round on his stool and turned to the bench. Although his body was partly shielding his actions, Carlyon saw that he poured a little water into a dish and carefully added a few drops of liquid from a bottle. Taking up a small hand mirror, with his other hand Friar Godfrey used a small brush to rub the solution into his short, straggly beard and over his head. Carlyon watched in puzzlement, but then he realised that the friar was applying hair dye. He almost smiled at the man's vanity.

When the friar was content with his appearance, he laid the mirror down and pushed the dish to one side. Stretching for another dish, he got ready to prepare a second solution. He reached out for one of his bottles, but suddenly stopped, the arm in mid-air. His head moved from side to side, like a suspicious crow's, as he peered at the bottles and boxes on the shelf. Carlyon was afraid that he had noticed that some of them might have been touched, but, as if satisfied, Friar Godfrey finished making up his solution. Reaching out, he took a small piece of cloth and put it into the dish. While it was soaking, he laid out on the bench to his right a piece of leather with tie-strings attached to it.

Carlyon wondered if this was being prepared for John. He wished that he had noted more carefully which bottles were used. His vision was restricted, and the height of the spyhole, which would have been ideal for the friar, was too low for Carlyon. His neck was becoming painful, as if gripped between pincers, and his bent legs had begun to tingle. Concentrating on what was happening in the chamber, he did not realise when he moved slightly to ease his stiffness.

He saw Friar Godfrey's head jerk up sharply and remain there, as if listening. The friar got up from the stool and turned his back to the bench. Thoughtfully he looked around the chamber, his hooded eyes probing. Carlyon was again struck by how familiar the friar seemed to be. Then the searching gaze settled on the tree trunk. Carlyon almost felt that the friar could see his eye at the knothole, but he was afraid to move. As if fists were clenching his lungs, he controlled his breathing. Still looking straight at the tree trunk, the friar began to move towards it.

10

From his hiding place in the artificial tree trunk, Carlyon watched Friar Godfrey move towards him. He knew that he was about to be discovered, and he prepared himself to brazen it out. Then suddenly there was a loud knocking on the chamber door. Friar Godfrey abruptly halted. He looked over towards the door with a grimace of annoyance pulling his face, as a voice called out for him.

Concealed in his tree trunk, Carlyon saw the friar go to the door to open it. He could not see the doorway, but he recognised the voice that spoke. It belonged to James.

"A blessing, Father. I must needs be shrived. I beg you to come. My soul is laden. I can wait no longer."

"Not now, my son, not now. I'm busy with my private prayers. I'll see you just before supper. Go in peace now and pray to St Michael until I come."

"Nay, Father, I can't wait. My heart's too heavy. I must be shrived now."

Carlyon now saw James. Using his extra size, the squire had pushed his way into the chamber and was now looking round curiously.

"Hah," he said. "Is this where you prepare your medicines and healing potions? Is that one you're preparing now?"

Friar Godfrey moved quickly to put himself between his bench and James. Then he held out his arms in a shepherding gesture. "Come, my son. It's better you poke not into things that concern you not. In those lie dangers for the unlearned and uninitiated. Come, we'll away to the chapel and there I'll hear your confession."

The tone of voice was calm and almost benevolent. There was now no trace of the asperity that had been in it when James first appeared at the door. Carlyon saw James turn and leave, closely followed by Friar Godfrey, who seemed to want to make sure that his visitor saw nothing else to rouse his curiosity. Silence fell, after the harsh sound of the closing door had died away. Carlyon was breathing more easily, but he was still controlling it. However, the silence continued.

Carlyon carefully came out of his hiding place. The room was empty. Friar Godfrey had not been waiting outside of Carlyon's line of vision. He took in a sharp breath and then went over to look at the patch soaking in the dish on the bench. Quickly also he glanced at the bottles and boxes, but he could make no more of them than before. It would be best to leave. He did not know how long James would keep the friar occupied, but he guessed that it would not be long.

When James came to find Carlyon a short while later, embarrassment was wrinkling the young squire's face. He was nervously licking his lips, and when he spoke, his usual measured speech had become fast and jerky. "Forgive me, sire," he began straight away. "I know not how it happened. You were almost caught. The fault is mine. Thanks be to Our Lady, you weren't caught. I should have been able to warn you."

"Let it be, James, let it be." Carlyon held up his hand, as if to ward off his squire's flow of words. "I'm safe, as you see. Tell me what happened."

"I was waiting on the stairs, keeping watch for any person coming up. I heard a noise in the passage behind me, so I peeped round the top of the stairs. I saw Friar Godfrey suddenly appear out of the wall. I'm sorry, sire, but I was afeared of his magic, and I pulled my head back, so he saw me not. I heard the door open, and when I looked again, he'd gone into his chamber. Oh, sire, I was so afeared that you would be discovered."

"Fear not, James. Our Lady blessed me, and I found me a hiding place."

"I hoped that was so, but I did think that mayhap he had done you some evil. I could think of nothing to do that would not make him suspicious. Then of a sudden a good spirit grasped at my ear and told me to ask to be shrived."

"And good for me you did so, I trow. I think he was about to discover my hiding place when you knocked. Friar Godfrey is not the holy man he makes himself out to be."

"Say you so, sire. Yea, it was no holy act that made him appear in the passage. There's magic there, I trow."

Carlyon thoughtfully scratched at his chin while looking at James. "Let's take a look at this place," he said suddenly. "I'd fain see where this was."

"Suppose Friar Godfrey sees us there?"

Carlyon shrugged. "He may be in his chamber, he may not. Whatever it be, we can walk about the passage, if we so choose. Come, we've seen magic enough in our time and we're yet here to tell the tale."

He led James quickly to the passage near Friar Godfrey's

chamber. There, despite his bold words, Carlyon made an effort to walk quietly, and when he spoke it was in a whisper.

"Where was the friar when you saw him?"

"I think me about here." James stopped and indicated a short stretch of wall. "He materialised out of the wall. I saw him do it."

Carlyon looked closely at the wall but could see little through the late afternoon gloom that filled the passage. He glanced around and took a rush out of a sconce on the wall. Striking his flint, he soon had a light. Now he could see more clearly, but there was nothing but bare stonework. Then it seemed to him that his rush was flickering when he held it by one place. Examining with the light almost against the wall, he found that there was a tiny gap running down the wall, through which a draught was coming. He turned his head to James. "You heard a noise, you said, which made you look," he whispered. "What kind of noise?"

"Scraping. Like a sword on a whetstone."

"Hm. Or like a stone on a stone. There's a door here. See how the flame moves. I think there's a chamber in the wall here. That's how the friar came unknown behind you."

"By're Lady! I can scarce believe it."

Amazement made James's voice louder, and Carlyon had to check him with a curt, "Shush!" He then felt around the stonework for some seconds, probing and pushing. "There must be some way of opening it. We need but find the place." He moved the light around to help him see but found nothing.

"Mayhap it only opens from the inside," James suggested.

"You may be right. There may be another way to enter. So, we'll leave it now. I'd talk with you in private."

Back in his chamber, Carlyon told James what he had seen in Friar Godfrey's room. James listened intently, screwing up his face as he considered what he was hearing. When Carlyon paused, he looked at James for a few seconds, waiting for a comment. He knew that James always liked to consider every angle before speaking. At last, his squire drew in a breath and pulled himself up a little. There was yet a very brief, almost instantaneous pause, while Carlyon saw words start to form. Then they came, unwinding slowly from around James's tongue.

"I think me you were right to doubt Friar Godfrey's intentions. When he shrived me, he questioned me straitly about matters other than the few sins I confessed. I thought me it was like to my catechism – about my father, my brothers. Nor was that all. Anon he asked close questions about you and the lady Patrina."

"Ha! An inquisitive priest! His chamber had a strange atmosphere. It had a sense more of evil than of holiness, and yet I know not why. Ah me, Friar Godfrey, what are you doing here, and what are you after? I like not the influence he seems to have on Lord John and his lady."

"I also have noticed that. And my lord John seems different. Much harsher than heretofore."

"He's a man with faults, I grant you. But he was never so greedy for wealth as he seems now. I fear me Friar Godfrey is at the back of that. He's after something, and doesn't mean good for anyone else, I trow." Carlyon nodded in satisfaction, as if to emphasise the conclusion to himself.

James had again screwed up his face in thought. At last, he said, "Is there aught we can do? Lord John is his own master. What can you say to him?"

"I don't know. But they are such dear friends that I'm loath to see them drawn onto rocks by a knave's light. I have me a strange feeling in my heart. I know there's something I must do, something unfinished. Mayhap it's here. This place will hold the answer."

"What are you going to do?"

"I'll have to think. I must needs investigate farther."

The next morning, John was in the yard, training a young hawk. He was pleased with the way that it was progressing. That day he had begun using the lure and his bird had quickly shown great promise. Again and again his manservant threw the lure, and the hawk left John's wrist to swoop onto the prize. John was looking forward to getting out into the field, but he knew that there was still some way yet to go. During a short break, while waiting for the lure to be repaired, he stroked an ungloved finger down the bird's neck. The dreamy softness seemed to pour against his skin like a silky scarf.

"If only I could kiss you and turn you into a human lady," he whispered. "This soft smoothness would fill my heart with its beauty."

"Beauty is as beauty does. And beauty can be stolen while a man looks another way."

Surprise pulled at John's body, and the suddenness of the movement disturbed the hawk. It hopped nervously on John's arm and would have taken flight had its master not laid a protective hand on its back. John turned his head and saw that Friar Godfrey had silently materialised beside him. He quickly recovered himself.

"Take you an interest in hunting now, Friar Godfrey?"

"I always take an interest in hunting, my son. There's always prey to be discovered. Look you, I've found a tenant who has some money buried in a corner of his cottage. I've sent out two of your men to collect it."

"By God's teeth! Is that so? I wonder he managed to evade our searches."

"You searched as men search. But nought can be hidden from me. And we must search hard. More money is needed."

"We have all the Michaelmas rents. I thought me to have a good feast before my guests leave."

"Your guests." The friar looked sideways at him, suspicion twisting his face. "Will they be leaving soon?"

"I fear me so. Sir Carlyon must needs get back to his father. I wish he could stay. He's such a dear friend and I find his company most pleasing."

"Your lady also, I ween. She'll find his company pleasing? Did the good knight not have a heart's desire to marry her one time?"

John laughed shortly. "A year or twain agone. Yea, he did profess his love for her. He and my lady were much smitten with one another, I trow. He undertook a quest for her, as you know, and they were like to marry, had I not gained the advantage. He lost her in his absence, and I doubt there's love there now."

"Think you so, my son. The human heart's a fickle thing. And words may not always say what the heart means. I saw the knight in the garden with your lady. They were closeted most privately, I thought. Mayhap he was making love to her. Look you to your lady's and your own honour, I say."

John looked piercingly at the friar standing humbly beside him, his cowled head bent so that John could barely see his face. The friar seemed unconcerned, other-worldly, but his words were burrowing into John like a wasp into an apple. John called his servant over. He gave him the falcon and told him that the practice was over for the day. Without looking at Friar Godfrey, he strode off across the yard and into the house. His intention was to seek Carlyon, although he was not clear in his mind why. He just knew that he needed to find him.

In the house, he was told that Sir Carlyon had been seen in the garden. There was no sign of John's quarry in the potager. Purposeful strides carried him through into the walled area. Just inside, he stood and moved his head from side to side to look around. Like a hawk's his head moved, his one good eye glittering as it peered about. Carlyon was there. He was sitting on a bench-shaped mound, partly hidden by a bush.

John wasted no time but set off towards him. Rounding the bush, he called out, "It boots nought to sit there, Carlyon. My lady won't be coming into the garden this day."

Carlyon seemed to have been abstracted, because he gave a noticeable start at John's sudden appearance. He moved, as if about to get to his feet, but settled and smiled at his friend. "I wasn't expecting anyone, John. I thought I'd be alone here. I was seeking peace and contemplation."

John's initial comment had been said almost as a friendly joke, but despite Carlyon's denial, the speaking of an interest in his wife had made the matter sharper. It slid into John's chest like an icicle, and he lifted his head to look contemptuously at Carlyon. "Seek you inspiration for a love poem?" he sneered.

"No, not at all. I have weighty things on my mind that I must consider. I fear I've written no verse since I left on my quest for the flowers. I seem to have no wish to compose. There's nought to inspire me."

"Can Patsy no longer inspire you? You sang her praises oft enough when she was a maid in Chertsey." Although John was little more than the length of a man's thumb taller than Carlyon, standing there, he towered threateningly over the seated knight. His fists were clenched, as determination drove him to extract a confession that he was sure would come. He saw puzzlement in the face that was turned up to him, and he thought it was because Carlyon did not know how to tell him the truth. He set his face and asked more directly. "Wish you not, you were married to my wife in my place?" Then he waited for the answer, poised like a fowler by his snare.

"No, John, I don't now." Carlyon seemed surprised. "Patrina made her choice, and I respect it. You won her, and there's an end. The love I have for both of you makes me glad for you. As for me, I don't know. I'll freely admit that there's a strange feeling in my bosom, as if something is missing there. I feel as though I've lost a deep love that I'll never find again. But so it be. I must perforce seek someone else to love, mayhap. It's in my mind that I'll go abroad to fight, to seek service with a foreign prince. It may be I'll find a new love there."

While Carlyon had been speaking, John's eye had been like a stone set in baked clay. He was telling himself that Carlyon was still in love with Patrina, and the more that he let it play on his mind, the more convinced he became that this love was being reciprocated by Patrina. The heat of his emotion was making him sweat in his groin, and unconsciously he scratched there. Yet despite himself, he was drawn by Carlyon's mention of going abroad to fight. The thought hovered in the background that he would like to join Carlyon in such a venture. It would be good to be fighting beside him. For a second or two this desire almost pushed itself into the front of John's thoughts, but his suspicions about Carlyon's behaviour were too strong.

"Yes, 'twould be well to go abroad," he snapped. "There'll be no lover for you here. Patsy is mine and there's no hope for you. Did you think you could come here, and she would still love you?"

"I did no such thing!" Carlyon stiffened and looked grimly at John. "I came here led by fortune, but glad in my heart to have found two old friends. You ask if I came in hopes that Patrina would still love me. I tell you true, John, I think she never did love me. I was only a young maid's fancy, a whim. For me, indeed I thought I loved her, but it was a dream, and on waking I found it no such matter. I swear to you, I no longer love her. I know not why, but I know my true heart's love is waiting for me elsewhere and I'll need to leave here to seek it."

He stood up and placed himself almost directly in front of John, almost touching. John tensed warily but relaxed in the warmth of Carlyon's smile.

"Come now, old friend," said Carlyon. "Let's not quarrel over old matters past and gone. I must needs be on my way soon. I'd fain stay here awhile more. There's something, a presence, I know not what. But it may be no business of mine. My soul's been so restless since I recovered my wits. Mayhap I should seek my peace elsewhere."

John had not been following all that his friend had been saying. His mind was creakily working, like the grinding stones and cogs in a mill when small pieces of rock had been put into the wheat to increase the weight. His thought processes did seem to have slowed and become harder since he had come to Leicestershire. His mind was still working over what Carlyon had said about love. Standing with him, John wanted to believe that Carlyon no longer loved Patrina, as he said, and his words were beginning to convince him. Suddenly, like a weathercock groaning round in a gust of wind, John's mood seemed to sway. He looked and saw his old friend in front of him. "Yea, Carlyon, let's not quarrel. I'd not wish to drive you away, but your father will be mightily pleased to see you again. An' you must leave, so be it."

He opened his arms and the two men embraced. John, with a hint of his old tolerant geniality, told Carlyon to stay in the garden as long as he wished and seek his contemplation. Then, feeling lighter in his mood, John broke wind, turned, and went off to the house.

Near the door he found that Friar Godfrey had appeared behind him. As he noticed this, he stepped into the shadow of the house out of the sun, but it was as if the friar had pulled his hood up over the two of them. John felt a shiver of coldness begin to tamp down the warmth that he had carried away from Carlyon. He hunched his shoulders and spoke quickly.

"I've spoken to Sir Carlyon – in the garden. He'll be leaving soon."

"I know, my son. I was there."

John's brow furrowed. Something was not right, but he could not think what. He stepped aside, to allow the holy man to enter the house first. "Sir Carlyon is my friend, Father. He'll do nought to harm me or bring shame on my family. I worry not about him and my wife. All is safe."

"I wish with all my heart that that was true, my son. Alack, I fear me things go not so well as you hope. Come with me. I wish to show you something."

They had been walking towards the great hall as they were speaking, but Friar Godfrey now turned and led the way to the main staircase. He said nothing as they climbed up, and his silence continued along the passage at the top. John, walking behind, looked down on the friar's slightly bowed head. He also said nothing. He seemed to be being pulled along, unable to resist or even speak. When Friar Godfrey stopped, John saw that they were outside

Carlyon's chamber. Momentarily he was confused as to why they were there, because he knew that Carlyon was not in the room. It seemed to be a wasted journey. Friar Godfrey opened the door and went inside. Holding the door, he turned and spoke at last.

"Come in here, my lord."

The tone was peremptory, and the words seemed to tug John into the room. He stood a few paces inside and waited for what would happen next. Friar Godfrey looked around the room with slightly screwed-up eyes, as if searching. John gazed at his face, wondering what was to come.

"Hah!"

John gave a start at the friar's sudden exclamation.

"Over there," Friar Godfrey continued. "Go and search in the bed."

John's legs moved, as if of their own accord, and carried him over to the bed. Suspiciously, he pulled aside the curtain. He had almost expected to find someone in the bed, but it was empty. The blankets were rumpled and turned back, as though replaced after a sleeper had hastily left. John grasped the edge of the blankets with one hand and lifted them. He was about to let them fall, when he noticed a pale blue cloth against the grey linen of the sheet. Reaching with his free hand, he pulled it out. He released the blankets and stepped back, so as to look in the light from the window at what he had found. It was a lady's wimple. He held it out by two corners, then let go of one and brought his arms down.

"See you that?" urged Friar Godfrey. "It's my lady the baroness's wimple. How came it there – in another man's bed?"

"She was here – in Carlyon's bed?"

"Indeed, she was. There is the evidence in your hand. See how limply it hangs. Like unto the lady Patrina's honour, it folds itself in for very shame. Who knows how often she has slipped in here unobserved, since you welcomed Sir Carlyon into your house? I feared me no good would come of that."

"I can't believe they would betray me that way. To behave so under my roof."

"We know not how long this infidelity may have been. Her Ladyship was much in love with the knight, to send him on a quest. I fear me she's cast your love onto the midden. Soiled and discarded."

"How can Carlyon do this base thing? I can't let this pass."

"Indeed not, my son. He's betrayed you, he's betrayed your hospitality, he's betrayed your honour. Such knavery should not go unpunished. Surely this knight must be put to death. Do it now, while this shameful bed is still warm from his lust."

"By God's teeth, he must be punished." Anger was making John tremble. He seemed to see Carlyon in bed with Patrina. His left hand came up to touch his scar. He wanted to kill Carlyon. "He'll die – and at my hand. But he's a knight even so, a lord's son. I can't slay him like a dog. He must fight me."

"Will it be wise to challenge him to a duel?" Friar Godfrey broke in quickly. "Is this a time to talk of knightly honour? You have but one eye. This knight will have an unfair advantage."

"I fear that not. I was always a better swordsman. And this time I'll have right on my side. He'll die by my hand, and my honour will be avenged. I'll go now."

"Wait! I've a potion that will help you." Friar Godfrey pulled a small phial out of his pouch. "Drink this. 'Twill give you strength and guide your arm."

He removed the stopper, and John took the phial. Without even giving it more than a glance, he drank it down. The taste was bitter to his tongue, making him grimace, but by then it was down his throat. He chewed but then felt a harsh heat spread out from his stomach. The hotness bubbled along his veins and into his muscles and sinews like a boiling oil. With it came anger. Anger at his betrayal. Anger at his wife. But most of all, anger at his false friend. By the time that the heat from the potion reached his head, he was almost blind with rage. A burning fury was shaking his body, but at the same time he seemed incapable of thought.

"You must act quickly now," he heard Friar Godfrey hiss into his ear. "Go to the garden and seek out Sir Carlyon."

As if the words had released bonds holding him to the spot, John now knew what he had to do. He stepped over to where Carlyon's sword in its scabbard was hanging on the wall. Taking it down, he turned, and without a word he left the room. Burning with urgency, he went off to his own room, to get his sword. Then he set off downstairs to go to the garden.

11

Carlyon was walking restlessly here and there in the manor house's walled garden. The sun, which had been warming him as he sat, had gone behind a large cloud and the resultant coolness had brought him to his feet. Worry was making him walk. The meeting that he had had with John had disturbed him. John did not seem to be the same person that he had known when they were bachelor knights together. Carlyon wondered that marriage could have such an effect, or perhaps it was his experiences in France? Distractedly, he shook his head. There was more to it than that.

It was the house. There was an almost tangible presence that seemed to have soaked into the very stones, to be hovering in the atmosphere like a midnight fog. Often when in the house, Carlyon felt that he was being watched by someone or something behind him or just beyond the edge of his vision, but when he turned there was nothing. He had told John that he was leaving, but doubts were now tumbling through him like pebbles in a millrace. While he was walking, he momentarily seemed to hear the rustle of a forgotten memory, and absently he fingered the ring on his finger, rubbing it lightly. Then unexpectedly he thought of Mary the thatcher's daughter, and how her calm and wise advice had helped him when he was seeking the flowers of the swan, and he and James were being pursued by the witch. He remembered also her pensive beauty, her soft-fringed eyes. Her face was clearly before him. It was such a pity that she was only a peasant and so he could never hope of having her as a wife. Even so, he wished that she were with him now, although almost immediately, in the midst of his mental turmoil, he smiled ruefully at the foolishness of the thought.

It went no farther. He was interrupted by the harsh sound of John's voice. Turning, he saw John coming through the gateway and moving towards him with long strides. His angry voice preceded him, as if his fury had driven him to speak as soon as he saw Carlyon.

"You've lied to me! You've taken Patsy into your chamber! I know what you've been doing. Your bed still reeks of your carnal lusts. You've lied to me."

Taken by surprise, Carlyon stepped backwards and moved his head from side to side, as if John's words were dagger-thrusts that he was parrying. Then he found his voice and broke in on John's flow. "What say you, John? What nonsense is this? I know nothing of what you claim. What are these false accusations?"

John had two scabbards tucked under his left arm. He lifted his right arm, and Carlyon saw that a piece of cloth was crumpled in his fist. John opened this out and let the cloth fall, until he was holding it by one corner. He triumphantly shook it, like a prized pennant. "There you are! I found it in your bed!"

"What?! I know nothing of this. What is it?"

"Do say, you know it not? It's my lady Patrina's wimple. In your bed, by God's teeth!"

"I know nothing of that." Carlyon had gathered his wits and now squared up to John, giving no more ground. "What is this wild nonsense, this fool's babbling? You're casting cess not only on my

165

honour, but also on that of your blameless wife. Retract it now, I say, and come to your rightful mind, in Our Lady's name."

"I know what's been happening beneath my blind eye. I may have only the one eye, but it's as good as any other man's two, and I can see now how things are. Thought you to take advantage of my infirmity? See how wrong you are. I claim the right to punish this dishonour." John pulled the two scabbards from beneath his arm. As he did so, his wife's wimple fell unnoticed from his hand and fluttered to the ground. Holding his own scabbard with his left hand, he laid Carlyon's on a stone bench seat, which was just to his side. He stepped back, accidentally trampling the forgotten wimple, and looked challengingly at Carlyon. "Take up your sword! Make ready to defend yourself!"

Carlyon put out his arm with his palm outwards, as if to ward off John's onslaught. Then from beyond John's shoulder he was distracted by a movement. Focusing quickly, he saw that it was Friar Godfrey, who had slipped in behind a bush. Momentarily Carlyon wondered what the friar was doing, covertly spying on them in the garden. His suspicions roused, he looked back at John and spread out his arms in a calming gesture. "Hold now, John, old friend. Do we quarrel this way? Let's not be so hot-headed. Calm, I say, calm. We must seek what this is all about."

"I know what it's all about, you rogue. Think not your silver tongue can sway me here. The time has passed for words. The time has come to act." John pulled out his sword and discarded the scabbard. "If you take not out your sword and fight like a man, by God's teeth, I'll stick you where you stand."

Carlyon looked at John's tensed body, the feet planted firmly apart, and the face twisted with fury. John's sword was ready for action, and Carlyon knew that he could say no more. He must defend himself. With a heavy heart he leaned over the bench and took hold of his sword's hilt. As the sword left the scabbard, sliding out as if from a woollen blanket rather than from between stiff leather, he felt a tingle in his fingers. The sword seemed to pull his arm into practice swings, and his body moved with an easy smoothness. Yet still he spoke softly. "Come now, John. Is this the end? Let's put up our weapons and go inside to take wine together. We can talk about this."

"You want your villainous tongue to persuade me I can't see what lies clear before me? I know what I've got to do. We'll take no more talk together."

Carlyon stood there irresolutely, his sword arm hanging down. John seemed to be under a spell, unable to hear reason. Then, as Carlyon was wondering whether to try more persuasion, John lunged at him with his sword. Carlyon jumped a step to one side, twisting his body as he did so. The attack, unexpected in its suddenness, only narrowly failed. Carlyon felt the flat of the blade slide against his abdomen. He accepted that the fight was on. Squaring his body, he lifted his weapon and prepared to parry further attacks. That was what he was hoping to do – to parry until fatigue set in or reason prevailed. He did not want to kill or seriously harm his old friend.

For some minutes he managed that tactic very well. He was finding it easier than he would have expected, given that John had always been the better swordsman. Carlyon's sword seemed to know where John's sword was going. It pulled his arm to meet the heavy blade. Part of Carlyon's mind noticed this. Thoughtfully, he tried at first to control it but then gave himself up to the absorbing power of the sword.

They continued to fight. Plants were trampled and twigs were broken off shrubs as they jockeyed about, John seeking an advantage,

Carlyon seeking to frustrate. The only sounds were of their grunts and heavy breaths, interspersed with the more strident clang of sword against sword. As time passed and the stalemate continued, Carlyon could plainly see that John was becoming angrier. It was making him more determined to kill Carlyon, and his anger called up greater reserves of skill. Carlyon had never seen him fight so well. He was almost admiring the skill that was on display. It was as if part of him had become detached and was watching from the side. But as they fought, he was still trying to think how to disable John without damage, to put an end to the contest.

His mind struggled with that, while his sword seemed to guide his arm, so that he remained safe from John's sallies. However, distracted as he was, he neglected to pay attention to what was around him. Moving backwards under a furious onslaught from John, he banged into the stone seat. Despite attempts to regain his balance, he fell over onto the ground. John gave a triumphant howl. He came forward in what was almost a leap, and his sword bore down on Carlyon. Again Carlyon's sword came to the rescue. John's thrust was parried and the force turned him slightly to the right, exposing his left side. As Carlyon used his free hand to push himself up off the ground, his sword slashed the sleeve on John's left arm. The blade ripped it open all the way up to the shoulder, exposing the leather patch.

This seemed to break John's concentration. He pulled himself back and glanced at the damage. This gave Carlyon the opportunity to roll to one side and spring to his feet. He took guard and was prepared again for defence. John was more cautious now, his sword held with both hands. Gently he moved the point to and fro in front of him, as if searching for an opening. His body, bent forward in anticipation, suddenly lunged. Carlyon was ready and twisted aside.

As he did so, his sword flashed and cut through the exposed tie that was holding the patch on John's arm. It did not even break the skin. The patch came away, as if the sword tip had pulled it. John grunted and stepped back. Flailing, he tried to catch hold of the patch with his left hand. However, Carlyon's sword indifferently tossed the patch away, and Carlyon was ready again.

John took guard, but then he paused. His brow wrinkled in puzzlement, and he shook his left arm. He briefly licked his upper lip and looked at his torn sleeve and bare upper arm. Carlyon waited, almost relaxing. He sensed that something was different, that they had moved into another field. John's head turned. He looked piercingly at Carlyon and then at his sword.

"Why are we fighting, Carlyon? What's happening here?"

Carlyon did not answer immediately. He straightened up, lowered his sword, and then warily said, "You have falsely accused me of staining Lady Patrina's honour."

John's brow furrowed again, and then, as if it were slowly coming back to him, he said, "Ah, by God's teeth, it was that. Friar Godfrey said you had been making love to her."

"He's lied to you, John. I swear by Our Lady in Heaven, I've nought but respect for Patsy and also for you, my oldest friend. Never would I abuse your hospitality. I've already told you that the love I once felt for Patsy has now gone, like the sparkling dew on a rose will fade as the morning matures. I swear on the honour of a knight that your suspicions are misfounded."

"I'd fain believe you, Carlyon. I will believe you. I know you well enough there. But see you that?" John indicated the wimple, lying where it had fallen. "I found that in your bed. How did it get there?"

"I know not." Carlyon was genuinely puzzled and thought it

strange that Lady Patrina should visit his room. "Why did you go into my chamber?"

"When Friar Godfrey told me you had been making love to Patsy, he said that we should look in your room."

"Aha!" Carlyon's suspicions were quickly aroused, and he wondered that he had not seen that sooner. "So, he knew where to look? A strange thing, but not of magic, I'll wager."

He remembered seeing Friar Godfrey as he and John were fighting, and he turned his head about, looking for him. This time there was no sign. He had left the garden. There were only a few of John's staff, who had been attracted by the noise of the fight. Carlyon waved his hand to dismiss them, and they began to move away. Then he turned back to John, who had sat down on the bench, as if nonplussed. Carlyon was about to speak to him when he noticed the patch on the ground, so he picked it up. As he examined it cautiously, John pulled himself together.

"Can it be fixed on again?"

"I doubt me that would be wise. This is not to cure your eye. It contains a magic potion, sure enough, but not to heal. It's to keep you under a spell."

"I can scarce believe that. For what purpose?"

"I know that not. But on my life, I believe that patch has some wicked magic, and I'll discover the purpose ere long."

John shook his arm, making the torn sleeve flap. He pursed his lips and furrowed his brow thoughtfully. Then he looked warmly at Carlyon. "Yes, 'twas a strange place to put a cure for my eye. I think me you have it. I confess, I feel different. My body is freer. My mind is clearer. How strange. It's as if I've returned from a long campaign."

"I sense a difference in you also. There's a calmness now. I thought it odd your moods should change so violently 'twixt calm and storm."

"Did you see that? I saw no change, and yet there did seem much to make me angry. I thank you for your swordsmanship. I knew something was wrong, you know. I could see the power that Friar Godfrey had over Patsy, and I was uneasy, but I seemed unable to do anything about it."

"I also saw the strange power he had over her. It must be a magic potion. Does she also wear a patch?"

"No, but she takes powders in milk, that Friar Godfrey gives her to cure her barrenness."

"So he does it that way." Carlyon glanced round and then lowered his voice. "Who is this friar? From where did he come here?"

John scratched at his crotch, while he spent a few seconds in thought. Then he also spoke in a quieter voice. "I can tell you nought of that. He was at the house when I brought Patsy here last Candlemas tide. They told me he had come the springtide before and was a priest for the household. I thought to keep him on. There seemed no harm. No man knew where he was from, yet his speech is that of a man from the north-west. I do know he has magical powers. With my own eyes I've seen him turn a stick into a viper. I fear what he may do if crossed."

"I think me you're right to be cautious. I also fear he may be capable of great wickedness. Yet what is a priest doing with such evil powers? What's he seeking?"

"All men are afeared of him and his powers. That's why they give up their silver and other goods, even if they are not always due. They've seen what Friar Godfrey can do if angered."

Carlyon wiped down his sword and placed it back in its scabbard. He was beginning to get a clearer picture of what was happening. He straightened up with his right arm crooked akimbo and the fist pressing into his side, and looked at John, who was putting his own sword away. "What do you do with all the money, the things you collect?"

John raised his head, and Carlyon saw his friend's brow furrow, as if he were surprised at the question. "I don't know," John confessed. "I don't have any of it. Friar Godfrey takes it. By God's teeth! I knew that, but until now, I thought nought amiss that it should be happening. And now I know not where it is. Unless perchance he keeps it hidden in the cellars?"

"We must go and seek this. Do you know the cellars?"

"Not since I was a boy. I remember me, they spread far – or so it seemed. But no one is allowed there now, by order of the friar. Yes, that'll be where he keeps his treasure. But it won't be easy to reach. He keeps fierce hounds down there and controls them with magic."

"We must deal with Friar Godfrey. I doubt me he's verily a man of holy orders. So there'll be no sin in laying hands on him. We can remove him and his evil influence from these parts. Life will be easier, I trow, and not only for you, but for your tenants also. I've seen how they live. It's not God's will they be so oppressed and ground down with such misery. The duty of lords is to take care of their tenants."

"Yes, we have our duties. Yet peasants are there to serve their lord. That's *their* duty." John spoke carelessly, as if his mind was on other matters. He continued, more positively this time. "I'd fain know where my money is being kept, and I doubt Friar Godfrey will surrender easily. I'll tell you true, Carlyon, we may have a fight, such as we've never faced before. His powers give me pause – they truly are great."

"I've met people with such powers before. They were overcome and I prevailed. With God's grace, it'll be so this time." Carlyon spoke confidently, but he remembered that in his previous victories over dark powers, he had had help. Suddenly, as his fingers unconsciously rubbed over the ring on his left hand, the image of Mary the thatcher's daughter came into his mind again. It was so clear that it was almost as if she were nearby. He wondered momentarily how she was faring and whether her life was happy. A great yearning seized hold of him, as if his mind were being pulled out of his head. Instantly the emptiness that he had been carrying around with him seemed to fill with gentle thoughts of Mary. He made a decision. After he had been home to see his parents, he would travel to the north-west and seek out Mary. And then… And then he thought no farther beyond that.

John had been silent for some seconds, moving his body restlessly, as he pondered over what to do. He seemed not to have noticed Carlyon's abstraction, and he sharply threw him a remark. "We'll have to rely on our swords. There's no other way." He picked up his scabbard, straightened his back, and set his jaw. "I fear no man – an' he be a wizard or nay. What say you, Carlyon?"

"In faith, we must put our trust in our swords and the rightness of our cause. I also can think of no other way." As Carlyon reached for his scabbard, he thought of his shield and wished that he had it with him. While fastening his sword round his waist, he wondered where he had lost the shield. It had been of great service to him, and he was sure that it would have helped him with what lay before him. "I wish I had that shield you gave me," he told John. "It was a good servant to me. It had magical powers to protect me, I trow. Where did you get it?"

"That shield?" John scratched himself. "Ah, yes. That was a well-crafted piece. I bought it from an armourer in Rotherhithe. He told me he made it from metal brought back from the Holy Land by a crusader. Yes, he said there was magic in it, but he knew not what. Mayhap it couldn't be broken by a knave's sword? I can't say. I had no occasion to use it. But it was of service to you?"

"Great service. It protected me well – and saved my life also, I warrant. But tell me, John, did you never notice aught of magic in the shield? Did you never hear it speak or see a face in it?"

Surprise struggled with puzzlement in the face that John turned to Carlyon. He seemed to be considering the question, but then shook his head, as if shaking it away. "I saw no magic. I only say what the armourer told to me. Saw you strange things with the shield?"

"I thought I did. I thought I heard it give advice in hazardous situations, but mayhap it was all in my imagination."

"Advice would be of use now, an' it be from a shield or from fancy. But without it, we must rely on our own mettle." John turned and looked fixedly at the part of the garden wall beyond which lay the house. "I'll order Friar Godfrey to leave immediately. You'll be with me?"

Carlyon nodded grimly, and John slapped the hilt of his sword in satisfaction.

Then he put back his head and shouted, "Ho! A man here!"

A servant appeared almost immediately, and John told him to tell Friar Godfrey to come to speak with him in the garden. As the man turned to do the bidding, Carlyon stopped him.

"Seek out my squire also. Bid him come to us here, fully accoutred and with all speed."

While they were waiting, John restlessly walked up and down. His fingers were twitching. His breath was being forced out of his mouth in angry gasps, like the steam from under the lid of a boiling pan. Carlyon watched him. He was standing more calmly, his right hand lightly fingering the hilt of his sword. Relief at how well things were going was like the taste of honey in his throat. Even so, he knew that he needed to keep his wits about him.

"We must be prepared for trickery from this knave," he said, almost as if thinking aloud.

John stopped his pacing and said, confidence crisping his words, "We two will be a match for anything he has. Standing shoulder to shoulder, you and I can withstand the world."

"You say the truth, John. Yet mayhap this time I should stand off to one side, ready to flank him. Also, any net of wiles that he has must then be spread the wider."

John peered at him, as if considering, and then nodded. Again he resumed his restless pacing.

At last his servant returned – without Friar Godfrey. John glared at the servant, but to Carlyon's surprise the man did not seem cowed. His stance was respectful, but it was more that of a servant towards a guest of the house. Carlyon well recognised the attitude. Now the servant looked straight at John and spoke in a clear voice.

"Friar Godfrey thanks you for your message, sire, and says he will be pleased to receive you and Sir Carlyon forthwith in the great hall."

Making a slight reverence, he turned and left the garden without waiting to be dismissed. Carlyon was astounded. The man had spoken as if Friar Godfrey was the master, not John. Carlyon also noted the mention of his own name. Friar Godfrey knew that he was involved, and Carlyon wondered why he was being called with John, what it boded.

John seemed unworried by that. He seemed more concerned with the insult to his rank. Gripping his sword hilt, while fury twisted his face, he cried, "Friar Godfrey will receive me?! In my own home?! Will he, indeed? I'll be master in my own house, by God's teeth. Come, Carlyon, we'll teach this turbulent friar a lesson he won't forget."

Without waiting, he strode off rapidly towards the archway out of the garden. Carlyon came immediately after him, but watchfully. As they approached the house, James came bustling out. Excited concern animated his face as he turned and fell into step with them. He listened while Carlyon briefly explained what was happening.

They entered the hall one behind the other. John strode confidently, the other two more cautiously. Friar Godfrey was standing below a window, strangely illuminated by the light. Carlyon saw that he would be unable to get behind the friar, but he moved away to one side. James took the other flank, and they crossed the hall like a three-pointed pincer.

"So, Lord John, you have come to see me?"

The voice sounded strangely hollow. It echoed through the hall, seeming to be coming from around them, rather than directly from the friar himself. The three of them halted abruptly. Both Carlyon and James glanced behind them and then back at the friar. Carlyon could feel the hairs at the back of his head bristling. He drew in a deep breath and carefully pulled out his sword. The other two drew theirs and prepared to advance again.

"Think you that swords will avail you?" said the friar. "I fear them not. But say now. You have your audience. What do you wish to ask of me?"

"Ask? You knave! I ask nought in my own house. I'm here to tell. I'm no longer in your power."

"Think you so? I tell you, that you have no idea what my powers are. You've not yet seen the smallest part of them."

"Enough!" John's impatience threw the word across the room like a piece of lead shot. "I'm a baron of the realm. I've fought and defeated many an adversary. I have no fear of you, Friar Godfrey. You'll leave my house and lands forthwith, taking with you nought but your staff and scrip, as befits a friar."

"Are you dismissing me on the persuasions of strangers, after all I've done for you and your household? Do you not wish to gain back your sight? Do you not wish to have an heir? I can do this. Can your friends I see creeping behind you?"

"Sir Carlyon is my oldest and my truest friend. I'd trust him beyond any man in the kingdom. And by God's teeth, my one good eye will suffice for me to see a rogue. You'll leave now, or I'll throw you out myself."

"I'll not be rid of like an old greyhound. I will stay in the house, and you had best beware that you put me not into a passion, or 'twill be the worse for you."

John snarled in his anger and raised his sword, ready for action. Almost in the same movement he stepped round towards Friar Godfrey. He had taken no more than two strides when the friar vanished. Carlyon had been about to move in support of John. Instead, he halted and blinked, disbelieving what he had just seen. But it was so. Friar Godfrey had been there but was there no longer. Disconcerted, the three men came together. Nervously they looked around, swords held at the ready. They exchanged a few words of surprise, but then the friar appeared again, just as suddenly as he had disappeared, this time at the other side of the hall.

"I'll not be dismissed so derisively." The voice was as echoey as before. "You will regret this foolish action of yours."

Before the three of them could react, he disappeared again. They looked warily around, standing back to back like the three sides of a triangle. A few seconds passed, but nothing else happened.

"What trickery is this?" hissed John.

"Magic," whispered James, sounding awed.

Carlyon licked his dry lips and said, "He must be hiding."

"Yea," agreed John, his confidence returning. "We must seek him out. To it now."

They spread out and searched the hall, which had several alcoves. Carlyon found a sheet of glass, held up by wooden props, where they had first seen the friar. John found the same arrangement at the other side of the hall, but of the friar there was no trace.

"We must search the house. Come, let's to his chamber."

They hastened upstairs, John boldly in the lead. Their haste was in vain, for Friar Godfrey was not in his room. Carlyon had not thought that he would be. He knew that they were dealing with a very wily character, magic or no magic. Thoughtfully he stood and looked around the chamber, while John vented some of his frustration by slashing at the curtains round the bed with his sword. To Carlyon it seemed that some things had been removed.

John may have noticed the same. "I think me this friar has left, in despite of his rantings."

"I would 'twere so," said Carlyon, shaking his head. "But I doubt we'll be rid of him so easily."

"I don't know why you want to be rid of him."

They turned at the sound of the voice and looked at the doorway. Lady Patrina was standing there. Her arms were challengingly akimbo, and she was looking accusingly at her husband. Carlyon was surprised at the firm intent in her voice, and he looked at her thoughtfully as she continued.

"What harm is he doing? He's a true man of God. If you send him away, who'll help me – and you – in our troubles?"

"He's no help to us," snapped John. "He's more a black mire, holding our bodies fast and like to swallow us complete."

"No, John, you mustn't send him away, I beg of you."

"She's still under his spell," Carlyon whispered at John's shoulder. "We must stop her drinking these potions of Friar Godfrey's."

John seemed to ignore that, but his irritation had a gentler expression to it than hitherto. Almost as if he did not mind his orders being opposed, he simply made a dismissive gesture with his free hand. "Tush, Patsy, leave these matters to your lord. I know yet more about this than you do. Get you to your chamber, my dear, and we'll speak of this later. For now, there's men's work to be done." He turned his head to look at Carlyon and James. "Come, we must search the whole house. We'll see if he's skulking here yet."

He moved quickly towards the door. Patrina stepped aside but stayed by the doorway. Carlyon shook his head when she tried to speak to him as he passed. He would have liked to comfort her, but he wanted first to be satisfied that Friar Godfrey was not in the house. Purposefully he followed John down to the hall, where John summoned his retainers. Search parties were organised, but by evening it seemed that the friar had indeed left.

Patrina did not join them for supper. She sent a message to say that she wished to stay in her chamber. Carlyon was suspicious, but

John said that she often did that. However, she did not appear at breakfast the following morning, and her maid, Matty, said that she was not in her chamber.

12

When Matty announced that her mistress was not in her chamber, John snorted derisively.

"It's not her fashion to rise and be about her business so early. I wish her to breakfast with us. Where is she?"

"I know not, my lord. Her bed's not been slept in. I saw her last when I took her some supper yester even."

"Most strange." John peered sharply at Matty with his good eye. "Have a search made. Hastily, now."

John resumed his breakfast, but it was not long before the searchers returned with no news of Lady Patrina. She seemed to have vanished as completely as Friar Godfrey had done. John made that connection.

"The silly woman has gone off after the friar," he told Carlyon. "She'll be wanting to serve as his acolyte. By God's teeth! When I find that knave, I'll kill him like the cur he is."

Carlyon pursed his lips, then thoughtfully pinched at his nostrils with his thumb and forefinger. He knew of ladies who were driven to leave their families and enter a convent, influenced by a forceful religious personality. He also considered that Patrina could be capable of such a capricious act. And yet, doubts scratched at him. "She may have gone willingly after the friar, John, and I doubt not but that he's at the back of this disappearance. Yet if she has been bewitched by him, mayhap she knows not what she does."

"In faith, I'll not want to believe she's gone willingly and defied me. But I'll still kill the cur. Come, we shall plan what we must do."

The three men had barely begun when their discussions were interrupted by the sound of a loud, "Ho!" The voice seemed to come from above, and looking about them, they saw that Friar Godfrey had appeared in the gallery. Seeing that he had their attention, he sneered, "So you plan how to find my lady Patrina? Pah! Weaklings such as you will seek her in vain."

"Weaklings, say you?!" roared John, his face so suffused with anger that the words had difficulty in forcing themselves out. "You'll feel the strength of my blade ere long. We'll find my wife, doubt you not of that. And 'twill be the worse for you if you've had a hand in any harm to her."

"She'll come to no harm from me, an' I get what I desire. I've taken her away to a secret place, known to no living man but I. She'll be safe there, until I choose to release her."

Hearing that, Carlyon recalled how a witch had taken Mary away, when he was seeking the flowers of the swan. A chill seemed to be pervading the air around him, as if a tangible evil were in the hall. It was on his skin, in his nostrils. He had needed a special power to release Mary from the evil force that had taken her. He knew of no way to discover such a power, so that they could free Patrina. He clenched his hands together, as they lay on the table in front of him. His fingers rubbed over his ring, and a vision of Mary seemed to swell out from his heart. She seemed so near to him. Her beautiful blue eyes were smiling at him, and he felt reassurance warm his head. He watched John get to his feet and step away from the table with his sword drawn.

"Release my wife, you rogue!" John cried. "You dare to lay hands on a lady?!"

However, the friar interrupted the threatening gestures. "You may see her again," he taunted. "Yes, she can be released."

"How is that to be done?" asked Carlyon. "What must we do?"

Friar Godfrey looked straight at him, as if noticing him for the first time, and then said, with a dismissive smile, "You'll only need to do one simple thing. If you wish to free Lady Patrina, you must go who knows whither and bring who knows what hither."

Almost while the words were still travelling from his mouth to their ears, the friar took a step back from the gallery rail and disappeared from their sight. With a shout of frustration John set off for the stairway, to dash up into the gallery. Carlyon followed him, but more slowly. He knew that they would not find the friar.

In the gallery, while John thrashed about in helpless fury, Carlyon carefully examined the back wall. There was no sign of anything, and yet he suspected a secret passage. He turned when John spoke to him directly.

"What did that cursed friar mean: 'Bring who knows what from where', or whatever he said?"

"We must go who knows whither and bring who knows what hither," said Carlyon quietly, as if musing to himself. "Strange words. No, I know not what they mean. We must think more on that." He sighed and stepped over to the gallery rail. Looking out into the hall, as his brain batted his thoughts to and fro, he remembered the panes of glass and how Friar Godfrey's voice had seemed to come from above them. "I think I know how Friar Godfrey did his vanishing trick yesterday. By some means he sent his image to reflect in the glass we found in the hall. Then he made his escape somehow, as he has done just now. Magic? Perchance only trickery and we need not fear this man so greatly."

"Pah! I fear him not, an' he be man or wizard. So, think you he is still in this house?"

"I believe so. He knows of secret passages within these walls. Know you of any such, John?"

"Oh," said John, after pausing in thought for a few seconds. "I recall now hearing of such when I was a lad. But I never saw any. Ah, no! I remember me now. I was shown a secret chamber. It's hidden behind a wall in one of the cellars. Of course! That's where this cur has hidden Patsy."

Filled with hope now, the three of them went down to the cellars, swords held at the ready. The air was thick with a fetid stench of dogs. Carlyon noticed here and there on the floor clumps of droppings and partly chewed bones. He remembered what John had told him.

"Does the friar not keep fierce dogs down here?" he whispered.

"He does. Mayhap they're in the shadows, but they'll be no match for us three. Haste now, and we'll catch the chief cur."

Carlyon could feel John's confidence and was heartened by it. He too had a feeling that something momentous was about to happen. Eagerly he and James followed John through the cellars, but they met no dogs. While Carlyon was wondering if they had been taken away for another purpose, John stopped at a small door.

"This leads to a small cellar, deeper than these. The secret chamber is behind its wall."

Putting his torch in a sconce, he opened the door. A damp, yet strangely fresh smell came out, as if blown by a fan. Carlyon wrinkled his nose but followed close behind John. As he straightened up after passing through the low doorway, he had to stop immediately, for

John, immobile, was blocking his way. John moved aside slightly, and Carlyon stood beside him at the top of a flight of stone steps. By the light of their torches, Carlyon saw why John had gone no farther. The cellar was flooded, and the steps disappeared into the dark water after two treads.

"We can't go," said John. "The secret chamber's in yon wall, but its entrance is under the water."

Carlyon had been looking about him, and he said, "This water is moving. Look! It seems to be coming in from that side and going out over there."

Sure enough, there was a slight eddying against the wall. It was as if a river were flowing through the cellar.

"That must have happened since I was a lad." John chewed his lip in frustration, then had a thought. "Well, if we can't get to the chamber, that knave of a friar can do so neither. He must be holding Patsy elsewhere. We must also seek him elsewhere. I won't let him escape me."

"I'll warrant there'll be other secret chambers within these walls. There's a passage behind the wall near Friar Godfrey's room, I trow. Let's go and search there. If we find a passage, it may lead us to Patrina."

John wasted no time in discussion. Carlyon sensed his urgency as he and James hurried behind him. Yet, looking at the tensed muscles in John's shoulders, he wondered if his friend's haste was more to seek revenge on Friar Godfrey than to rescue his wife. He dismissed such a thought when they came out onto the first-floor landing. It was important that they find Lady Patrina. No doubt, that would then lead them to the friar.

At first, they were unsure what they should be on the lookout for. Carlyon told John of his search the previous day.

"There must needs be a doorway hereabouts. We should look for a place where there is a chink in the mortar."

They began to search. Carlyon tried to remember where he had found the gap, but for a minute or so there was no success. Carlyon bit at his lip. Desperation was now beginning to creep through his body. He knew that there had to be a passage, but he was fearful that perhaps the door was an exit only. Perhaps it could only be opened from the inside? However, he said nothing of that fear to the other two. John was muttering frustratedly as he searched, and James was commenting as much to himself as to the others.

Carlyon ran his left hand over the wall, as gently as if caressing it, almost willing it to give up its secret to him. He was looking, however, at his right hand, where his dagger was unavailingly probing the mortar. He sighed and pressed his body against the wall. His left hand swept up, to go above his head. Slowly it moved, and the probing palm was caught by an irregularity in the stonework. His hand had moved on before his brain caught up with the possible significance. He moved his hand back to check, although without excitement. It took him a second or two to find the spot, just higher than his head and a little to his left. He fingered the place and peered intently at it.

It looked to be a pebble set into one of the stones. A thumb's length in diameter, it barely protruded. Carefully Carlyon tried to run the point of his dagger round the pebble. It seemed to penetrate a little, but not in any way far enough for him to be able to prise out the pebble. He tried to get a grip with his fingers. Using the tips and gripping as firmly as he could, he tried to pull the pebble towards him. There was no movement. His fingers kept slipping off. So he tried to turn the pebble, first clockwise, then anticlockwise. At first, he thought it was moving, but again his fingers were simply slipping round the polished surface. He thought of pushing it inwards. Probing with his fingers, nothing seemed to happen, but he put the base of his palm over it and steadily began to exert pressure. Almost immediately he felt it begin to give way, and as it did so, he heard a muffled clump behind the wall. He pushed again, but nothing more happened. He pulled back and looked. Then he put his palm back on the pebble. To get more leverage, he pressed his knees against the wall. To his surprise, he felt the wall give way there. He continued pushing and saw that a small portion of lower wall had pivoted, opening out a narrow gap.

"Here we are!" he cried. "Look at this."

John was already moving towards him, having heard the creak of the newly found door. As he bent to peer into the dark opening, excitement bubbled through his voice. "By God's teeth! There is a passage here. More light, I say!"

A servant, who had been standing nearby, handed a lantern to Carlyon. Another servant had been striking a flint, and he handed a candle to John, who had impatiently gone up to him. When John turned back, Carlyon was at the gap, holding out his left arm with the lantern into the passage. He poked in his head.

"We can pass through it," he said. "This will be how Friar Godfrey flits about the house so secretly. Come, let's go."

"Yes, now. There's no time to lose. My blood is boiling."

John was pressing closely on Carlyon, and Carlyon felt John's breath on the back of his head. Hunching his shoulders, he turned sideways and squeezed himself through the open gap. Almost pushed by John, he stepped forward along the passage that lay before him. It was narrow, barely more than shoulder-width, and so low that Carlyon had to bend his neck. There was a strong musty smell, but the atmosphere was breathable. There were frequent cobwebs, but

Carlyon could see evidence of many having been recently broken. It confirmed to him that Friar Godfrey had been using the passage. He moved along it and soon came to steps leading downwards. Warning John and James, he began to descend. The passage continued at the bottom of the flight, but Carlyon had only gone a few steps when he saw something sticking out of the right-hand wall. He stopped to examine it. It seemed to be a narrow lever, about a hand's length.

John tried to peer round him to see. "What's this?" he asked. "Another door?"

"Mayhap."

Carlyon was cautious. He held up his lantern to look along the passage. It became a little wider but otherwise seemed no different. He examined the lever, and then at John's impatient urging he tried to pull it towards him. It was fast, so he tried to move it up and down, without success. Finally, he pushed it forward. This time it moved. As it did so, a wooden barrier, studded with knife blades, swung quickly out across the passage and was caught with a bang by the opposite wall. Carlyon saw it coming. He instinctively jerked back, knocking into John, but his upper left arm was caught by one of the blades. Had he not been turned sideways, examining the lever, it would have been more serious. John cursed, frustrated by the narrowness of the passage. Carlyon felt that he should be the one to curse, but he put his lantern on the floor and looked to his wound. It was not deep, and James made a pad and bound it up with a kerchief. Then they examined the trap. The lever was set to be pushed by someone walking along the narrow passage. This released a spring holding the studded gate. Had Carlyon not spotted it, he could hardly have failed to brush it with his arm in passing. The blades would then have gone straight into him. He looked at his bandaged arm when he realised that and breathed a silent prayer of thanks.

"A devilish trap, I trow," said John, who had had the same thought as Carlyon.

"In faith, I wonder that Friar Godfrey should have constructed such a device."

"Nay, not he. Look at the rust and dirt. This's of ancient construction. I wonder what my forefathers needed to protect, to lay such a trap."

"Friar Godfrey also. See, this grease on the spring is fresh. He's set it to protect something. We'll on and see."

Carlyon pushed at the gate, and with John's help, in despite of the confined space, they got it back against the wall and were able to fasten it. It came into Carlyon's mind to wonder where in the house they were, but he thought that at least they were now on the ground floor, and thankfully the ceiling was high enough now that they could walk without bending the neck. He was about to set off, but John said that he would take the lead. Pressing his back against the wall, Carlyon let John squeeze past and followed him with James bringing up the rear. John strode forward confidently, making the flame of his candle flicker and his shadow dance on the wall behind him. He was moving so purposefully that within a few steps he was two to three yards in front of the other two, who were following more cautiously.

Suddenly, Carlyon saw John throw up his arms and seem to slide down into the floor. For a second he blinked. Then he realised that a section of the floor had tipped, and John was slipping beneath it. As he moved forward, John disappeared, and the stone fell back into place with a bang. Carlyon almost jumped back, but he collected himself and warily crept forward, bending low, to shine his lantern on the floor. He saw nothing to show that the floor was unsafe.

"Is this another trap?" James asked hoarsely. "Has Lord John been taken?"

"It's a trap, to be sure. And Lord John is held in it. We must seek how to rescue him. Here, hold my hand."

Carlyon sheathed his sword and offered his right hand to James, stretching out his arm. Telling James to be prepared to pull him back, he gingerly moved forwards. Inch by inch he slid his feet along, his body turned sideways. After only a short distance, he found that the floor was beginning to tilt beneath his feet. He drew back, then, keeping his balance, he gently tested it. This confirmed to him that a slab of the floor was on some sort of fulcrum. "John is under here," he told James. "We must find some means of keeping the floor open, so that we can get inside. By God's mercy, John will be safe."

He thought for a few seconds. James screwed up his face while he also thought, but Carlyon spoke first.

"I'll move forward and tilt the floor. When it comes up behind me, you put the hilt of your sword into the gap. Then the two of us will be able to lift, I trow."

When James was crouching down ready, Carlyon inched ahead, resting his hands on the wall at each side. Over the fulcrum he leaned forward with his weight on his front foot, until the floor began to tilt. James called that he had done his part, and Carlyon thankfully moved back onto solid ground. Kneeling by James, he saw that light was coming out of the narrow slit that had been made. Hopeful, he and James put their hands into the gap and pulled upwards. The slab tilted smoothly, although it seemed ready to fall back if they released their pressure.

Looking down, they saw that John was still holding his candle, and its illumination showed them that he was in a small pit. He was almost up to his knees in water, and although the pit was not deep, his outstretched arm was beyond their reach.

"By God's teeth!" John shouted, as soon as he saw their faces peering down at him. "Praise be, you fell not in also. Get me out of here now. Haste you, in God's name."

Carlyon had been about to ask John if he was injured, but he gathered that that would be an unnecessary question. Instead, he wondered how they would get John out.

This time it was James who provided a suggestion. "How would it be, sire, an' you put your good shoulder against the stone, while I reach down for Lord John with my surtout? I can help him out, I'll warrant."

Carlyon glanced at James and nodded. He turned and put his shoulder under the edge of the slab. Then, taking the strain, he tensed himself, while James carefully let go. The weight pressed on Carlyon, but he was able to hold it. James leaned back and quickly took off his surtout, while John urged him to hurry.

"Almost there, my lord," said James, lowering down the linen coat.

"Thanks be to God! I thought me I was like to be left to rot in here."

John doused his candle, and with both hands he took hold of the dangling surtout. It was not easy for James in the restricted space that he had next to Carlyon, but he pulled. His muscles strained and Carlyon saw the sinews bulge in his jaw. Then John was high enough to grab the lip of the floor, and tugged by James, he managed to get out. With a grunt of relief, Carlyon let the slab fall back. He got to his feet and turned to look at the other two.

"This is a place of traps," he said. "For what purpose? And how did Friar Godfrey discover them?"

"Someone in the household will have shown him," said John shortly, as if his mind was concentrating on whom that person might be. "Old Ned, I'll warrant. He'll have told him shortly before he died."

"He's dead? His knowledge would have been useful also to us."

"Ah, he fell into the moat one night and was too old to pull himself out."

"Say you so?" Carlyon pulled in his lips, thinking how convenient the death could have been for Friar Godfrey. However, he shook away his suspicions, for he knew that there was nothing to be done now. "Friar Godfrey has made good use of what he learned. We must take care. God knows how many more traps there may be."

"We must hurry. Too much time has been wasted. How do we get past this snare?"

"One of us will have to stand as a counterweight, while the others pass. Then he must needs jump and hope not to be caught. James, you're right nimble, I ween. Will you balance for us?"

"Right so, sire. I'll do that."

James stood on the pivoting slab, and Carlyon stepped quickly over. There was a slight movement under his feet, but the hole did not open. John was next. He took James's candle and crossed with a broad stride. The slab moved more than under Carlyon's weight, but John was safe. He turned and looked at James.

"Move quickly now, James, and I'll catch you."

John held out his arms ready. James took a breath, tensed himself, and began to move forwards. As the slab began to tilt, he took a standing leap. It was enough to carry him to solid ground, and he was in John's arms.

"Well leaped, James!" John cried. "You're a good man to have alongside. I'll not forget your work this day. But at it now – we can't spend long wandering around like this. There must be an end soon."

He used James's light to put a flame back on his own, and once more they set off. Carlyon was in the lead again. He knew of the need for haste, but he wanted to move cautiously. However, John was pressing close behind, urging him on, seemingly driven by anger at Friar Godfrey and a determination to succeed.

Carlyon held up his lantern as he probed forward, looking for snares. John was telling him that he would grab him if there was any danger. Distracted by that, Carlyon suddenly realised that the floor felt strange. It was overlain with a thick layer of dust, which had not been the case farther back in the passage, but what drew Carlyon's attention was the feel of the floor. There were low criss-crossed ridges. He turned his head to look back at John. As he opened his mouth to say that they must stop and examine the floor, he felt something against his shin. Quickly, he looked down. While he saw a thin rope stretched across the passage, he saw that he had tripped it. Before he could do anything, the floor rose up around them. Now Carlyon realised that it was not the floor. It was a net, which had been spread out and hidden by deliberately scattered sand. As the three of them had been walking so closely together, they were all three caught in the toils. Thrown together, they struggled. John's candle, pressed against his body, went out. Carlyon, looking up, saw that the net was attached to a beam. He saw it begin to move. It knocked open a wooden shutter in the wall, and light burst in from outside. The beam swung out, dragging the net and its contents, and lifted them over a stew pond. Limbs were poking through the net. One of them was Carlyon's arm holding his sword. As the beam jerked to a stop, it also jerked his arm. The sword flew out of his grip and landed on the bank.

The net began to sink into the water. James's candle had blown out. John was at the bottom of the heap of writhing bodies and limbs. Carlyon could hear him cursing loudly as he fought against the enfolding net and the pressure of his two companions. Carlyon was struggling to get his hand to his belt so that he could pull out his dagger. He knew that they had to cut through the net. John went under the water, but he managed to get his head out again by clawing at James. Then the weight of the net inexorably began to drag them all down into the pond.

Suddenly Carlyon felt a strand of the net give way near his arm. Then another. He battled to turn his head and look. The net was being cut by his sword. Glancing up, he saw that the sword was being wielded by a young peasant woman. She was kneeling on the bank and stretching out her arm. Her head was covered by a hood, which made it difficult to see her face, but Carlyon was now concentrating on his escape. The sword moved as if it knew where to cut, and at last Carlyon was free. He splashed his way to the bank, where he held on to the lip, while he caught his breath. He looked back at the other two, squirming in the water little more than an arm's length away. Just as Carlyon was about to push off and go to help, John broke free of the net and spat out water as he shook his head. He seemed to grasp the situation immediately and, grabbing at James, he hauled the squire with him to the bank.

"By God's teeth!" he growled. "That was a bath I didn't choose. I thought me it was all over." He turned his head and looked out over the stew, which had been dug deep to hold fish for the house. "I'm keeping away from water hereafter."

Despite his discomfort from his soaking and his wounded arm, Carlyon smiled at John's bluff cheeriness. "I thought me we were like to join the fishes. I also will leave them to fishermen hereafter. But see, we have a rescuer to thank."

He looked over to where the woman was. She had laid down the sword and walked round the side of the pond. Now she was looking up at the wall of the house, as if searching for something. She seemed oblivious as the three men hauled themselves up from the water and onto the bank. Huffing, and at the same time laughing at their escape from death, they got to their feet and began to squeeze water out of their clothes. Their rescuer turned and walked towards them, dropping down her hood as she did so. She was some five and a half feet tall and walked with a stately sway. Her long, very light brown hair was twisted into braids, tied round her head, and covered with a linen cap. Her warm blue eyes seemed to mirror the joy in her welcoming smile.

James was the first to recognise her. "Mary!" he whooped, delight and surprise leapfrogging each other in his voice. "Mary! How glad I am to see you. How could you be here so opportunely?"

13

As James greeted Mary, Carlyon also recognised her, and for a couple of seconds he was unable to move. His heart began to beat faster in his chest, seeming to bang on his ribs. His pleasure at seeing her rushed through his body as if he had swallowed an elixir. He smiled broadly and opened his arms in welcome, almost as if for an embrace.

"Mary! It's you! What are you doing here so unexpectedly? How have you been since we parted?"

"I came looking for you," she said softly, in the lilting accent that he remembered so well. "When you didn't return from Warrington, I sensed danger, and so I set off to search for you."

"By're Lady, it's most fortunate for us you did. And that you found us at this time. I am right glad to see you, Mary. I've often thought of you and wondered how you've been faring."

Mary was smiling brightly, as if sunshine were illuminating her face. She seemed about to speak, but Carlyon had turned to John, who was trying to dry his sword.

"See now, John. This is Mary the thatcher's daughter. I rescued her while I was on the quest. She was very helpful to me. She saved my life. Who would have thought she'd be here, when most needed, so far from her home? She has saved my life again. And yours also, I trow."

John pulled himself up and, somewhat loftily, said, "My thanks for your service, wench. You'll be well rewarded for it, fear you not."

He was clearly speaking to her as if she was a peasant. Seemingly he assumed that she had been a servant to Carlyon, and although imperious, he was wanting to show kindness. Carlyon, accustomed to John's offhand treatment of lower orders, caught the condescension in John's behaviour and was offended by it on Mary's behalf. It was true that he, Carlyon, was a knight and she was a peasant, but he could well remember all that they had been through two years before, while he was seeking the flowers of the swan. Mary had been more to him than a servant, and even now he had a fond feeling for her that he could not explain. He wanted to tell John how special she was, but before he could find words to do so, John's mind had already moved on to a more pressing problem.

"We must get back into the house. So much time has already been lost. We'll to the front."

He strode off immediately without looking back, as if expecting the others to follow without question. Carlyon thought that it would have been easier to try to enter the house through the rear, but John seemingly was too proud to sneak into his own home like a wandering vagrant. Carlyon also wanted to speak to Mary, to tell her all that had happened to him since he had last seen her: how he had found the flowers, brought them south, and then travelled about the country for many months with his mind lost in darkness. However, there was no time for that. He had to support John. Taking a firm grip on his sword, he set off straight away at John's heels. James and Mary followed.

At the front of the house, they gathered before the main door, while John hammered on the stout oak. There was no response, so he banged again and shouted for attention. At last, a casement in the wall above the door scraped open. They stepped away from the door and looked up. Friar Godfrey's head was peering out at them.

"Bang away, as you will," he said. "This door is closed to you."

"You rogue!" roared John. "Open this door straightway! Do you dare to keep me out of my house?"

"This is no longer your house. The house and all within it are now mine. Get you gone away."

John's face twisted in anger. Blood suffused the skin, turning it a livid red, and he could scarcely get his words out at first. "You say... that...you say, you rogue. You'll not take mine from me. Where is the lady Patrina? Tell now, caitiff, where she is. An' you release her not, it'll be the worse for you."

Friar Godfrey laughed and said, "Rattle on, you empty cask. I fear you not. As for my lady, she'll serve me henceforth. If you like that not, then you must rescue her. But be warned, I keep what's mine."

While these exchanges had been going on, Mary had been looking carefully at Friar Godfrey. After a few seconds she leaned towards Carlyon. "Do you not know him?" she asked quietly. "He's Thomas the forester, the man who held me in his cottage."

Carlyon realised why the friar had seemed familiar. The robes and the dyed hair had confused him, but now that he had been told, he could see that it was the man who had held Mary prisoner, to force her to marry him. Carlyon could guess what would have been her fate, had she not been rescued. "I can scarce believe it, but it's true," he told her. "He's brought his evil here and bewitched another woman, a lady of high rank this time." He turned to John and spoke boldly, so that Thomas could overhear. "This one is not a friar, I trow. His name is Thomas. He is a forester from Lancashire. I know him well. How he came here as Friar Godfrey, I can't tell, but I know him to be a wicked man."

The unmasked friar poked his head out farther and gripped the window frame with one hand, as if about to pull himself through. His thin face twisted into a sneer as he surveyed the group in the courtyard below him. "My name matters not," he spat out at them. "My dress matters not. You, Sir Knight, know of the magic I possess. Yet even though you bested me once, this time I have the power to take all I want. And you, Mary, I confess I had not expected to see you in these parts. You should have stayed at home with your babe."

Surprise jerked Carlyon's head round to look at Mary. Sadness rippled down his back at the thought that she had a baby and, with that, a husband. He shook his shoulders to dismiss such a feeling. It should be nothing to him that her life had moved on, for it was over two years since he had last seen her, and she was a comely woman. He moved his mouth into a smile as he looked at her, but she was not looking at him. She had stiffened at Thomas's words, and she shouted back spiritedly, pointing at Thomas in emphasis.

"D'you dare to speak about my babe? He's nought to you! He's safe with my mother. I've no fear of you. It's you, should have fear of us."

Thomas seemed somewhat taken aback. He pulled his head back but immediately came forward again. "Hah! Fear? You know nought of what fear is. Get you back to your babe, before it's too late and you lose all you have. I no longer need you. I have better."

He abruptly jerked back and closed the window. It was as if he had never appeared. John put his hands on his hips and glared at the window, as if expecting Thomas to reappear. Carlyon's brow was furrowed, as thoughts made his brain revolve like water in a millrace, tumbling over a racing wheel. There was much to consider. He made a decision.

"This house was made for defence," he told John. "It won't be a simple matter to get inside. This Thomas has your men in his power and working for him. Look you." He pointed to the two wings of the house, where archers could be seen behind balustrades on the roof. John, who had not noticed them, bridled, but Carlyon continued. "We'll need to plan out how to get into the house. You'll know the weak spots, I'll warrant. Let's retire awhile. We can dry these wet clothes and consider what would be the best attack."

"Retreat?! I'll not give this cur that satisfaction. I'll beat down this door myself." John stepped up and gave the door a bang with the side of his fist, but then immediately seemed to reconsider. "No, we need men to take this house. Let's away. I know where to go." He moved his arms at the others, as if herding geese, and then set off across the courtyard. Once through the gateway, he led them down the road without hesitating.

Some fifteen minutes or so later they were at an inn. It was part of John's estate, and on entering he peremptorily ordered three rooms to be made available for them, changed to four at Carlyon's insistence. Then he called up robes.

"We have clothes to be dried. See you have a good fire. For me, bring some dry clothes straightway. I want breeches and a chemise. And a tunic. To it!"

"Alas, we've nought here as befits Your Lordship to wear. We're but simple folk," said the landlord, wringing his hands.

John made no attempt to hide his irritation. "By God's teeth! Am I to be held here by that?" He petulantly sliced downwards with his right arm. "I won't wait. Bring me what you have. Straight now, knave!"

When some clothes had been brought, John dressed as he could and then put on his own trimmed surcoat, sodden though it was. He was eager to start seeking a force of men, to help him attack and enter his house.

"I'll away now," he told Carlyon, striding into his room without ceremony. "This Godfrey – or Thomas – may have taken control of my house men, but there are many more of my tenants I can gather. This very night we'll let this rogue taste my cold steel."

Carlyon would have preferred that they spoke more about the layout of the house and any weaknesses, but he knew that there was no holding John at that stage. He let him go and thoughtfully turned to cleaning his sword. After replacing it in its scabbard, he sat and considered the situation. Daggers of worry were pricking at him as he thought about the powers that he feared Thomas possessed. He knew also that Thomas had a deeper knowledge of the house and its secrets than John would have. Their task would not be an easy one.

He was not sure how long he sat there, but almost a score of minutes fell through unnoticed. Then unconsciously his fingers began to rub the ring on his left hand. Almost immediately he began to feel a sensation of calm grow in his body, as if his head were being caressed to the sound of a soothing lullaby. Almost imperceptibly, his worries were replaced by a calm confidence. His lips tightened as he drew in a breath, which he let out straight away and got to his feet. Glancing down, he saw that his hand was resting on his ring. He took it away and could not stop himself from looking at the ring. It was as if a force were pushing him to examine it, to think about it. His brow furrowed, and he wondered yet again how he had acquired the ring, but, as always, there seemed no answer. Then he forgot the ring, for he was suddenly seized with a desire to see Mary. Belting his borrowed robe about him, he went down to the private parlour set aside for John and his guests. Refreshments had been provided, and Carlyon, James and Mary sat round the fire. Carlyon turned immediately to Mary.

"Well, indeed, Mary," he said. "I thank you once again for your glad arrival. I can't say how pleased I am to see you, my heart's too full. But pray tell, I must know, what have you been doing since I left you and your dear mother, to go for the flowers of the swan?" He said nothing about the baby. He wondered if she would give details but did not want to show how his emotions were affected. Why should a peasant girl's marriage cause him to feel such a sense of loss?

Mary looked at him with her brow furrowed, as if unsure thoughts were pulling at the muscles. "Do you not know, Carlyon?"

He was taken aback at her familiar use of his name, but before he could speak, James broke in with a laugh.

"He knows not what he himself has been doing these past eighteen months. Is that not so, sire?"

"In faith, it is," Carlyon acknowledged with a rueful nod of his head. "Mayhap I should tell of my adventures first? I did find the flowers of the swan, thanks be to your mother's directions. I came back and looked to find your cottage, but somehow, I went astray. I know not, but it was as if it had all been a dream. Right glad I am to find it not so. I set off on my journey south and met James, that I had thought dead, but who had been cared for by monks."

He paused, which allowed James to say, "There is a tale to tell, when my turn comes."

Carlyon smiled indulgently and continued. "We travelled on to Chertsey, where I learned that the lady who had sent me on my quest had not awaited my return, but had married Lord John – he that you have but now made acquaintance of. Sad at heart, I threw the flowers into the river and thought to seek other adventures. But strangely, I had an accident. I know not what. I can remember nought after that, until one morning I awoke in a quarry near the town of Warrington. How I got there, or why, is a mystery yet to be disclosed."

"Indeed so." Mary nodded. "I spoke to the quarrymen when I went in search of you, after you did not return."

"It's God's mercy that you should have found the quarrymen. But why did you come after me, so long after I'd left? And you have an infant, it seems. How have you left him and your husband, to seek me?"

Mary looked at Carlyon, and he saw sadness pass over her face like the shadow of a cloud passing over a pool of water. He assumed that there had been death, and sympathy with her loss made his fingers tighten. He was about to express this sympathy, but Mary spoke, smiling with an unexpected, regretful knowingness.

"I had to leave my babe to find my lost husband. So it is. This is what has happened, I tell you truly. When you left to go for the flowers of the swan, I thought me I'd never see you again. I'll tell you, my heart was sad, but I knew you had your duty. Then one day my mother told me you were lost and a danger lay in wait for you. She has these powers of sight, and so I knew her words to be true. I travelled to the south, and I found you in Oxford. You were with a goliard who had rescued you from drowning near Maidenhead, yet you had no memory of that, nor of your life before that. You did not even know your own name."

"So that's what happened, how I was rescued. And now I have no memory of this goliard, although I can remember everything until I fell into the river. What tricks our mind plays with us. Tell me, when did you find me in Oxford? And where have I been since that time?"

"I found you in early summer last year and took you to my home. My mother hoped to bring back your memory, but even though we told you who you are, none of her mixtures prevailed. So, you lived with us, and ere long your heart turned fondly towards me. You took me to wife, and nigh St John's Day last, I bore your son – Stanford."

James had been greatly interested in Mary's tale, listening to the latter part with his mouth partly open. He screwed up his face in thought, as Mary paused, and he looked at Carlyon.

"Do you remember nought of this?" Mary asked, hope brightening her face.

Carlyon did not speak immediately. He struggled with what he had just learned – it made no sense. It was as if Mary had been relating a tale about someone else. But he must remember, especially if he had a son. He moved his arms, as if trying to dandle a baby, and still there was nothing. "I know nought of any of this. Say you, we were wedded?"

"Yea, we are wed. Many in the village came to witness it."

Carlyon's eyes widened. If the marriage had been in front of witnesses, then it meant that the child, his son, was legitimate. This would need much more careful thought. He nervously rubbed his thumb over the ring on his left hand. Suddenly there was a memory in his mind like the echo of a distant song, but then it was gone. He shook his head. "Alas, I remember none of it. I wish I could, yet if you say 'tis so, then so it must be. We must talk more on this matter, for the more you tell me, it may be I'll remember. Even so, we must leave it for the nonce. We have a dark cloud hanging over us, and that must first be blown away. I little thought me I should see Thomas again."

"His ambition has grown," said James forcefully, "but like a jackdaw flying high, he'll be no match for an eagle. We'll tear his feathers, an' we get inside the house."

"Yea, however bright the sun may be when it rises, it can always set behind a cloud. E'en so, I worry me about Lady Patrina," said Carlyon, glancing at Mary. "She'll be safe, so long as he desires her, just as you were. Yet, and he feel his life in danger, he'll use her to bargain, I trow."

"He'll not want to have his prize taken from him a second time," Mary told him. "He'll fight to keep such a high-born lady, and we must be prepared for more tricks than he's yet shown."

"He's a man of tricks. We must meet him with tricks of our own. But first we must gain entry to the house. I'll warrant we'll need to fight past those servants of John that he's bewitched. If John finds good men, we'll be able to do that, I ween. My sword is an army on its own."

"I also have your shield," Mary suddenly said. "I think me it was eager to return to you, for it acted as a lodestone, to lead me here."

Carlyon's face lit up, as if he had suddenly come into sunlight. His hands moved, as if about to touch Mary's arm. "It pleases me to hear that, Mary. With my sword and my shield, I fear neither man, nor beast, nor wizard. We shall fight and we'll prevail."

Feeling surer of himself, he led the talk about the struggle that lay in front of them. It was as if he wanted to concentrate on that, rather than consider the implications of his relationship with Mary, a peasant girl. His father, his family, would find that hard to accept. Yet he himself was oddly taken by it, as if he were holding junket in his hands. He knew that it would be delicious, but it was like to slip out of his fingers at any moment. He did not know whether to taste, whether to hold, or whether to let it slip. It was better to talk of something else.

John was not away for long, and when he returned, Carlyon decided to say nothing about the thunderclap of his marriage and fatherhood. As it was, John gave him little chance. He burst into the room, followed soon by a boy with ale. John had already begun his tale as James and Mary moved aside so that he could sit nearest to the fire.

"God's teeth! There're some rogues about! This cursed friar seems to have everyone under his cloak. All my precious things are now nought but a post that passing dogs defile." He banged into a chair and looked at Carlyon, as if hoping to be proved wrong. "These are *my* tenants. They owe their livelihoods to me and my family. If I call, they should all come running, ready to serve. It seems they loved me only when they thought to get something from me. These lapdog loves, that wagged their tails as they chewed, will find another dish ere long."

He broke off, for the boy was approaching, and he shouted at the lad to be quick in pouring out ale. Carlyon pursed his lips and his brain chewed over what he had just heard. He had thought to have a reasonably sized force in their support, when they got into the house. There would need to be a rethink. It was obvious that people in the area were either afraid of Thomas or accepted that he was now the stronger power. Even so, it would have been expected that they would be willing to back Lord John in removing Thomas. Instead, it seemed that John had lost his popularity, and any love that his tenants might have had for him. Carlyon considered the matter, while he watched John take a long drink from his mug.

Temporarily satisfied, John belched and continued his complaint. "I'll not forget this. These cowards will rue that they came not to my aid. By God's teeth, I'll make them smart."

He drank again, and Carlyon spoke.

"They're but simple folk, John. They've been living in fear for too long to be able to toss it away like an old breechcloth. If we have no fighting men, then we must necessarily do it all ourselves."

"Oh, we're not on our own. I've found a dozen men who'll take my silver to fight. They're not trained, and their weapons are but clubs and sickles. Yet I think me they'll look fierce enough."

"Could we not go to the sheriff?" James offered a contribution. "If a warrant is sworn, the sheriff will provide men to take back the house."

"My lord high sheriff?!" John spat out the words and pushed his head forward to peer angrily at James with his one good eye. "I'll not give him the satisfaction of knowing I was kept out of my own house by a peasant, who even took my wife from me. I'll deal with this myself, and all will know I've done so. We'll attack the house on the morrow. Then all will see I'm not a man to be scorned."

Carlyon saw the anger flaming up in his friend and realised that the ale was not dousing it. He tried to calm things down. "Yes, there's no time to go to the sheriff. We shall take your house, fear not. And this Thomas will face justice, an' it be summary or not. Yet I wish me we had more sure knowledge of where Patrina is, where this fiend is holding her."

"I'm sure Her Ladyship is in the house," said Mary, speaking for the first time since John's return. "She's being held in a dark chamber known only to Thomas."

Carlyon nodded. "I agree she'll be in the house. There she can easily be kept close from any man's eye. But we must consider our attack carefully, lest it put her life in danger."

"Pah!" snorted John. "An' we attack speedily and stick my sword through this rogue, he'll have no time to do aught to harm my lady."

"And yet if Thomas were to die before telling where Her Ladyship is hidden, it may be she'll not be found." Mary said these words softly but firmly, with the confidence that Carlyon remembered well.

John, however, looked at her with irritation marking his face. "Why's this servant girl sitting with us, as if she is an equal? I'm not accustomed to being spoken to without permission."

At John's words, Carlyon jerked his body upright in his chair. It was almost as if he himself were being attacked, and he put out a hand to halt John. "Nay, John, you speak hastily. I wish to have Mary's advice. Her wise words have shown me a clear path in the past, and I'll warrant she'll be of good service to us now."

He wanted to protect Mary, and would have said more, but John carelessly waved his hand. He seemed to have calmed down a little.

"You had always a soft heart for the lower orders, Carlyon," he said. The words were dismissive, but the tone was affable. He lifted a buttock and broke wind. This seemed to relieve him. Although he ignored Mary, he smiled at Carlyon as he put his ale mug to his lips. After drinking, he spoke again. "Very well. I wish not to put Patsy's life in danger. But we must get into the house first."

"Verily so, John. We must get into the house. Thomas has many men to defend it, but though the leaves of the tree are many, the root is one. If we but take Thomas, the house is ours."

"You say right. We must take this cur into our hands. He thinks to scoff at me! I'll once get my hands on him and then I'll make him scoff."

"We can do that, John. I remember me how this Thomas disdains those he thinks to be in his power. He likes to play, to amuse himself, sure in his own mind that he'll prevail. His arrogance will be a lever for us to tip him into a pit."

"Do you recall what Thomas said about Her Ladyship?" James asked diffidently. "He said that if we wished to free her, then we must go who knows whither and bring who knows what hither. What did he mean by that?"

"Pah! The ramblings of a madman," sneered John.

"I doubt me that," said Carlyon. "Thomas won't taunt without reason. He's told us what to do, because he's sure we can't do it."

"And what is it we must do?"

Carlyon shrugged. He did not know, and John contemptuously blew out his breath. Stung, Carlyon struggled to find some meaning in the words.

"We must make a journey – a quest, if you will. At the end of it we'll find something, who knows what, that will help us to defeat Thomas and free Patrina. We must all bend our minds and try to discover the secret in the words."

John looked somewhat incredulously at Carlyon, but he said nothing. For some seconds the four of them sat in silence, until John burst out.

"This's nonsense! We can sit here like ninnies, when we should be planning our attack. Why waste we time like this?"

"I know not, John. I only know that Thomas is a man of great cunning, and he says nothing without purpose. There is a meaning hidden in his words, can we but find it."

"They're simple words. They mean nothing."

"I think me my lord speaks truly – they *are* simple words." Mary spoke this time, and as all turned to look at her, she flushed but drew in a breath and continued. "Thomas has said the words but to confuse, to provide a false mystery. He's telling us truly what we must do. You must go who knows whither and bring who knows what hither. We can guess what you must bring hither. What else can it be but only Her Ladyship herself? The task Thomas has set is to find out where she is."

"And we must go who knows whither to answer that riddle," said Carlyon.

"Not so far, I trow. Her Ladyship will be close confined in the house."

"There you are: we must get into the house." Impatience had been shaking John during the preceding exchanges, and his words were forcefully spat out. "Patsy will be in a secret chamber somewhere. When I get my hands on this rogue, I'll make him tell. For now, we must plan our campaign."

He told Mary to call the landlord and have more ale brought. Then he led a discussion with Carlyon and the occasional contribution from James, to consider what lay ahead of them. Fuelled perhaps by the ale, their planning went well, because John grew more confident. Carlyon also was confident that they would succeed, once they were inside the house. His big doubt was over their ability to get inside. In the end, this was the only point that was without a confident solution.

During their discussions Mary sat quietly, offering no opinion. Carlyon frequently glanced at her, for although he was concentrating on their proposed assault, part of his mind was still probing what he had learned from her. He knew that it was a matter that he could not evade. Fortunately, John's forceful optimism kept his mind focused on the main issue. Then, as he had begun to be distracted by thoughts of supper, his attention was pulled by the sound of voices from beyond the window.

John also was drawn by the clamour. "Something's happening out there!" he snapped out, twisting his body in his chair to look towards the window. "Mayhap we have more men?"

He got up from his chair to go and see. Carlyon's initial thought was that Thomas had sent armed men in search of them, but he got up and followed John to the window, to look out into the yard. It was indeed a small crowd, but it had been drawn by a man who was holding a bear by a chain around its neck. The bear was sitting on its haunches and moving its head slowly from side to side as it sniffed the air. The man was calling out, trying to attract a larger crowd.

"Come," said John. "Let's go and see what happens here. I'm in need of entertainment. And we may get ourselves some more men from this crowd."

Somewhat surprised at John's sudden decision, and yet pleased at the chance of a break, Carlyon paused, but then, indicating to James and Mary to come, he went out into the yard with John. They pushed through the crowd, which had grown a little larger. The man seemed satisfied with his audience and announced that he would make the bear perform, as if human. Holding the chain with his left hand, he began to play a small pipe, which he was holding in his right hand. As the first notes sounded, the bear got to its feet and, lumbering forward, began to move in a shuffling dance. To and fro it went, round and back again, keeping time with the slow tempo of the music. After the dance the bear got down on all fours, put its head on the ground, and lifted its hind legs into the air. When it came down, it rolled, making the crowd scatter fearfully in that area.

The man laughed as the bear got back to its feet. "You do well to be afeared," he warned. "I control him, but and I let him go, you'd see a more fearsome dance. A bear is the most terrifying of God's natural creatures. Why, I've seen a bear crush a man to death in less time than it takes to doff a hat. No man can defeat a bear in combat. A bear can kill anything it meets. Are you not afeared?"

"Not I!" shouted John. "I fear neither man nor beast. Nor will a bear kill me, by God's teeth!"

Carlyon jerked his head round to look at his friend. John was swaying, and Carlyon realised that he was more drunk than he had suspected while they were sitting inside the inn. He smiled and shook his head at his friend's bravado. Then, just as he was about to turn back to look at the bear, he was surprised to see John draw the sword that he had belted round his waist on leaving to come out into the yard. John waved the sword about and took a step forward.

"I'm not afeared of your bear," he cried. "I can show it who's master."

"Hold now, John," hissed Carlyon, stretching out a restraining arm.

John seemed not to hear. He stepped forward again, nearer to the bear, and made two quick feints, as if about to run the animal through. The bear handler cried out in his alarm, and this seemed to disturb the bear. It reared up to confront the aggressor. Its jaws opened, showing its teeth. A rumbling growl came out, and it raised its arms, ready to crush. The crowd began to draw back again, and the handler pulled the chain tighter, calling out his words of command. Despite this, the animal lunged forward. Carlyon gasped, but John instinctively drove his sword up. It went into the bear's ribcage and the tip of the blade appeared at the back. As the animal fell forward, its arms clasped John. The handler pulled on the chain with both hands, but the weight of the dying bear pulled John onto the ground. Carlyon and James leaped forward, daggers in their hands. Carlyon was not sure at first what he was going to do. He stabbed into the bear's neck, but John's sword seemed to have done its work. The bear was already still. The distraught handler moved to pull it off John, and Carlyon hastened to help. The handler was crying out in his distress, tears glistening in his eyes, as if he had lost a family member. Carlyon was worried about John, but when the bear was rolled over, he saw John lying on the ground, grinning triumphantly.

"By God's teeth!" John slurred. "That was a warm blanket."

Carlyon realised that John's drunkenness had made him unaware of how close to harm he had been. "Are you hurt?" he asked, bending over to examine him.

"Not I, not I," John replied, pushing himself up to a sitting position.

Carlyon looked closely at him. There was blood on the left forearm, where John had raised it to protect himself from the bear's teeth, but otherwise he could see little else of concern. "Why did you kill the poor beast?" he asked. "It was meaning no harm."

John looked over at the bear and frowned, as if he needed to think what had happened. "I needed to kill something. It's only a bear. 'Twill do, until I can kill the caitiff who's stolen my house and chattels."

Carlyon sighed. He could understand John's anger at what had been happening to him. He had seen John take out such feelings on uninvolved objects and creatures in the past. Even so, he felt sorry for the bear's owner. "This man has lost his living," he said. "It would have been well to leave him be."

"He'll find another. He's but a strolling entertainer. I must take something to drink now. My head is like a bees' nest. It needs to be sweetened."

John got to his feet and swayed his way towards the inn door. Carlyon, concerned for his friend and yet sorrowed at his lack of remorse, watched the unsteady progress, as John shambled off, almost like the bear that he had killed. Carlyon tightened his lips and swung round to go to the bear handler. Parting the small crowd which had gathered closely round the bear, now that it was no longer dangerous, he stepped up to the crumpled beast. Its owner was sitting on the ground with the bear's head in his lap and stroking it.

"What will you do now?" Carlyon asked.

"What *to* do, my lord?" The man's voice was forlorn yet resigned. "I must sell Panser for his meat and his hide. He was a good animal. We've been together now for many a year, since he was a cub, and he's been a truer companion to me than any man. I'll not see his like again."

"Will you not get another bear to continue your act?"

"No, not now. I'll play my pipe, as I did before. And, God willing, I'll make a crust."

Carlyon looked at the bear and thoughtfully rubbed his lower lip with his thumbnail. An idea was forming in his mind. "I would have this bear's skin myself," he told the man. "Flay the animal most carefully, so it be a whole skin. Bring it to me on the morrow and I'll tell you what else you can do for me."

The man nodded, and Carlyon turned. The curious crowd parted to let him through, and he went back into the inn with James and Mary.

As they walked, James asked about the skin. "Is this to be a trophy, sire?"

"No trophy, James, but a powerful tool, I hope. I have me an idea to help us gain entry to my lord John's house. We'll discuss this privily and lay our plan."

14

Peter, the bear trainer, brought the skin to Carlyon early the next morning. All the flesh had been scraped off, and Carlyon examined it with some satisfaction. More work was required on the head. He wanted to retain the snout and the teeth, because he knew that the bearskin would need to look as realistic as possible for what he had in mind.

Most of the morning had passed before he was content. And this content was mostly due to Mary. She had gone out shortly before dawn and collected some herbs still damply pearled with dew. To these she added salt and spices from the larder. When everything was made into a potion, she rubbed it on the inside of the bearskin.

"This will preserve it for a few days and will also give a sweet odour. There'll be no discomfort in wearing."

Carlyon smiled at her words. A warm surge of happiness buoyed him at working so closely with her again. She seemed to fill him with optimism, and he was confident that they would be successful. He needed to be active, for there was more to be done in planning the attack, and yet it was giving him great pleasure even to be near her while she was working on the skin. Silently he watched her deft and skilful movements, marvelling at how she worked away in soft beauty and unconscious delight.

He was interrupted when John joined them. John had been training his small force, putting them through some paces, and he was now eager to finalise his plan to retake his property. He had been unable to think of anything better than a direct assault, so it was with evident pleasure that he received Carlyon's plan.

"A man will garb himself in the skin. He will seem as if a bear to other men. He'll be led to your house, and his handler will seek entry, saying that he wishes to entertain the household. Inside the house, our man will seek an opportunity to open the gate to us. Once we are in, we'll not be ejected so easily this time."

"No, by God's teeth! I'll not leave this time. I'll have my revenge. But wait! Suppose the door's not opened and our bear handler is turned away? How know we he'll be admitted?"

"We know not. Yet the trick is worth the hazard. I think me this Thomas will be intrigued by a wild beast controlled by a man. He'll want to see it and find out if aught differs from his way."

"We'll do it! When will it be ready?"

"This day, I trow. Mary is sewing up the skin and preparing it for use."

"Good. I'll wear it and no bear will look so fierce as I. Mayhap I'll have my chance, and I'll be able to slay this Thomas before he knows aught of it. Then I can take control once more."

"As it may be, John. We need more thought yet." Carlyon had not planned that John would wear the skin, and he was not sure that someone so hot-blooded as John would be the best choice. A calm, careful man would be needed, in order not to rouse any suspicion in Thomas's mind. He sighed and told John that they would speak again after dining.

When Mary had finished her work on the skin and a frame had been provided to shape the head, it did not, in fact, fit John.

Carlyon hid his relief that the baron was too bulky to get inside and instead consoled him.

"It will be better an' someone else acts the bear. You'll be needed to lead the men into the house."

"Likely so, Carlyon. I'll do that and you can wear the skin."

"I fear not. I thought me the bear looked taller when alive. Yet the skin will fit James, I trow, and could we trust any man more than he?"

James was keen to take on the task and lost no time in trying on the skin. It was a good fit, except that he found it difficult to see. This required more work by Mary, but at last hidden eye-slits had been made. Carlyon and John walked round the bear, looking closely. The cuts made in the skin when the bear was being killed had been expertly darned and were not visible in the fur. To Carlyon's eye, James now looked just like a bear.

Peter, the bear's former owner, was not so sure. "It's not the Panser I knew. He's standing wrongly. He moves too much like a man."

"Then you must teach him how to move," said Carlyon. "You know how it must be done. James will practise. If you go to the manor house this even, 'twill be dark enough to hide any imperfections."

Peter furrowed his brow, but he seemed to relish the challenge. He was left alone with James, and the two of them practised how James should move like a bear and how he should dance and perform to his handler's calls. Late in the afternoon they gave a demonstration before Carlyon and John. Carlyon, even though he knew that it was not a real bear, found it convincing.

John whooped his delight. "We have him. We'll be in the house this night and the sly snake will wriggle his last. Let's be away now."

"Are you ready, James?" asked Carlyon. "Will it go well?"

"I'd as soon it were over quickly," replied James's muffled voice. "But first, I fain would take some refreshment. This skin is somewhat stifling."

Despite John's impatience, James was helped out of the suit. His face was flushed, and although the skin had no rank odour, he himself smelled of sweat after being wrapped so closely all afternoon. John took the opportunity to go and speak to his men, and when James went to visit the privy before taking some refreshment, Carlyon asked Peter for his opinion of James's performance.

"It will go well, sire, I'm sure of it. No man can tell the truth of it. We'll get into His Lordship's house, and we'll play our part."

"It gladdens my heart to hear that. You'll be well rewarded on the morrow."

"I thank you, sire. And may I beg also that I can take Panser's skin with me? An' I can find a partner, I think me I'll be able to put on many a show."

Carlyon chuckled at the man's enthusiasm. It was a surprise to him that even more good might come from John's wanton act.

When James was ready, Mary sewed him back into the skin and he and Peter set off for the manor house. At the gate, James waited docilely, while Peter asked for entry. It was not immediately granted, and James was thinking that the plan would fail, but Peter spoke persuasively.

"Come now, good fellow. Here's an amusing thing. I've got me a ferocious beast and yet I've trained him to obey my commands. I've heard tell that the master of this house has an interest in such things. He'll want to know of this and will perchance be angry if he hears I was turned away."

The gatekeeper paused a few seconds, then told Peter to wait. When he returned, he opened up. "Come in," he said. "My lord would fain see your animal."

James would have preferred not to go into Thomas's presence, but he was thankful that they had gained entrance. The last few embers of the day were glowing in the western sky, but the courtyard was full of shadows that accompanied them as they walked across to the house. Inside the house it was even gloomier, for few lights had been lit. James was glad that he was being led, because he could see little. In the hall, Thomas was sitting alone at the table. Dishes here and there indicated that he had just finished taking supper. James looked around cautiously, moving his head as little as possible. Thomas was still wearing his friar's habit and was lolling in the carved wooden armchair that John had used. There was no one else in the room, except a servant standing to one side, and an armed man who had stayed by the door after they came in.

Thomas looked sideways at the bear and its handler for a few seconds, as they stood in the centre of the hall. "What do you want of me?" he asked at last, the words snapping through the silence.

"Forgive my intrusion, good Father," said Peter, bowing obsequiously. "I have here a bear, a wild and ferocious beast, and yet through my skill I have made it gentle as a lamb, subject to my bidding. See its teeth, see its claws. Yet it will show neither teeth nor claws, unless I command it to do so."

"I too can control ferocious beasts. And I have seen a larger bear than your creature. No matter. You interest me and I'm in need of amusement. How do you control this animal?"

"I've trained him, good Father. I began when he was but a cub. I used a mixture of kindness and firmness, and he now relies on me for everything."

"Hah! I have potions to control my beasts. I've had no use for kindness. Let that be. I would see your show. Be sure to entertain."

James thought that he detected a hint of warning in Thomas's voice, but he was feeling more confident now that they were in the house. He held himself ready and looked at Peter, awaiting the signal that they had practised. Peter put his pipe to his lips. Giving one stamp with his foot, he began to blow, and James started to dance. Thomas watched with a bored air until the music stopped but said nothing. James began to worry and sweat seeped uncontrollably from his body as he grew uncomfortable in the confines of his suit. He wondered how long they could continue to amuse Thomas. Peter took him through a few simple tricks that they had practised. Still Thomas seemed unimpressed. The fingers of one hand were coolly drumming on the table. Peter gave the command for rest, and while James took his relaxed position, Peter bowed to Thomas.

"Those were tricks that will amuse the ladies of the household," he said. "Now I shall let the bear loose, and yet withal I shall keep control."

Thomas looked directly at Peter, but his eyes still had a narrowness that displayed suspicion. James waited. The chain was removed from his neck, and at the command, he raised himself up and moved menacingly towards Thomas, who began to watch closely. At another command James turned and moved towards the servant, arms reaching out. He gave a low growl as he moved close, and the servant turned and fled towards the door with a howl of fear. James stopped at the command and came back. He saw that Thomas was smiling, seemingly with pleasure. Peter sent James again towards the table. Thomas seemed to tense himself, but James was called back and resumed his relaxed position, while the chain was fastened again to his neck.

"Interesting," said Thomas, getting up from his seat and coming out from behind the table. "Even I, though I knew I was in no danger, felt a little afeared. You've trained the bear well. I would control this beast. Tell me the commands."

"This's not an easy thing, Father. I know not that he'll move to another man's call."

Peter was clearly reluctant, and he stepped back a pace. James also felt a tremor of worry release sweat in his armpits. It would not be good for Thomas to come too close. The plan was that they would provide a show and then retire to the stable for the night, during which James would open the gate to let in John and the attacking force. Thomas's sharp interest was an unforeseen development to the plan.

"I will learn to control the bear," said Thomas, the firmness in his voice banging at the atmosphere like a hammer. "Teach me the commands now."

"At once, Father," Peter hastily agreed. "Yet come not too close to the animal. An' you hold the chain like so, it will keep a space, so that the bear sees no threat."

James breathed a little easier at Peter's quick-witted ploy, and he listened while the commands were explained to Thomas. When Thomas tried the commands himself, James carried them out, hoping to satisfy Thomas quickly. There were not many commands to be taught, for Thomas did not seem interested in dancing or tricks. He wanted to learn how to make the bear threaten and seem fierce. It did not take long, to James's relief, but Thomas's next words tightened up the tense feeling in his chest.

"This is good," he heard Thomas say. "I have me now a small task for this beast. A show for the lady of the household indeed." He laughed derisively. "I'll take him away for but a short while. Wait you here for my return."

"Nay, Father," said Peter, "I think it not wise to take him away from me. He'll be nervous."

"Nervous? See how gently he waits. I know of handling wild beasts, and this one will be no different. Worry you not. I'll bring him back safely and you'll be well paid for this little task."

"But, Father, I'm still afeared. I must come with you."

"Stay!" The word came out like an arrow, reinforced by Thomas's pointing finger. "I will do this, and 'twill be the worse for you, an' you cross me. Stay you here and we'll be back ere long."

James listened to the exchange and wondered what wickedness Thomas was planning. He was not expecting anything good, and yet he knew that he would have to follow as he could. When Thomas pulled his chain, he obediently padded along behind. He was led towards the cellars, Thomas not glancing back to check on his bear more than once. James kept himself to the length of his chain. He did not want to get too close to Thomas, even though the light from Thomas's candle did not illuminate him too brightly. However, if Thomas did realise that he was not a bear, then James was determined to attack as best he was able.

When they reached the cellars, Thomas carefully closed the access door behind them. He seemed to be making sure that they were alone. Seemingly satisfied, he glanced at the bear, before setting off again, and James saw that they were going to the flooded cellar. As before, it was full of water, rippling gently in its brooding blackness. James stayed in the doorway, while Thomas let go of the end of his chain. It had come into James's head that Thomas was planning to make him go into the water for some devilish reason or other. He made up his mind to refuse, knowing that it would be difficult to swim in the bearskin. He would pretend to be afraid of water.

However, that did not seem to be Thomas's intention. James watched tensely as Thomas placed his candlestick on the floor and then took an iron bar from an alcove by the door. The bar was about half a man's height and had a crossbar on one end with a hook on the other. Thomas went to the top of the stairs leading under the water and put the hooked end of his bar down the side. He hooked it onto something in the water and began to turn it. James heard a grating noise, after which there was silence except for a slight gurgle of water. Thomas unhooked the bar and placed it back in the alcove. Then he picked up his candle and stood looking out over the water. James looked also, and soon he saw that the water level was going down. As it did so, he was able to see that a sluice gate in the wall had been closed, and he realised that the iron bar had been used to turn some sort of spindle. For some minutes the two of them stood there. James, still in the doorway, was watchful, but outwardly relaxed. Thomas, at the top of a slowly appearing flight of steps, gazed impassively at the water, with an occasional backward glance to check on the bear.

Eventually the water was all but gone. Only puddles remained. Thomas picked up the chain and pulled James forward. They went down eight steps, and James saw that they were in a small pit, a little over two yards or so square, and which was, he supposed, originally built to store ice. Certainly, it was cold enough, even now. James could feel the damp chill through the bearskin, but his nervous doubt at what was to come was eased somewhat when he saw a door in the wall and began to suspect that he was being taken to where Lady Patrina was being held.

Thomas opened the door and pulled James inside after him. It was a short, low passage, dank and cold. James could smell the musty dampness, and he shivered at the thought of being held prisoner in this place. Thomas halted at a door, which he unlocked. It gave access to a small, low-ceilinged room, that held no furniture except for a low truckle bed. Lying on the bed was a figure wrapped in a fur cloak. The figure stirred at the noise of the intrusion, and a head appeared from beneath the fur, blinking in the candlelight. James's heart bumped to see that it was Lady Patrina. Her head was uncovered, and although her hair was dishevelled, it was still fastened up. Her face was vacant, as if she had woken from a deep sleep and did not know where she was.

Thomas lit a candle in a holder on the wall and set down his own candle. He put his hands on his hips and surveyed his prisoner. "Well, my fine beauty, have you slept enough for the nonce? How long will you stay here?"

"What am I doing here? I feel most strange. There's a noise in my head, as if bees are buzzing. I feel fastened down, trapped in a sticky net. What is all this?"

"Nought but a potion of mine to keep you here. You've been in my power this many a month now, an' you but knew it. Now you are completely mine."

"This will not be so. I demand you release me forthwith. I like not this place."

"Truly, this be a dismal dungeon and I honour the mind that devised it. Yet it can be made worse, and it will be, my fine lady, an' you refuse my bidding."

"What mean you, Friar Godfrey? I can't stay here. I say again: release me forthwith."

"Release you, my pretty? Yea, I can release you. But release will only come when you agree to take me as your husband."

"What nonsense is this? I already have a husband. He will kill you for laying your hands on me, even though you be a man of the cloth. It would be meet were you to release me and make your escape. Even were I free, I could never marry a man such as you, base of birth and nature."

James had been standing motionless during these exchanges, outwardly relaxed and unaware. In fact, he was struggling to contain himself, as his mind fought with the prickly flame of what he was hearing. He saw now what Thomas was after, and yet he could not see how Thomas would achieve his end. As Lady Patrina had said, she was married, and her husband was not standing idly by. James peeped at Patrina through his eye-slits. She had pulled herself up somewhat on the mattress. Despite her drugged state, James could see a gleam flickering in her eyes in the candlelight. Her strength of will was driving her to fight, though her body's struggles were futile. James sensed a maturity in her that had been totally absent when he'd known her before her marriage. His heart went out to her, and he resolved to lay down his life for her, if he had to.

Thomas was laughing. "Brave words, I trow. They mean no more than a puff of smoke on the wanton breeze. I've taken possession of this house, and I'll take possession of you. As for your husband, the bold baron – it will not prove so easy for him to kill me. I'm protected by magical powers greater than aught he has. He must needs look to himself. I tell you this – he'll die in battle anon against wild animals I've trained for this very purpose. You must decide soon. Marry me or stay forever trapped in a nightmare you can't imagine." He held out his arm and pointed his finger at her threateningly. Then he stepped to one side against the wall by the door, leaving a clear space. "I'll show you a little of my power over animals."

He gave the necessary command, and James raised himself up. Then Thomas gave the command for the bear to become fierce and to move towards Patrina. James hesitated momentarily but thought it best to do as commanded. It was one more thing for which Thomas would pay, and the payment date was imminent. James lifted out his arms and seemed about to attack, so that Patrina flinched back, and was unable to prevent a scream of fear escaping her throat. But it was only a few seconds. As if unwilling to go too far, Thomas ordered the bear to stop and sent him to a corner.

"See you now?" he said, almost gloating. "I can make this wild beast act at my will. I could do the same with you, but I would you come to me willingly. And you will do what I wish. Mayhap I'll leave the bear with you. He'll be in need of companionship to satisfy his natural desires. It'll be nought to him that you be a human female. Think on it. But now I must leave. Your husband has been trying to gather men, and he plans to attack on the morrow. I must away to check my defences. When I next come to see you, you'll be a widow. You will give me your answer then."

He pointed to Patrina, and then at the bear. After a brief pause, as if to give time for reflection, he stepped over to Patrina, and James saw that he had taken a tiny phial from his pouch. Kneeling down by the bed, Thomas firmly gripped Patrina's head and held the phial to her lips. Whatever was inside it was put into her mouth. Thomas lowered her head and got to his feet. For a moment he looked down at his prisoner, then, as if satisfied, he turned and moved over to snuff the candle on the wall. Picking up his own candle and James's chain, he left the cell, pulling James after him. Without even looking into the cell again, he closed the door and locked it.

James wondered what was next but was hoping that Thomas had no other plan for him. He worried that Thomas might become suspicious of him and discover that he was not really a bear. He had been lucky so far that the light was so weak. He could not be examined closely, but the longer that he was with Thomas, the greater the risk.

The chain round James's neck tightened as Thomas began to move, but it was only for a few steps. Thomas stopped outside another door and unlocked it. As if he were alone, he opened the door and went into the room. James, in the doorway, saw that the little cell was full of money – mainly silver, but some gold. It was in piles, seemingly in no arrangement, as if thrown there from time to time. James was unable to estimate how much there was. In the flickering candlelight, he also saw pieces of jewellery glinting. Thomas stood and looked. Nothing more. It was as though he were breathing in strength, simply by looking at his ill-gotten wealth. James, behind him, thought that it would be a good chance to kill him. His arms twitched, but sewn into the bearskin, he could not easily get at his dagger. Also, fear of Thomas's powers held him. He was alone in that dank, dreary place. It would be better to wait and follow Carlyon's plan. At least Lady Patrina had been found, and once Carlyon and John had been let into the house, it would be easier to deal with Thomas.

Thomas did not stay long with the treasure. It seemed that he simply wanted to check that it was there. Satisfied, he abruptly left the cell and locked the door. Moving quickly, he pulled James into the sunken cellar and, after securing the door to the passage, climbed the steps out of the well. Thomas barely glanced at James, as he let go of the chain. He appeared to be driven by a fiery haste. James sensed the agitation in Thomas's body and knew that the false friar was eager for the coming fight. He leaned against the wall and watched, as Thomas used the iron bar to open the sluice and let the water run through once more. Without even waiting for the well to fill, Thomas picked up his candle and the chain and hurried out of the cellars.

When Thomas got back to Peter, he said brusquely, "A man will show you where to keep the bear this night. Hold it close, for I'll have work for it on the morrow."

Thomas then left them just as brusquely, and James saw Peter's mouth move as he let out a breath of relief. A servant took them out to the stable block and Peter was shown a secure stall.

"This will be safe for your beast. See how it locks. You can sleep in the loft above."

"My thanks, but I'll stay with my bear. He'll rest easier with someone he knows."

The man nodded, accepting it as normal, and left Peter to it.

When they were alone, Peter turned to James and said, "It's right glad I am to see you safe. I feared me much, while you were away."

"I had fear also, yet fortune favoured me, and I've discovered more than I expected. But come now, take me out of this skin and I can rest before I go to open the gate."

Peter worked quietly and pulled open the stitching. At last James was free, and he shook himself to loosen his shift that had become stuck to him with sweat. Pleasure at being out of the confinement was like a cooling breeze on his skin. He turned to Peter, who had opened up his pack and brought out James's boots and other clothes. Once he was dressed, Peter handed James his sword, which he belted round his waist. Thus properly accoutred again, he flexed his muscles and took in deep breaths.

"Rest you there, Peter," he said, indicating the straw at the back of the stall. "This night's fighting will be fierce, but with God's grace, we'll be victorious."

15

*J*ames sat in the stable with his back against the wall, waiting for the household to settle for the night. There seemed much activity outside, as men were ordered about and James assumed that a guard was being set. But he did not have to wait long, for it was late in the evening and shadows were already noiselessly creeping in as night gently rolled over field and wood. When it became quiet outside, he heard two stable boys moving in the loft above them for a short while, but the creaking of the boards soon stopped. Before long there was only the occasional snuffle from the animals in the other stalls.

At last James decided to move. In the darkness, he felt his way to the door. Peter had earlier pulled it slightly open, and a faint glimmer round its edge guided James. He pulled it open enough to peep out. There was some light, as a skittish moon dashed through the clouds. The breeze in the yard was rattling a loose shutter somewhere, but there seemed to be nothing else. After reassuring himself, James slipped through the gap to stand in the yard with his back flattened against the stable wall. Again, he stayed where he was and carefully looked around. From what he could see of the house, it was in darkness, all windows shuttered. The yard was empty, but Thomas had posted guards on the wall. James counted two but knew that there would be others on the far side of the house. He waited for some minutes, seeking to assure himself that the guards were only on the wall.

Drawing in a breath, he began to move cautiously along in the shadow of the stable. At the end there was a clear space that he had to cross to get to the wall. He looked around and saw nothing. Then the moon was behind a cloud once more. Tensing himself, he moved quickly across the narrow space and was in thick shadow again. For a few seconds he paused, listening. No one seemed to have seen or heard him. He nodded to himself – the guards would have been looking out over the wall, not into the yard. He began to move again, creeping along towards the gate. Carefully he moved, one hand touching the rough stone of the wall as a guide. Suddenly he bumped into something. Fortunately, he was advancing so slowly that the knock on his knee brought only a low gasp from his throat. He felt with his fingers and then realised what it was. It was a narrow area that had been fenced off to store sharpened stakes. He remembered seeing it. Tightening his lips, he crept round it and continued his progress.

At the gate, he waited. He could hear two men talking above his head. Almost immediately, one of the men set off to walk along the wall. James heard the other stamp his feet, but there was no sign that he would move away. Hunched tensely in the darkness, James decided that he would wait no longer. He felt for the bar that was holding the postern gate closed. Carefully he began to lift one side out of its hook. There was the slightest of scrapes, which to James's ears seemed as loud as a screeching raven, but he had to continue. He lifted the other end clear and, cradling the bar in his arms, turned his body to lower it to the ground. In the darkness, one end thumped on the gate as he turned. It was not loud, but it attracted attention.

"What goes there?" A voice spoke from above his head. "Be that you, Henry?"

James stiffened but said nothing. A man jumped down into the yard, and James saw a shape peering at him.

"Henry?"

"Hold, friend," said James at last. "Fear not. There be nought to worry."

"Who are you? What goes on?"

As James bent to let the bar onto the ground, his head moved into the moonlight and the man said, "I know you. You're squire to the knight who's been here these few days. How came you here now? What do you here at the gate?"

"Nought amiss. I'm leaving now, that's all. But what do you in this wise? Are you not ashamed to be so disloyal to your liege lord the baron?"

"The baron was a bad lord. He was cruel and recked little of us. We be well rid of him, I trow. Friar Godfrey will be a better lord and more powerful to protect us, I'll warrant. He'll reward me well for holding you."

The man, who had had his hand on his sword hilt, now began to pull it out of its scabbard. James had been on the watch for such a move. He was quicker. His sword was out, and he had slashed at the man before he could take guard. The man leaped back with a howl. He shouted out for assistance, but James ignored him. Turning, he lifted the latch on the postern and dragged it open. He gave a loud whistle and then took guard, ready to defend the opening.

The wounded man made no move to attack. He continued to shout and merely skipped out of reach when James lunged at him. It was not for long. Almost immediately another man, sword in hand, had run up. Now the two of them advanced on James. Superior swordsmanship told, and by the time that two others had arrived, one of the guards was dead. Three men now launched themselves at James, who parried them skilfully. For several seconds he held his own. Suddenly John burst through the open gate, quickly followed by Carlyon and their other men. This shifted the balance, and in the cold moonlight two of the men were quickly dispatched. The third broke off and ran over to the house, closely pursued. John was the first inside, after the man, who had tried in vain to close the door. James was immediately behind John and bumped up against him. His eyes, which had become accustomed to the outside, now met what seemed like total blackness. He understood why the baron had stopped. Then James was jostled, as others came in through the door, and there was confusion.

"Have a care with that sword!" someone cried.

"Ho! Strike up a light here," called John.

James heard a flint being struck, and at last a rush was lit. At the same time, he saw that lights were being lit up farther on in the house, as men got ready to deal with the intruders. Now that they could see better, John began to organise his force properly, splitting it into two groups to take two sides.

"We must seek out Thomas," said Carlyon, touching James's sleeve to get his attention. "John and I will go now. You take charge of the men and seize the house. If we can find Thomas, then his men will have no cause to fight."

James nodded, but had no time to consider, for they were already under attack. Shouting encouragement, he led a charge.

Carlyon had been surprised at how easily they had got into the house. It was almost as if they had been invited, as if they were wanted. If that was so, then he had no doubt that they were wanted for a reason. Thomas's men were fighting fiercely and Carlyon wanted to engage with them, but he knew that they were only the body. Thomas was the heart and mind, and there would be no success until he was taken.

Carlyon followed John, who ran down a side passage which led to a staircase. John took the stairs two at a time and was at the top, while Carlyon had almost a third yet to climb. John, however, had to wait for him, because Carlyon was carrying the candle in his left hand. Impatiently John urged him on and took him round to the passage where Thomas's room lay. Here there were lights burning in sconces on the wall.

"These lights are freshly lit," said Carlyon. "I think me they've been placed to lead us on."

"An' they lead us to that black-hearted caitiff, it matters not."

"I doubt me it'll be so straight. If Thomas is leading us, then he'll want us for some fell purpose, I'll warrant."

"E'en so, we must press on and be ready for aught."

John strode off purposefully towards the door to Thomas's room. Carlyon followed watchfully. Without even looking round, John lifted the latch, pushed open the door, and went into the room. Carlyon kept as close behind him as he could, to guard John's back. Sword held ready, he glanced to each side as he stepped in through the doorway. There was some light. A single candle was burning on the far side. Carlyon saw almost immediately that there were animals in the room. At first, he counted three dogs. They were large, well-built bandogs. Their jaws were open to growl, and flecks of foam were bubbling on the sides.

As Carlyon and John moved into the room, the dogs leaped in to attack. It was then that Carlyon realised that there were three other dogs in the room. They came snarling from the side. Twisting to meet this new threat, Carlyon's feet slid. There was something slippery, almost smoothly ice-like, on the floor. Carlyon's feet went from under him, and he fell to the floor. As he did so, he banged his head on the edge of the open door. The shock made him disoriented for a second or two. The dogs immediately sensed a fallen prey. They leaped at him and began to try to rip at him savagely with their teeth, as if they had not eaten for some time. Carlyon struggled, but his senses were mazed, and the weight of the dogs round him made it difficult to move. He felt teeth go into his arm and into his legs, kick as he would. Then there was the fetid smell of one dog's breath, as it came to rip his face. Carlyon pulled up an arm, to try to grab the dog's jaws, but suddenly he felt the dog jerk. John had run one dog through with his sword and then had seen what had happened to Carlyon. He stuck his sword into the dog that was at Carlyon's face, but the animal still lived, as if it were a phantom beast. Frustration drew a growling roar from John's mouth. Leaving his sword in the dog, he grabbed hold of the animal with both of his hands behind its shoulders and yanked it off Carlyon.

John bent over Carlyon, and two of the dogs turned their attention to him. Ignoring their attack, John pulled Carlyon up and half-dragged, half-carried him out of the room and into the passageway. Carlyon had been bitten, but his senses were rapidly returning. John was blocking much of the passage, keeping the dogs away from Carlyon. They were jumping at John's back. He straightened up with an effort and pulled out his dagger. Banging his back into the wall to try to dislodge a dog, he slashed at another. This yelped but continued its attack. The weight of the dogs began to pull him down.

Now Carlyon had pushed himself to his feet. He was bleeding where he had been bitten, but his head had cleared. He could see what had happened. Holding his left arm with his shield against his chest, he gripped his sword more tightly. As if diving, he lunged at the dogs. The blade of his sword flashed in the rushlight. He had struck before the animals even had time to catch his scent. This time the advantage was with him, and the dogs were dead.

The passage was splashed with blood. It was becoming slippery underfoot. Carlyon felt a moment of unsureness grip his feet, as he twisted round to look at John. To his surprise, John was lying on the floor. Blood stained his tattered clothing. One sleeve was all but ripped off, the arm red with gore. His surtout had long rents, revealing the chain-mail vest beneath which had protected his body from the sharp teeth of his attackers. Carlyon knelt beside John and saw to his dismay that not all the blood on him was from the dogs, as he had thought. When he put an arm under John's shoulders to lift him up, he was able to see a stream of blood pulsing urgently out of the side of John's neck. Carlyon put a gloved hand over the small wound, pressing with his fingers to try to staunch the flowing blood.

Without turning his head, John moved his eyes to look at Carlyon. "This's bad," he said, his voice sounding hoarse. "I fear me I'm dying."

"Not so, old friend. We've been in more direful fights than this one, and we'll get through this."

"My head seems far away. I'm swimming to a different shore. Ah me! I dreamed of dying in battle, but I never thought me the battle would be in my own house."

"Cease such foolish talk. The only one to die here will be that foul traitor, Thomas."

"Yes, die he must. I'll not be able to do it now. You must find him and kill him. Then you must rescue Patsy, wherever she may be. You must be the one to look after her when I'm gone. I leave her in your hands."

"Not yet, John, not yet. You've saved my life here, and I'm going to save yours now."

Quickly Carlyon pulled out his silk kerchief. His fingers fumbled in his anxiety, but he made a pad with a few folds and pressed it over the wound on John's neck. John's eyes had closed, and his breathing had become so shallow that Carlyon feared that it had stopped. Then he saw John's mouth opening, as if in a yawn. The breathing continued, but no more reassuringly than before. Blood was staining the kerchief.

"Rouse you now, John, there's still work to do," Carlyon urged. "Your sword will be needed."

John's only response was to open his eyes, but there seemed little recognition in them, despite Carlyon's continued urging. At last, his mouth opened to speak, but the voice was so low that Carlyon had to strain to catch the words.

"I would I had me cool water to drink."

Carlyon looked around, but it was of no help. Keeping his left hand pressed to the pad on John's neck, he used his teeth to tug off the glove from his other hand. He brushed that hand on John's brow, thinking to wipe away the sweat, but the skin was cold and clammy. Fear pulled his hand to John's shoulder, as if to shake him. "John! John!" he called hoarsely. "Fight this battle! Fight hard!"

He could feel his friend's body tremble. Then he saw the mouth open slightly. There were no words. A weak breath came out, as if John's soul were escaping. Suddenly Carlyon knew that his friend was dead.

"John! John!" he called again, but he knew that it was hopeless.

He could hear the noise of fighting elsewhere in the house, but where he was, there was no sound, except for the strange gasping of his own breath. He bent his head and murmured a line of prayer. Looking up again, he set his jaw. He would find Thomas and take vengeance for John.

Painfully, he got to his feet. He was still bleeding from where the bandogs had bitten him, but it was only seeping as he moved. Shaking his head to clear it, he replaced his glove, put his shield on his back, and picked up his sword. Quickly, he went into Thomas's chamber. This time it was empty, and now that he could look around, he saw that it had been cleared of Thomas's things. Thomas had moved elsewhere in the house. Almost without thought, Carlyon knew that Thomas had moved into John's room. He presumed himself to be the lord now. Carlyon wasted no more time. As if pulled, he jerked round and went back out into the passage. It was imperative to act quickly.

He hurried across the house towards where John had his privy chambers on the other side of the great hall. Darkness soon brought him to a stop. The further passageway was unlit. He snatched a candle out of a sconce on the wall and set off again. Doubts were now pricking at him that perhaps that side of the house would be empty, but he had no better immediate plan. The doubts were eased somewhat when he drew nearer to John's chamber and saw a light. One single candle guttered on the wall, its flame moving in the draught, as if enticing Carlyon nearer. Reassured in a way, Carlyon pressed on down the passage. Then movement caught his eye, and caution slowed his steps. Forward of the candle, and just within its circle of light, a dark shape was lying on the ground. It was as if a sack of vegetables had been dropped there. Lying against the wall where it was, Carlyon would not have noticed it, had it not moved, seeming to be disturbed by his approach. The shape now unfolded, and Carlyon saw that it was an animal getting to its feet.

Carlyon paused and peered through the weak light. It was a wolf. Its eyes glittered, and Carlyon saw its lips pull back from its jaw to reveal its untameable teeth. Placing his candle on the floor, he quickly slipped his shield round off his back and onto his arm. Tightening his grip on his sword, he held it out ready and moved forward. He had taken two steps when he saw the wolf lift its head, and then he heard it speak.

"The intruders are being beaten."

Carlyon stopped, almost as if the words were threatening daggers aimed at him. The voice had a slightly echoing sound, but he recognised it as belonging to Thomas. His tongue moistened his dry lips, and he listened as the wolf continued.

"Only you remain, and you will fail. I will not be defeated."

Carlyon was trying to look closely. Now he was not sure whether the voice was coming from the wolf or from the air around it. Yet he believed that Thomas could turn himself into a wild beast. While he was wondering what evil trick Thomas would try next, he saw that the wolf had tensed its muscles and gone back onto its haunches. Carlyon braced himself, knowing that the animal was about to attack.

The wolf launched itself. As if shot from a catapult, it came through the air over the short distance to Carlyon. Carlyon turned sideways and stepped backwards. At the same time, he held out his shield, twisting it to use the wolf's own impetus to knock it away. The wolf rolled over. Carlyon's sword came up. It went directly into the animal's underside, ripping through the heart and other internal organs. The sword slid out, as the wolf thumped heavily onto the floor. Carlyon poised to strike again, but after a few twitches the animal was still. Carlyon saw blood spilling over the floor, and he bent to examine the wolf. Warily at first, he grasped the head and shook it. He pursed his lips thoughtfully. It was a real animal. There was no magic there now.

He straightened up and continued down the passage. The door to John's chamber was not far. Squatting in front of it was a large eagle. Carlyon gave his shoulders a hunch and held his shield ready. Looking sharply in front of him to check for anything else, he strode purposefully forward, his sword arm primed for action. The eagle drew itself up, spreading out its wings to increase its appearance of size. Again, Carlyon heard Thomas's voice, coming as if through the bird's beak.

"So, Sir Knight, still you advance. Perchance you have slain one manifestation of me? You will fail this time. I can take whatever shape I desire. Can you slay them all?"

Carlyon had stopped. His brow furrowed at this further example of Thomas's magical powers. He gathered himself and determined not to be intimidated or daunted. He would continue to the end. "I can slay any evil, be they as numerous as a nest of ants. Do your worst. Right will prevail."

The eagle shot towards Carlyon before he had finished the defiant sentence. Almost taken by surprise, Carlyon moved up his shield to protect his face, as if the shield itself had pulled his arm up. The eagle clattered against the shield and its talons clutched at the lower part of Carlyon's tunic, getting a purchase for support. The bird's weight pushed Carlyon back. He staggered two steps and barely regained his balance. Drawing in a deep breath, to try to drive out the sudden weakness that was pulling his body down, he tried to push the shield outward. His previously wounded left arm was bleeding again and seemed to lack strength. A wave of nausea rippled through him as the eagle tried to move its beak round the shield. Carlyon staggered again and feared he was about to fall. Then his right arm moved. It drew back and brought the sword forward and upward. Slicing into the eagle, as if into a woolsack, the sword sheared off a wing. The bird squawked and its grip loosened. Carlyon twisted his sword round. The eagle bent its neck to attack, but it was too late. The sword went into its heart.

Carlyon pulled back his arm and the sword slipped out of the eagle as the dead body flopped to the floor under its own weight. Carlyon drew in a deep breath. Gently he moved his head from side to side, to try to clear the buzzing dizziness that flowed over him like a billowing silk sheet. He glanced down at his left arm, where blood was showing through the torn sleeve. The wound did not seem too serious. He could still hold the shield. Drawing in a new breath, he stepped over the eagle and put his hand to the latch of the door that the bird had seemingly been guarding.

Carlyon pressed the latch and warily pushed the door open. Placing a foot over the threshold, he held his shield in front of him. There was a burning candle, but the room was gloomy. It was almost as if he was expected. After pausing for a moment or two, listening intently and sniffing the strange odour that seemed to be seeping out of the room, Carlyon stepped fully through the doorway. A pall of silence was heavy in the room, and Carlyon stayed where he was. Holding his body still, he moved his head so that his watchful gaze could sweep the room. The point of his sword, held out before him, moved as his eyes did, prepared to meet any danger.

Carlyon saw no immediate danger, and yet he had a sense that he was not alone in the room. Moving his shield up slightly to cover the lower part of his face, he peered over the top and examined the room again. He realised that it was not John's privy chamber.

Yet it was the door that the eagle had been guarding. There was a curtained bed, and he could make out a bench under the window. He remembered now that John had mentioned to him that Friar Godfrey had also taken a room next to his, so that he could pass through easily to discuss affairs. There was a doorway in the wall to Carlyon's left. He supposed that John's chamber lay beyond it, and that hopefully he would find what he sought there.

He took a step towards it, leaving the shelter of the entrance door. A dark shape caught his eye. Thinking it to be Thomas, he turned swiftly towards it, on guard. Then he relaxed. It was only a tree trunk, the one in which he himself had once hidden. Then it crossed his mind that Thomas might now be hiding in it. In one fluid movement, without pulling back his arm to give warning, Carlyon drove the sword into the simulated bark covering. It passed through and into an empty space within the frame holding up the covering. There was no one there.

More confidently now, but still cautiously, he began to walk towards the connecting door. Suddenly a low cackle made him jump. He stopped and turned to look at the corner. A dark shape had materialised there. This time it was moving, and as light fell on it, Carlyon saw that it was a human figure. It was wearing a grey woollen shift that came down to the floor, and had a hood pulled low over its face. The back was stooped, and after two faltering steps the figure stopped. A hand came out of the long left sleeve, reached up, and pulled back the hood. It was a woman, and Carlyon's immediate thought was that it was the witch whom he had killed in Lancashire, but then he saw that she was much older. Her right hand came up, as if she was about to throw something, but Carlyon spoke first.

"Where is Thomas, old Mother, Thomas, who calls himself Friar Godfrey? Do you know where he is?"

"Thomas is gone, who knows where? He's where he can't be found, and he's left me here." The voice was thin and quavery, but the words were clear.

"Who are you?" Carlyon asked peremptorily. "Where've you come from?"

"I've been in this house for many a moon, though I've kept myself close from man's sight. But I've seen much. Now I'm looking after my lord's business."

"You'd do well to do that, an' it be the true lord. So, you've seen much, old Mother? Well now, you must know where the lady baroness is."

"In faith, sir, I've seen her. She's in danger but may yet be saved. Give me your arm, sir, and help me out into the passage. I'm such an old and feeble woman, I can barely walk."

Carlyon was about to sheathe his sword, his nobility guiding him to help the old woman, but the sword suddenly seemed immovable. Stiffened by suspicion, Carlyon pulled up his shield and took a step backwards. "Soft awhile. I've but now killed a wolf and an eagle that I thought to be Thomas. Mayhap you also are here to deceive?"

The old woman cackled and put her head to one side like a crow. "Were you impressed by Thomas's magic? Hah, it was not entirely so. They were wild beasts he had controlled with special potions. He can make such beasts as meek as lambs or more ferocious than the mind of man can conceive."

"That may be so, but I heard those beasts speak with Thomas's voice. That was no potion, I trow."

A smile seemed to move like a shadow over the woman's face, and she hobbled the few steps to the wall. She held her hand over two small wooden funnels that were protruding from the wall and looked sideways at Carlyon. "Here's Thomas's magic voice. He was neither the animals, nor was he in them. He but spoke into these tubes and a credulous fool would believe that an animal spoke."

She cackled again, and Carlyon tightened his lips. He recalled other times when Thomas's voice had seemed to come out of nowhere and he had believed in magic. Impatiently he let out his breath and the sound rasped through the room.

"Enough of this!"

He was about to bid the crone to tell him about Lady Patrina, but, as if she guessed, she interrupted him.

"Come closer, sir, and examine these. Perchance you'll be able to speak to the lady baroness?"

The mild words temporarily disarmed him. With his mind fixed on Patrina and her rescue, he laid aside his caution and stepped over towards the old woman. She was standing in the wavering light with her back stooped and her bent right arm pressed into her body as if crippled. Suddenly the right hand came up. In one swift movement the fist unclenched, and a powder was thrown at Carlyon. He was caught off guard but recovered immediately. His shield came up. Even so, a few grains of the powder landed on his face. He licked his lips, but there was no other time to think. He thrust with his sword, and the glinting blade went deep into the woman's chest and through her heart. As he pulled out the sword and the woman fell to the floor, the light from the candle caught her face. There was a look of shocked surprise in her eyes, and yet strangely also a spark of triumph. Carlyon stepped back, ready for any treachery, but the crumpled body lay motionless, face down.

Releasing his shield, Carlyon moved across to the candle and brought it over. He held it above the woman and then used his foot to turn her over. For a few seconds he stared. Satisfied, he straightened up, prepared to move on and face whatever else lay before him. But he stopped and looked again at the body. There was something abnormal about it. He knelt down, put the candle on the floor, and felt amongst the woman's clothes. It took him but a moment or two to discover that he had killed not a woman, but a man. There was no mistaking the wiry chest – it was male. He looked closely at the face. It seemed odd in some way, and he probed at it with his fingertips. It felt somewhat strange to his touch. At first, he thought of a snake or a frog, but then he realised that it was a close-fitting vizard fastened over the head. Feeling round for the edge, he pulled it off. Underneath he saw the narrow, pinched features of Thomas. The sallow lids were closed over the eyes, hiding their suspicion forever.

Carlyon turned the mask over in his hands, examining it. It seemed to have been made from bark and coated with an oil to keep it supple. In the dim light it had been a good enough disguise. Carlyon got to his feet and sheathed his sword. Disappointment tightened his throat as he looked down on Thomas's body. It was good that he was dead, and yet there was now no chance to make him tell where Lady Patrina was hidden. Carlyon almost drew back his foot to kick the body in his frustration, but he knew that that would be no help. He needed to move quickly now. Hanging his shield behind his back, he took hold of Thomas and dragged him into the passageway.

From there it was not far to the gallery overlooking the great hall. Fighting was still taking place, but it did not seem to be going well for the small force that John had recruited. Those that were left had been driven to one side with the doorway at their back and were slowly being forced to retreat. Carlyon shouted for attention, again and yet again. At last men paused and looked round at him.

"See!" he cried, holding Thomas up against the railing. "The man who gave himself out to be Friar Godfrey is dead. The wicked tyrant will oppress no more."

Weapons began to be lowered, as men drew back and looked.

Carlyon pressed his advantage. "Fight no more! The battle is over. Lay down your arms."

Men relaxed at the words, but some looked questioningly at each other, as if unsure what to do next. One, bolder, raised his head. "Where is His Lordship the baron?" he called. "Will he show mercy?"

"Your lord the baron is dead, fighting bravely to free you from dark evil. You must serve the lady Patrina now. She'll show mercy to all who serve her loyally. I give you my pledge. But first Her Ladyship must be found. The wicked friar has imprisoned her, I know not where. Seek now – search every nook and corner of this house, until she be found."

One man immediately shouted, "Yes, we must find Her Ladyship!" and he was echoed by others. Quickly, those without serious wounds dispersed.

Carlyon caught his breath and looked for James. He had not been noticeable amongst the combatants, and cold fear gripped Carlyon as he hurried to the staircase. Down in the hall, he moved quickly amongst the dead and wounded bodies lying about. It was not long before he came upon James. He was lying partially covered by the body of another man, as if both had perished in mortal combat. With the hot breath of fear in his throat, Carlyon pulled the dead body away from his squire. Kneeling down, he cradled James's head sorrowfully in his lap. It was then that he realised that, although unconscious, James was still alive. Relief made his hands grip James more firmly, as if afraid of losing him. Carefully he examined him.

His clothes were badly stained with blood and there was a gash to the side of his head. Carlyon thought to tear off a strip of his own silk shift, so that he could bandage the wound, but was stopped by a hand on his shoulder. He looked round and saw that it was Mary.

"I've brought in a physician," she told him. "He'll dress the wounded."

"Good! Our Lady's blessing on you. I need him here forthwith. James is sorely wounded."

Mary returned her restraining hand to Carlyon's shoulder and said, "No, Carlyon, don't give James over to him. An' you find us a room, I shall salve James's wounds myself."

Carlyon wasted no time. He got to his feet and called out for two men. They carried James away to the room that he had been using during his stay in the house. Carlyon, standing by himself, shook his head. There was a fuzziness clogging it which would not go, so he tightened his lips and went to look for William, John's steward. He had seen the man earlier, fighting with Thomas's supporters, and had remarked how he had quickly sent men in search of Lady Patrina when the fighting ended. Carlyon came upon him at the back of the house and the steward hastened to speak first.

"All the men are searching, sire. The women of the household also. Pray God, we'll find Her Ladyship ere long. Ah me, what a time we've had, but by God's blood, I'm pleased that rogue has gone."

The words were clattering out like turnips from a sack, and Carlyon could almost physically feel the steward's tension. He cut him short. He had no time for recriminations. The important thing was to find Patrina. It would then be for her to call people to account for their actions.

"Search well. Her Ladyship must be hereabouts in the house. Make sure men pry into every corner of the cellars. Time is short.

Also, the baron's body lies by the friar's chamber. Have it taken and laid out as befits a hero of his rank."

The steward obsequiously said that he would do all that straight away, and would have said more, but Carlyon again cut him short. Telling him to be about it, he turned and moved away. He wanted to see how James was, before joining the search for Patrina.

James was lying on the bed in his chamber, the linen sheets stained with blood. However, Mary had cleaned his wounds and salved them with herbal potions that she had in her pouch. When Carlyon came in, she looked up and smiled but continued her binding up of the wounds.

"How goes it?" he asked. "Will he live?"

"God willing. His wounds will heal, I trow. Yet he has taken a grievous blow to his head. See him senseless still. I know not when he'll awaken."

Carlyon looked down at the unconscious James. Mary tied off the bandage round her patient's head, and as Carlyon watched her sure movements, he was suffused with relief. The sensation flowed through his body, as if he had drunk a spiritous liquor. Then it left him, and unconsciously he relaxed. Suddenly his head began to swim. The walls of the room started to shimmer, and a rushing noise came into his head like a wind through a forest. He seemed to see a darkness rising slowly towards him, watching. As if from far away, he heard Mary's voice.

"Carlyon, you have a strange look. What's amiss?"

He heard a muffled voice, that sounded like his own, coming through the speaking unreality of a dream. "I'm not here. There's no rest yet. What's this hole?"

He felt himself float, slowly, smoothly down. Then there was only blackness. Nothing.

16

ames was lying in his bed with his head on a pillow. His eyes were closed, and he was trying to recall a dream. There was so much that was blank. He remembered being moved, lifted, turned. There had been pain, and then an easing. He was sure that he had seen Mary, but perhaps that had been in his dream. As consciousness returned, so did the pain, but not so fiercely. His arms were sore when he tried to move, and there was a throbbing ache in his head. He decided to open his eyes, but his muscles refused to obey. He was too weak, and it was better just to lie there.

Then he realised that his mouth was dry and that he had a raging thirst. For some seconds he struggled with that realisation, and then finally he made a great effort. His eyes opened. His head was propped up on a pillow, and he saw that he was in his own room in Lord John's house. There was the sudden sound of a snort. Slowly he turned his eyes to one side towards the sound. An elderly dame was sitting on a chair by his bed. Her head was bent, her chin pressing into her chest, and her regular breathing showed that she was dozing. He recognised her as one of the household retainers.

"I'm thirsty. Give me to drink, I pray."

His voice was hoarse and the sound that came out of his mouth was lower than he'd expected, yet the dame's head jerked up into wakefulness.

"You're awake, sir! Praise be! Yes, I have drink here." She left the chair with a nimbleness that belied her age and picked up a beaker from a small table by the bed. "This is a potion given by Mistress Mary. She's said to give it you when you awaken. It'll help you. Oh, she'll be so pleased to know you've awoken."

While prattling on, she had pushed an arm gently behind James's head to raise it and had placed the beaker at his lips. He began to drink. It was slightly bitter, but not unpleasant. He drank it all and then let his head rest back on the pillow. His thirst was gone, and he was beginning to feel better. Now he tried to think. He knew that there was something important, but it was as if it were a wraith fluttering behind him. There had been fighting. He could remember that.

"I must rise and dress. I have things to do."

"Nay, sir, nay! You must rest. All's well. You've been sore wounded and lost much blood, they say. You fought valiantly and inspired your men. Victory was yours and the evil friar is no more."

James was somewhat reassured, but he still felt that there was something important that he yet had to do. He asked after Carlyon.

"He lives, but he has been bewitched and lies in a swoon these past two days. Mistress Mary is caring for him."

"Where's the baron? I must speak with him."

"Alas, sir, the baron's dead. He was killed by savage beasts while seeking the friar."

The improving feeling that had been flowing through James was abruptly checked. A black cloud seemed to push into his head, but the dame was still talking and her words filtered in to him.

"Mistress Mary has taken charge of everything these last two days. William the steward and Henry the bailiff are putting all in order under her direction. The people are so pleased that the evil power is no longer around them. Our only sorrow now is that Her Ladyship the baroness has not yet been found, e'en though men still search day and night."

"Her Ladyship? Lady Patrina?" Shock jerked at James's body, as if he had been knocked off a horse. "Ah me! She's locked away. I must go to her!" He had remembered what he had to do, and horror at the thought that two days had passed unknown pulled him upright in the bed. He moved back the blanket and the sheet, and despite the dame's protests, he swung his legs over the edge of the bed. His head was swimming, but he took deep breaths and used his hands on the bed to push him to his feet. He swayed but stayed upright. "Help me to put on a robe!" he said. "We must lose no time."

"Oh, sir, I'm sure you should not be out of bed yet."

"Do as you're told! Help me now."

He would have done it himself, but his bandaged arms were stiff. However, the old woman, although still advising against it, helped him to put a robe on over his shift and then put leather-soled stockings on his feet.

"Now, call two stout fellows and tell them to meet me at the cellars with torches straight away. Go to it! Her Ladyship's life depends on it."

This seemed to strike home, and the dame waddled quickly out of the room. James followed more slowly. At first, he moved with painful difficulty, and often he needed to put a hand to the wall for support. When he reached the entrance to the cellars, two men were already waiting. Walking between them, James directed them down the stairs. At the bottom he paused for a few instants, while he made sure of his direction, then set off.

On the small landing in the flooded cellar, he had no trouble finding the iron rod. Urgently he instructed one of the men how to insert it in the spindle and turn it to close the sluice gate. The minutes dripped by as the water level dropped. James leaned against the wall, trying to conserve his strength, and kept on his feet by an iron determination to rescue Lady Patrina. At last, he could wait no longer and led the men down the steps. They sloshed through the remaining water, and one of the men unbolted the door to the hidden cells. The dank, earthy smell hung round them like a miasma as they hurried along the passageway.

"Not far now," said James breathlessly. "The door at the end."

The men did not need to be told to unbolt it. Then James pushed it open himself. Taking a torch, he bent his head and entered the cell. The light scampered in before him, dispersing the darkness. Against the far wall he saw the low plank bed, and, on it, a body wrapped in a fur cloak. Stifling a groan, he bent over it, then almost swayed in his relief as he saw that Lady Patrina was breathing. He handed back the torch and sat on the edge of the bed. Carefully he raised Patrina's head. The cheeks were cold, but he could feel warmth in the head.

"Your Ladyship," he said softly. Then, a little more loudly, "Your Ladyship."

Patrina's eyes opened. Fear glittered in them, sparking her face with lines of terror. But only momentarily. She recognised James almost immediately and closed her eyes as she relaxed.

"Wine here," said James. "Quickly now."

A man handed over the small flagon that they had brought, and James held it to Patrina's lips. She took a little, and then, as if her dry mouth had been primed, she took a longer drink.

Moving her mouth away, she said croakily, "I've been alone

here in the dark so long. I thought I was like to go mad. It seemed I'd been left here to die."

"Mayhap so, my lady. I had discovered your prison, and had I not been so grievously wounded in the battle for your house, I would have come the sooner. But thank God, I pray I've come in time. We'll get you to your own chamber now and Matty will see to your needs."

"But Friar Godfrey. What of him?"

"Fear you not, my lady. He was no friar. Sir Carlyon has slain him, and his power is at an end." James turned his head to look at the taller of his companions. "Take you Her Ladyship and carefully carry her."

He gently released Patrina's head and got to his feet. He was anxious to get her out of the oppressive atmosphere of the cellars, before she asked about her husband and had to be told of his death. Fortunately, she seemed too overwhelmed with what had been happening to her to think of further questions. James followed the men out of the cell and along the passage. He glanced at the door of the cell that held the treasure but did nothing. While Patrina was being taken to her room, James went to his own. His body felt as though hot blades were being laid on him in places, and he had a great desire to lie down.

He remembered nothing of sleeping, but suddenly he was aware that Mary was standing by his bed.

"Here, James," she said, when she saw his eyes open, "drink this. It were well you found the lady Patrina when you did."

"How is she?" he asked, concern making him pause before drinking.

"She rests. Fret you not. I've spoken to her about my lord Cerrenore. She was distressed, yet not so sorely, I trow." She pursed her lips and went on. "You too must rest. I'll return to Carlyon."

"How is he? What's happened?"

"He was put under a spell by Thomas. I'm fighting it as best I can. He's in great danger. For two days and two nights now he's been lost as one dead, but if he lives through this coming night, then he'll be saved."

"Pray God you're right. And, now that she's free, at last he'll then win his ladylove, the baroness Patrina. And so his quest will end."

Mary looked at him with the hint of a rueful smile on her lips. "Yes. If that's to be, then so be it."

Carlyon could feel that his brow was being wiped with a damp cloth. The sensation was pleasant, and at first, he thought that it was part of a dream. Slowly he opened his eyes and saw Mary's face above his. She smiled her warm, beautiful smile with lips that were lovelier than the lips of roses, and his face crinkled in pleasure. He thought that he was in bed in her mother's cottage, having fallen ill after rescuing Mary from the witch. Then he realised that he was lying in a bed with silk sheets, and the full memory of what he was doing in John's house jerked back into his mind. There was still work to do, and he started to get up. Mary restrained him with both hands on his shoulders.

"Gently, my lord. You've been gravely bewitched for three days and three nights together now. I thought me your soul might not return. It was a powerful spell."

"It was Thomas. Before I killed him, he threw a powder at me. I thought some grains landed on my face."

"Ah, that will be it. I knew it must have been of such sort. I had to try many things to save you, but all will be well now."

"I owe my life to you yet again, Mary. Our fates are bound together, it seems, like vines growing towards the sun." Then, quietly, almost as if to himself, "It would be bootless to fight against it."

He was about to say more, when a manservant came into the room and stood expectantly by the door.

"Yes?!" said Mary, somewhat sharply.

"Her Ladyship has sent to ask how Sir Carlyon is, mistress."

"Tell her he is but this instant now recovered, and the danger is past."

Carlyon was surprised at the man's deference to Mary, and also by her air of authority. He looked at her thoughtfully, as the man left.

"Her Ladyship has been found," she told him, as if he had asked. "She's safe and well but mourning her husband."

Pleasure at the news of Patrina's rescue warmed Carlyon, but he was saddened at the reminder of John's death. "Where is Lord John's body?" he asked.

"It lies in state in the chapel here. The funeral will be in four days from now."

"A sad time, and I would it were not to be. John died to save my life. He was a true friend. I'll not see his like again." Carlyon sighed and shook his head sorrowfully.

Mary laid a gentle hand on his shoulder, as if to comfort him. Then she said, in a matter-of-fact way, "Thomas's body has been laid in a pit outside the churchyard wall and covered with quicklime. He'll trouble no one again."

"It gladdens me to hear that. He caused trouble enough. It was his doing that caused Lord John's death and put Lady Patrina into mourning. But tell me, how was she found?"

"James discovered where she was imprisoned, while he was disguised as the bear. It was a secret chamber beyond the cellars. She was much weakened by her ordeal, but she is recovering well now."

"Thanks to you, I'll warrant." Carlyon smiled at Mary, and she smiled knowingly back. "I must away to her and comfort her."

A shadow of disappointment flitted briefly over Mary's face, as if someone had passed between her and the light, but she made no attempt this time to restrain him when he sat up in the bed. "Her Ladyship is now a rich widow with much property," she said, as if by the way. "There's much work to do to manage everything here on the estates. I've been doing what I can. Her Ladyship will need a helpmeet who can shoulder her burdens."

Carlyon glanced up at her and gave a short laugh. "Even so. Yet that'll not be for me. A great evil's been defeated here, and at a greater cost than I would wish had not been paid. But so be it. My work here is done, I trow. I'll not stay."

"The lady Patrina is your love, is she not? You undertook an arduous quest for her, and even now you've served her like a true knight."

"Ah me, Mary! I've served Patrina as any knight would serve a lady. In faith, I thought me one time I could see her as my ladylove, but the glass of time is brittle, into which we peer for such a brief while when young. I can see now that that love was only as the rainbow's hue – strong at the first but soon fading. It was as insubstantial as the bubbles churned up by a seething millrace. My heart's in calmer waters now, and I can see more clearly what true love is. And I know that it flies without effort, as a bird flies when it ceases to move its wings."

He was about to say that true love was nothing to do with family alliances and rank, but he brought his lips together and cut off the words. Suddenly it seemed to him that such words would demean Mary. He had come to understand that Patrina, for all her good qualities, was light and flighty. The lady that would call to him would have strong and capable characteristics, and he realised that he had been seeing those in Mary, peasant though she was. His eyes heavy with love, he looked at Mary standing by his bed. She was smiling at him, as if aware of his thoughts. He smiled back, uncaring that she might be able to see into his heart, and even hoping that she could.

"I still have no memory of the past year," he said. "I remember nought of what you told me has happened. I wish me I could remember. When did we marry?"

"A year gone this week." She told him all about it, and when he asked about their son, she described his appearance and his little actions and expressions. "I miss him sorely, but he's safe with Mama. And I knew that you were in need of me, though you knew it not yourself."

"That's so. I was lost, although I knew it not, but it were good for me that your love found me. Think you I shall ever remember all this?"

"It may be you will, but I can't know such things."

Carlyon's intended reply was prevented by Patrina's entry. She was supporting herself on James, but she was smiling graciously.

"How now here, Carlyon," she said. "It does my heart right good to see you looking so well. We were much afeared for you."

"I thank you for your good wishes, my lady. I also am right pleased to see you so safe and sound." He was in fact surprised at how well she was looking after her ordeal. Emotions seemed to be bubbling within her, and he wondered at the excitement that he could sense crackling around her. "Mary has told me how James found you."

"In faith, sire," James said, "Thomas unwittingly showed me where he was keeping her concealed – and much more beside."

Patrina broke in then, unable to wait any longer. "I'd surely been left to die in that dark and dismal place. Had I lived, it would have been as a slave to that vile toad." She hunched and shook her shoulders in a shiver. "Horrible, oh, horrible! Yet how romantic an ending! I was rescued by my noble knight." She looked fondly at James and seemed to hang on his arm even more securely.

James smiled shyly and looked down at his feet, as if embarrassed. "It's true I rescued a lady," he said, "but I am only a squire."

"For but a while. I shall speak to my father about your investiture and tell him to arrange it. He won't refuse me."

"I also will support it," added Carlyon, with an encouraging smile for James. Then, to Patrina, "Will you be staying here, or returning to your father's?"

"I'm an independent widow. I can do as I wish. I now have much property – many people are in my care. I must look after them. There are many wrongs to be arighted. But I'll not be alone. I'll have a brave knight to marry ere long."

She looked at James with an arch smile, and James smiled down at her. Carlyon suspected that Patrina's words had not come as a surprise to James. He nodded, genuinely pleased for the two of them.

"And you, Carlyon," asked Patrina, "will you be seeking new adventures?"

"That may be so. I have my sword and my shield and my good right arm. Perchance an adventure awaits."

"Yet first you will return home?"

"Home? I have a home, I trow, although I can't recall it. I also have a wife and child, and I must see to them first."

The muscles on Patrina's face tightened in her surprise, and James's expression seemed to indicate unsureness. Carlyon smiled briefly. He glanced up at Mary, who was standing nearby, but with her back against the wall, as if she were not part of the group, and he told Patrina what Mary had told him. As he related how it had happened, both Patrina and James kept looking from him to Mary and back again. When he finished, Patrina pulled her eyes closed and then smiled.

"How romantic!" she said softly.

James screwed up his face thoughtfully, before saying, "Mary is a woman worthy of any man." He paused, and then went on hesitantly, "Yet if you were not aware of what you did, is it truly in God's sight? An annulment can be sought."

"I say not, James! It's true, I remember nought of such a marriage, yet I can hold no doubt I was aware of it at the time. In sight of God and the world I have a lawful wife. And I have a lawful son and heir." Carlyon paused and looked at Mary, who had straightened up and was looking at him intently. "I'm married to a woman I love, and you also are now witnesses to it."

He put out his hand towards Mary, and she stepped up to the bed to take it. Her eyes were sparkling brightly, as if her delight could only be expressed like sorrow – with the glint of tears – and her warm, enfolding smile lit up the beauty of her face. Her head nodded slightly, but she did not need to speak. Carlyon pulled his eyes away from her tender bonds and looked at Patrina and James.

"I know not if my memory of that time will return. I must carry the hope of that like milk in a beaker, but, and it does or no, I now know what I want. We'll to Lancashire with all speed, so I can get to know again my wife and son. Before that, Patsy, can you take Lady Mary away and have her dressed as befits and is lawful for her rank? And you, James, as your final act as a squire, help me from this bed and see that all is ready."

www.ingramcontent.com/pod-product-compliance
Lightning Source LLC
Chambersburg PA
CBHW030533030726
47495CB00004B/971